DARKNESS
CALLS

DARKNESS CALLS

AN INSPECTOR CECILIE MARS THRILLER

MICHAEL KATZ KREFELD

Translated from Danish by Ian Giles

Podium

SAGA
EGMONT

For my beautiful wife and best friend, Lis

Copyright © 2018 by Michael Katz Krefeld

English translation copyright © 2023 by Saga Egmont

Cover design by Podium Publishing

ISBN: 978-1-0394-2497-5

Published in 2023 by Podium Publishing, ULC
www.podiumaudio.com

DARKNESS
CALLS

And I will execute great vengeance upon them with furious rebukes; and they shall know that I *am* the LORD, when I shall lay my vengeance upon them.

—Ezekiel 25:17

1

COPENHAGEN

Fie could still picture the dragon. It had stared at her from the side of his neck, mouth wide open, moving in time with his body as he forced his way into her. Deep, penetrating thrusts. Over and over. The dragon had looked down upon her mercilessly with the same reptilian gaze as its owner. It was an old dragon. Much older than her own eighteen years.

She staggered away under the dim streetlights, heading for the concrete silos of Bellahøj. The run-down tower blocks loomed as they encircled her, and she supported herself against a lamppost to avoid falling. The cool metal under the palm of her hand reminded her of the gleaming knife he had held up to her eye. *This is what cock teases get.* She continued along the deserted street towards her door some way ahead. She passed the basketball court with the netting fluttering from the hoops. Her hands were shaking uncontrollably, and it was with some difficulty that she managed to retrieve the key from her jacket pocket. Once she had let herself into the building, she went to the lift and slid open the door. The cramped space stared back at her, and she gasped for breath. She could still feel his weight on her and his iron grip on around her throat. It had all gone black and her cry for help had died away before it had even reached her vocal cords. *Bebe . . . bebe* was all she had managed to say. A word that had made him laugh. It had turned him on so much he'd ripped her trousers off. Cold blades of grass under her buttocks.

Rough, nicotine-stained fingers at her opening. *You're soooo wet.* Then a cutting sensation down there. All the way up to the diaphragm. For a split second, she'd thought it was the knife that was inside her rather than his member. *Take it. Take it, you nym . . . pho . . .* In his excitement, he stumbled over his own words.

She let go of the lift door and turned towards the stairs. Every single step was agony. They reminded her of his thrusts, each accompanied by a grunt—a sound that now filled her head and echoed around the stairwell. Six storeys. One hundred and eight steps. An eternity—just like the one she had experienced in the park's dark landscape, together with the dragon.

She locked the flat's front door behind her and tiptoed through the hallway. From the bedroom she heard her mother's sleepy voice.

"Fie, is that you?" That was followed by: "Ugh, it ended up being a late one then?"

Fie dumped her bag and denim jacket in the hall. A light was switched on inside the bedroom and she heard the bed creak as her mother got out of it. Fie hurried down the hallway and into the bathroom. She quickly shut the door, ensuring she locked it, too. A moment later, she saw her mother's silhouette through the frosted glass.

"You not feeling well?" she asked.

Fie didn't reply.

"Are you okay?"

"Yeah . . . yeah," she managed to stammer.

"Are you pissed?"

"No . . . I mean, only a little."

There was a groan from the other side of the door. "Fie! We promised Grandma we'd arrive early."

"Yes, yes . . . Good night, Mum."

"G'night, sweetheart." A moment later, the bedroom door closed.

Fie stood in front of the basin and examined herself in the mirror. There was extensive bruising on her neck, and below her left eye she had a cut from his knife. Blades of grass sparkled neon green in her matted black hair. Her face was swollen with tears. The shock was still there in her vacant stare and the open mouth, the trembling lips. She disgusted herself. *How pathetic.* That was what the sight made her think. She lowered her gaze from the mirror and quickly undressed. There were traces of fresh blood in her knickers, and she rinsed them before dumping all her clothes in the laundry basket. She spotted the little pearlised purse sticking out of her trouser front pocket. *You're not gonna grass, right?* He'd taken her health insurance card with her address on it. Warned her not to tell anyone. If she did, he'd stop by with his knife. She'd promised him she wouldn't say a word. He'd smiled and shoved a two hundred kroner note into her purse. *A little something for the taxi, sweetie. Or for something tasty tomorrow.* None of it had made any sense. He'd winked at her—or perhaps it had been the dragon on his neck that had done that—before they both disappeared into the darkness. She took the banknote from the purse and tore it into tiny shreds that she threw into the basin. She removed the plug and watched the scraps of paper vanish in the swirling water. Tomorrow, it would all be gone. Tomorrow, she would wake up and have forgotten everything.

2

It was early evening and the sports bar on Vester Voldgade was packed. The big venue resounded to the sounds of 80s hits and the yells of patrons watching the Champions League matchup on the big screen. At the far end of the bar, there were two rows of pool tables. They were all fully occupied, and there was some heavy drinking taking place around them as players awaited their turn.

Cecilie Mars was standing by the table at the very back, taking aim with her cue. She was slight, not especially tall, and she had to stand on tiptoe to reach across the table. She swept her fringe out of her eyes. The three men around the table watched her silently, each clutching a beer glass. Cecilie struck the white hard. With a clunk it hit the purple, which in turn rolled in a straight line towards the most distant hole in the corner. The collision simultaneously dispatched the white sideways, causing it to clip the black. "No, no, no," Cecilie said as she watched the black's trajectory towards the middle hole. "Shit!" she exclaimed when it was swallowed by the pocket.

"Guppy, looks like the next round is on you, too." Lasse, who was three heads taller than she was and far more powerfully built, let out a booming laugh. He pulled her into an embrace which made her disappear into his striped shirt. Cecilie affectionately stuck her elbow in his side and liberated herself.

"Benny, Henrik. You on the Hoegaardens like Lasse?" She pointed to her two colleagues' glasses with the cue. Both nodded, and Benny raised his glass to her from the far side of the table before draining it.

She set down the cue on the table and headed for the bar at the far end of the venue. En route, she spotted Andreas Bostad sitting at the corner of the bar together with two middle-aged men. The trio were the only people in the whole sports bar wearing suits, and she guessed they all worked for the Prosecution Service.

"Good evening, Mr. Special Prosecutor," she said with a smile, stopping beside Andreas.

Andreas returned her smile and ran his hand through his curly blond hair. Then he placed his hand on her shoulder and she felt the warmth of his palm through the thin fabric of her T-shirt. "Good to see you. Everything alright?" he said.

Cecilie averted her gaze. It already felt as if she had been looking at him for too long. There was very little resemblance between Andreas and a typical prosecutor, usually about as sexy as a tin of liver pâté. Instead, he was reminiscent of the hero in a John Grisham movie, in a somewhat Matthew McConaughey-esque fashion.

"This is my colleague, Jesper Lund," he said, gesturing at the middle-aged man standing closest to him. "And that's Steen Holz behind him."

"Might I offer the young lady a drink?" Jesper Lund asked in a dialect that revealed he came from north of Copenhagen. He smiled suggestively, his eyes cloudy with booze.

"Another time perhaps. It is definitely my round." She caught the barman's attention. "Four Hoegaardens for me, and three shots of whiskey for the lawyers."

"It just so happens that I'm a psychologist, but since you're buying . . ." Steen Holz quipped, grinning.

"Steen is our expert witness. Not that it helped us much today," Andreas said.

A roar erupted from the patrons around them, leaving them in no doubt that a goal had just been scored. Cecilie stood as squarely as possible to avoid being shoved to the floor by the men nearest to her, who had begun to jump up and down in jubilation. At that moment, the barman returned with her order. She slid the three shots of Jack Daniel's towards Andreas, who distributed them.

"What are we celebrating?" Steen Holz asked.

"Does there need to be a reason?"

"In my experience, most people have a reason."

She nodded appreciatively at him. "Well then. Here's to us all being alive, and it being a Tuesday." She grabbed the four beer glasses and turned around. "Have a good night."

When she returned to the others with the beer, Lasse raised his glass. "Cheers to my partner, who is one hell of a talented investigator but the world's worst pool player."

"Hear, hear!"

"And let's not forget congratulations on the promotion, Guppy. You, of all people, deserve it."

Benny and Henrik chorused their agreement and she was actually touched. "Right, let's get to it. I'm going to have my revenge on the winner." While Benny set the balls, Cecilie turned back towards the bar. Andreas was sitting sideways, staring towards her. He raised his glass and she did likewise in return.

Benny and Henrik began their game, and Cecilie sat down to watch.

"I think I'm going to get off home soon," said Lasse. "What about you? Fancy a lift?"

She shook her head. "Can't leave until I've beaten Benny."

"Then it'll be a long night."

She smiled and sipped her beer.

"I meant what I said before," Lasse added. "Bloody well done, Guppy. Papa's proud of you."

She couldn't help but guffaw. Lasse was a couple of years her junior, and despite his abundant beard, he still resembled the thing he was: a happy lad hailing from Aarhus. "Well, thank you, Papa."

"I hope we can remain partners. Hopefully, you won't skedaddle too soon."

"Nothing's changed, except a little more paperwork for me."

He stared into the middle distance. "You'll go far, Guppy. Right to the top. You'll be in the commissioner's office one day. Just wait and see."

"I may have been on the force for ten years, but I've yet to see that office from the inside. Anyway, homicide suits me fine."

They clinked glasses again. Twenty minutes later, he departed and she played Benny, followed by two games against Henrik and then another against Benny. She lost them all. Eventually, the two of them had had their fill of free beer and thanked her for going several rounds with them. Not long after that, they said their farewells and staggered out of the door.

Cecilie returned her cue and looked around the sports bar. The football match had ended long ago and the patrons were beginning to thin out. Only the most tenacious of them remained at the bar. Andreas had apparently split from his own party and was checking his phone. Cecilie slung her jacket over her shoulder and sauntered over to him.

"What did you tell your entourage?" she said with a smile.

Andreas quickly returned his phone to his jacket pocket. "That I needed to watch the match until full-time."

"Who was playing?"

"No idea. What about you?"

"I had to play an extraordinary amount of pool until they'd had enough."

"Do you even know the rules?"

"I know that you aren't meant to pot the black until last."

"Same place?" he said, looking at her searchingly.

Cecilie, naked, straddled Andreas, and pressed herself down onto his cock. Slowly, she moved up and down, fully in control of her tempo. She could feel him sliding in and out of her. She could feel him filling her and how he was trying to push further in. She dug her nails into his chest, increasing the tempo. She heard him groaning loudly underneath her. His grip on her rump tightened, and together they found their rhythm. It felt intoxicating. It was as if she were floating slightly above them while looking down. She saw them fucking in the shabby hotel room in the yellowish hue of the street lights as the roar of the traffic forced its way through the open window. It felt dirty and raunchy and it was good.

Their movements grew faster, and his grip got even tighter. Finally, he came inside her and she heard him give a long sigh. She wished she could have lost herself forever, but she could feel her body drawing her back. A little later, sprawled on his chest, she noticed that his heart was racing. He smelled pleasantly of sweat, perfume, and her sex all over his face. He held her close, and for a moment she almost relaxed in his embrace.

"Damn . . . Cecilie . . . Damn it," he mumbled.

At that moment, she got out of bed. He watched her in surprise. "Are you okay?"

"Yep." She found her panties on the floor and put them back on. Then she retrieved her jeans.

"Maybe we should find another place next time?" Andreas asked.

"Why?" she said, pulling her jeans up to her waist. She went over to the window and looked down at Istedgade below. A group of homeless men were standing by the hostel doorway on the opposite side of the street. They were on the brink of a fist fight.

"I was thinking maybe a better hotel?"

"This one fits the bill just fine."

He let out a hollow laugh. "You're a cynic, Cecilie."

"No more than you are. It's just that I don't pack as much in as you."

"Then why don't we see each other at yours instead?"

She turned around to see whether he meant it. Judging by his expression, he did. She pulled her T-shirt over her head. "Or we could screw at your house?"

He looked away. "I don't think that would be well received. Even if the separation *has* been finalised."

She bit her lip. She hadn't meant to be catty. Andreas's domestic arrangements were irrelevant to her.

He got out of bed and began to gather his clothes from the floor. "Why exactly do they call you Guppy?"

"It's only Lasse who does, and a few friends."

"But why?"

"It goes back to my time at Police School. Cecilie got shortened to Sille, and then it was Silver Darling, like a herring, and then Lasse made it Guppy. A little fish. Clever, isn't it?"

Andreas buttoned up his shirt. "So as of today I'm supposed to call you *Inspector* Guppy?"

"I told you. It's just something my friends call me. Have the two us turned into friends, Andreas?" She wriggled into her leather jacket and smiled at him.

Andreas's perfect smile faded a little.

3

A couple of days later, Cecilie walked along the long narrow corridor leading to where the Division for Crimes Against Persons and the Homicide Unit detectives were based. She cast a sidelong glance out of the tall windows, contemplating the quiet waters of the Teglholm Canal.

"Guppy!" Lasse called out, rushing towards her from the far end of the corridor.

"Where's the fire?"

"I've been . . . trying to . . . call you," he said breathlessly.

"I've been at the shooting range all morning," she replied without stopping. "It's in my calendar, too."

"The shooting range?" he said, following her.

"Yes, the annual test."

"Did you pass?"

"Of course. I bagged twenty-eight points."

He raised his eyebrows. "If I recall correctly, the minimum for a pass is twenty-seven. It seems we should have been getting you some target practice."

"What is it that's so urgent?" she asked, stopping outside the door to the Division.

"Do you remember that rape case from January? The bodybuilder guy with the shiny knife and the hoodie?"

She nodded. "The one we have under suspicion for a string of other cases?"

"One and the same. We've just received another report. This time in Rødkilde Park."

"Northwest of the city centre?"

"Yes. The victim is a young girl who was drunk."

"Same modus operandi?"

"Down to the letter. He threatened her with a knife, carried out the rape in a deserted spot, and then afterwards he stole her ID."

"So he knows where she lives," Cecilie said, nodding. "Did this happen last night?"

"No, nine days ago," he replied.

"Shit." She bit her lip. "So once again we won't be able to secure any DNA?"

"Not a fucking chance."

"Thanks to him terrifying them so much. So what do we have?"

"A scared girl in room three with her mother and an advocate," he said, pointing back towards the room.

Cecilie sighed heavily. "Has the girl been able to give anything resembling a decent description?"

"Yes. It matches the others. Male, Danish, thirty-five plus, muscley, stank of booze."

"Was he wearing a hoodie and a scarf across his mouth like before?"

Lasse screwed his eyes shut. "Hoodie, yes. Scarf, no."

She perked up. "Has she identified him?"

"Not yet. We're about to take a look at some pictures. I was just on my way to fetch a code for the system."

"Great," she said, giving him a playful punch in the chest. "So the arsehole got cocky."

"And stupid."

"That's just how I like my criminals. Who's the victim?"

"Young girl from Bellahøj. Just eighteen years old."

"My neighbourhood?"

"Yes. Her name is Fie Simone Simonsen."

Cecilie stopped smiling and took the notepad from him.

She inspected his scribbles, interpreting them. "Fuck."

"You know her?"

"In a manner of speaking. From my social outreach work. She's in my self-defence group."

"I'm fine handling this by myself."

She shook her head and returned the notepad to him.

"Come on," she said, continuing down the corridor towards the interview room.

Although it was just a couple of weeks since Cecilie had last seen Fie at training, she barely recognised the girl. Then, Fie had been smiling and full of energy; now she was sitting there with a dead gaze, staring at the table. Her lower lip was trembling, and it looked as if she was about to burst into tears. Sitting to Fie's right was her mother, Tina, who was around forty and robustly built, her lips painted dark red. Cecilie remembered her well from the neighbourhood at home. On Fie's other side was Mona Krog, a legal advocate. Cecilie had met her previously on other similar cases. Krog was okay, but she could be a little manic, and Cecilie suspected she had a drink problem. She greeted them all and took a seat.

"Fie, I need you to tell me in your own words what happened that night. Please take your time."

Before Fie could manage to say a word, Mona Krog leaned across the table. "Fie's already given a statement several times, including her first one at Bellahøj Police Station. As it happens, I intend to lodge a complaint on Fie's behalf in relation to the duty officer's conduct, which was beyond contempt."

Cecilie calmly raised her hand. "I think that is a very good idea, especially if you believe there are grounds to do so. But right now, it's important for me to hear Fie's account. Then we can concentrate on the investigation. Do you think you're up to that, Fie?"

It took a long time for Fie to react. Then she looked up briefly at Cecilie before casting her gaze back down as she described the night she had been raped in an almost inaudible voice: There had been a party at high school, and afterwards she and five others from her class had gone to a local pub called Klovnens Bodega. They'd had beers and played rounds of Mia. This was where he'd approached them.

"The guy who attacked you?"

Fie nodded and explained that while he was much older than them, he'd flirted with both her and two of the other girls there. He'd also bought them a round.

"Then what happened?"

Fie said that they had left just before closing time at around one o'clock. Since she was the only one of them who lived in Bellahøj, she had set off home on her own. On the way she had encountered him again. Near Rødkilde Park. He'd hit on her right away.

"How?"

"Compliments. He asked if I had a boyfriend. Whether I liked older guys. He tried to . . . hug me."

"What did you do then?"

"Pushed him away. Walked more quickly."

"And what happened in Rødkilde Park?"

Fie didn't reply.

"Take all the time you need; it's absolutely okay."

"He got a stranglehold on me. Called me all sorts of names and dragged me into the bushes. He held that knife up to me and said that he was going to . . . going to . . . going to stick it up me if I didn't do as I was told." She buried her face in her hands and began to sob.

Tina put an arm around her daughter and stroked her hair. "That fucking swine raped her, then he took her health insurance card so that he knows our address. You *have* to catch him. Do you understand?"

Cecilie nodded. "Fie, when you're feeling a bit better, I've got some pictures I'd like you to take a look at. It's fine if you don't recognise him. Actually, it's just as important for us to rule suspects out so that we don't waste time investigating the wrong people. Do you think you can help me with that?"

A quarter of an hour later, they gathered around Cecilie's desk, which was towards the back of the open-plan office that housed the Homicide Unit. She turned on her computer and logged in to their image index.

As part of the investigation into the previous attacks, a number of suspects—convicted sex offenders—had already been indexed. This meant
that Cecilie was able to show Fie a limited and precise search.

After they had gone through about twenty profiles, Fie suddenly put
her hand to her mouth. Tears began to trickle down her cheeks.

"Is that him?" Cecilie asked.

Staring at them from the screen was a man with dead, reptilian eyes.

"It's . . . it's . . . it's him," Fie said.

"And you're sure about that?"

"I'll never forget that tattoo."

Cecilie took in the dragon with its jaws wide open, twisting its way up
the man's neck. Her eyes narrowed and she breathed through her nose
in small, controlled inhalations. Then she half-turned towards Lasse.
"Right, time for us to bring him in."

4

Cecilie pulled the dark blue Golf back into the inside lane of Borups Allé. The rain was coming down hard and the wipers were struggling to keep the windscreen clear of water. Following behind her was the Tactical Unit's personnel carrier, which was in turn followed by one of the dog team vans. Lasse had suggested that the two of them bring him in themselves, but she was taking no chances. Neither in relation to the suspected rapist nor in relation to the tense neighbourhood they were heading towards.

"Ulrik Østergård, thirty-six years old," Lasse said, leafing through the printout he'd brought with him. "He's got several convictions for violence starting back in 2002. In 2013, his career peaked when he was convicted of rape and sent down for fourteen months. The judge ordered treatment and sent him to Herstedvester Prison."

"What about the last few years?" Cecilie asked, pulling onto Lundtoftegade.

"Most recently, he did six months inside for assaulting his live-in partner. This time in a proper prison. He got out in August last year."

"So, in terms of the timeline, Ulrik could easily be our rapist in all four cases where we've got him under suspicion?"

"Oh yes," Lasse replied. "Let's just hope that the address in the population register is current."

Cecilie peered up at the dreary high-rise flats on which satellite dishes were affixed to each and every balcony like overripe pimples.

"Pull in here," Lasse said, pointing to a large car park between two buildings. She parked the car and got out. The dog handlers and the six members of the Tactical Unit stayed put. A couple of young lads on scooters had already spotted the police cars and were watching them from a distance. Cecilie tapped on the side window of the personnel carrier and the officer lowered it. "Be ready to grab the target if he comes rushing out of the building." She pointed towards the doorway to the nearest stairwell. "And make sure you keep an eye on our young toughs over there."

"Roger that," the officer replied, directing his gaze towards the growing group of lads.

A couple of minutes later, Cecilie and Lasse were in the cramped lift, which stank of urine. "Nice spot to take a slash," Lasse muttered.

When they reached the eighth floor, they got out and made their way to the first door on the external gallery. It said Østergård on the front. Beneath this was a faded sticker which cryptically read Vinnie Larson. Cecilie knocked so hard that it resounded around the open-sided gallery. A moment later, the door was opened by a woman in her late forties wearing a pink tracksuit. Her grey hair bristled in all directions, as if she'd just got up.

Cecilie noticed the blood leaking from the woman's right eye. "Are you Vinnie?" she asked over the racket of the television, which was on at full blast inside the flat.

"Might be," said the woman, taking a drag on her cigarette. "Who's asking?"

Cecilie and Lasse introduced themselves, showing their IDs. "Is Ulrik at home?" Cecilie asked.

"What if he is?" Vinnie exhaled a cloud of smoke at them.

"Well, we'd like to have a chat with him." Cecilie tried to see past her into the hallway, but Vinnie was blocking her view.

"Well, he's not home. Was there anything else you wanted?"

"Any idea where he might be?"

"Nope. None at all. No."

Cecilie leaned forward and took a closer look at Vinnie's extravasation. "What happened, Vinnie?"

Vinnie looked away. "Can't fuckin' remember. Slipped in the bathroom or summit. Was hammered." She smiled nervously.

"It's not anything you'd maybe like to talk about? Maybe even report?"

Vinnie put her hands to her side. "I told you, I slipped. What's to report?"

"Fair enough. You still sure you don't know where Ulrik is? Gone to the shops? At a friend's? At work?"

Vinnie spluttered with laughter. "I can't remember the last time he had a job." She took a drag from the cigarette. "Fuck's sake, it's not like it's a state secret. He's at Klovnens. Just like he always is. Probably with that slut Lonnie. Please may I be left in peace to watch my show now?"

"Of course. Would you like my direct line in case . . ."

Vinnie slammed the door shut.

Lasse shook his head and headed for the lift. "So Ulrik rapes a girl that he meets at his regular haunt. How bloody stupid can you get?"

Klovnens Bodega was on the corner of Rantzausgade and Jagtvej. Despite the sign on the gable end depicting a jolly clown, the place looked dismal in the pouring rain. Cecilie headed inside, closely followed by Lasse and two officers from the Tactical Unit. The dog handlers stayed in their van and judging by the relaxed vibe inside the bar there would be no need for them on this occasion. Cecilie looked around without spotting Ulrik. She approached the bar and introduced herself to the barman, who was obese, elderly, and wearing red braces. At the sight of her police ID, he instinctively crossed his arms over his chest.

"We're looking to talk to this guy," said Cecilie, flashing a photo of Ulrik on her phone.

The barman hesitated, but then he glanced towards the back of the pub. Cecilie led the officers through the bar into the games room, where she spotted Ulrik right away. He was standing by one of the pinball machines together with a man of the same age and a woman in a denim skirt. Ulrik was pressed up closely against the woman as she played the machine. "Ulle, you little terror . . . I can't concentrate!" she said.

The two men laughed.

"Ulrik Østergård?" said Cecilie.

Ulrik gave her a visual once-over. "Do we know each other, sweetheart?"

"Cecilie Mars, Copenhagen Police. We'd like a chat with you."

He tilted his head to one side. "And I'd like a blowjob, but that's life."

Both the woman and Ulrik's friend laughed.

"Wrong answer." Cecilie glanced at her watch. "The time's 13:22 and you're under arrest." She retrieved the handcuffs from her belt and took a step towards him.

Ulrik clenched his fist and raised his arm. But before he could do anything else, Lasse stepped between them. He spun Ulrik around, laying him flat on the floor. The two officers from the Tactical Unit kept the other man and woman at a distance from the scene. Cecilie slapped the cuffs around Ulrik's wrists. "I had him," she snapped at Lasse.

"Of course," he replied, heaving Ulrik off the floor.

"This is fucking police violence. I'll sue you. Do you hear me? You vile Nazi scum!"

"Sure, we hear you: police violence, Nazi scum. Now let's be on our way, pal," Lasse said, nudging him without being gentle.

Ulrik bellowed all the way through the bar and into the car, where Lasse put him in the back seat.

Outside the car, Cecilie stared through the side window at the dragon on Ulrik's neck. She felt her stomach constrict.

"We've got him," Lasse said with a smile as he patted the roof of the car.

5

It was 22:30 and the air in the small interview room was hot and stuffy. Across from Cecilie and Lasse were Ulrik and his lawyer, Phillip Vang, who wore a bright pink open-necked shirt and a pricey Rolex on his wrist.

Cecilie had spent the best part of four hours asking Ulrik to repeat how he and Fie had met, and what had happened after that. She had endeavoured to be polite, but it was apparent that Ulrik didn't care for being questioned by a woman. When she yet again asked him to say when he had arrived at Klovnens Bodega, Phillip Vang interjected: "I think we've *got* an answer to that question by now."

"I'm just trying to form an overview of Ulrik's movements," Cecilie said, gesturing vaguely.

Phillip Vang smiled coolly. He was nicknamed "the Terrier," a name that less civil tongues suggested he had given himself. "My client has now been answering your repeated questions for several hours. He has described how he met a group of young people at Klovnens Bodega, and how he bought them a round of drinks because he thought they were funny. He's also outlined that there was subsequent flirtation between him and Fie Simone Simonsen. He also acknowledges having sex with her, but naturally this was with her consent."

"If so, why was it necessary to threaten her into sex with a knife?" Cecilie looked at Ulrik, who gritted his teeth.

"It's her word against his," Phillip Vang interjected. "Have you actually found a knife?"

Cecilie didn't respond to the question, and Vang smiled. He had good grounds, too. They had found neither the knife nor Fie's health card at Ulrik and Vinnie's flat.

Phillip Vang held out his hands. "Ulrik even gave her cash for a taxi to make sure she'd get home safely. I do hope she included that part in her statement?" Cecilie still didn't answer and Phillip Vang smiled again. "Thought as much." He leaned across the table. "There's no case here. The only reason my client is here is because a young woman regretted a one-night stand, and the police are judging Ulrik based on his past. Let's shut this whole thing down right now and we can all go home."

Cecilie leaned back in her chair. "Sorry, but that's not going to happen. Tomorrow, your client will appear in court for a preliminary hearing, and we'll be making an application for remand."

Phillip Vang made a small grunt. "Let me be up front with you: You're wasting your time."

"As is your right to say—but as I said, that's what's going to happen." She continued to meet the lawyer's gaze until he looked away.

"Very well. I suppose I'll see you all in the morning," Phillip Vang said, extending his arms. "I hope you brought your toothbrush, Ulrik."

Ulrik looked at him, dumbfounded. "Er . . . wot? Am I being banged up or something?"

"Yes, you'll be spending a night in the cells. But tomorrow you'll be a free man again. Promise."

"Fuck—all because of what that whore says?"

Phillip Vang hushed him and stood up. "I said you'll be back home tomorrow. Consider this a mini break away from the wife."

After the officers had escorted Ulrik to the cell and Phillip Vang had departed, Cecilie and Lasse lingered in the corridor outside the interview room. He smiled at her. "We've got the right man. And not just in Fie's case."

"I just hope that we've got enough to hold him on," said Cecilie.

Lasse shrugged. "With his rap sheet and Fie's statement, this should be a stroll in the park. Why didn't you ask about the other cases?"

"We're not giving that gift to the Terrier," Cecilie replied. "For the time being, we want Ulrik remanded for Fie's rape alone. Once that's sorted, we'll dig into the rest of it."

"How long do you think we'll be able to hold him?"

"We'll have to ask Andreas about that first thing in the morning. Right now, I'll take anything the judge gives us."

They parted ways in the corridor. Lasse went home, while Cecilie made for the office. She was on the brink of collapsing with exhaustion, but there was still a lot of groundwork to do ahead of the preliminary hearing in the morning.

6

The usher opened the doors to courtroom four at Copenhagen City Court a little after 11 o'clock the next morning. The preliminary hearing had just concluded. The few members of the public who had been in the gallery—comprising largely of law students and pensioners—trudged out of the room. Shortly after them came Phillip Vang, clutching his briefcase in one hand, his mobile pressed to his ear in the other. Following him was Ulrik, struggling energetically to put his leather jacket on. "You're the man! A true king of men! You reckon there's any chance we can apply for compensation?"

"Calm down. You're still being charged. If I were you, I'd maintain a low profile. But give me a call if they proceed with the case. See you around, Ulrik." Phillip Vang was already en route to his next hearing down the corridor.

Cecilie emerged from the courtroom together with Lasse. "Tell me that didn't just happen."

"Sorry, Guppy. It did. They let the bleeder go." They both watched Ulrik's receding back as it disappeared through the large main entrance. "We'll get him."

"Hopefully before he rapes anyone else." She was trembling with rage. "This investigation takes top priority. I don't give a fuck what else Karstensen tries to throw at us. And I want Henrik and Benny on the team, too."

"Of course. I'll brief them."

"Fuck it. I've half a mind to put twenty-four/seven surveillance on him."

"We won't get that through—not after this."

"And don't I damn well know it?" She looked down at the long colonnade, thinking. "We need to bring Ulrik back in as soon as possible. I want a detailed investigation of the crime scene at Rødkilde Park. We need to prepare a list of his possible hiding places: basements, bike sheds, allotments, his car. Anything that we'll be given permission to search when there is a justified suspicion."

"What are we looking for?"

"The girls' health cards."

Lasse looked at her in surprise. "You think he kept them?"

"I'm sure of it."

"But none of the victims have subsequently been contacted. Despite reporting what happened to the police."

"Which might indicate that he actually takes their health cards as trophies."

At that moment, Andreas appeared in the corridor. He loosened his tie and came over to them.

Cecilie gave him a look. "We could have done with a remand on this one."

"And I could have done with a better prepared case."

Cecilie sighed heavily. "That's what we had, and I didn't hear any protests from you."

"Which was my fault," he said irritably. "By the way, next time I'd appreciate it if you told me that you know the victim, so that I don't have to hear it from the opposing side in open court."

She shook her head. "It's all just a load of shit from the Terrier. Fie's trained a few times as part of a group that I teach. Just like a whole bunch of other young girls in the neighbourhood."

"Nevertheless, the Terrier managed to convince the judge that it might have affected your judgment in relation to Ulrik's arrest."

She lowered her voice. "Yes, because Judge Mogensen is a stupid, sexist pig."

"Easy now," said Andreas, a smile playing on his lips.

"Don't you think I know all the stories about how he treats the female employees around here?"

"Which don't necessarily have anything to do with his professionalism."

"No?" she said, looking Andreas in the eyes.

Andreas turned to Lasse. "Anyway, the way things stand, you need to find more on Ulrik Østergård. Simple as that."

At that moment, Andreas waved to Steen Holz, who came over to them. The middle-aged psychologist briefly greeted Lasse and Cecilie. He wore a white linen lounge suit, which went well with his suntanned complexion.

"Steen and I have the pleasure of the Terrier again in less than four minutes' time."

"So we have to see whether we can let justice be done," said Steen, smiling kindly.

"Speak later," said Andreas as he and Steen Holz left them.

Lasse watched Andreas go. He was now some way down the corridor. "He's got one hell of an arse, that Andreas has. But he's a bit too leggy for my taste. What do you say?"

"Don't mix work and pleasure," she said, looking away. "Anyway, aren't you married?"

"*Happily married*, thank you very much. To the world's nicest man. But there's no harm window shopping."

"Come on," she said.

When Cecilie and Lasse returned to the Division, she looked up Fie's number. It wasn't that she felt like calling, but she still felt a certain obligation to notify her of the poor outcome at the preliminary hearing.

It was Tina who answered her daughter's phone, and Cecilie asked to speak to Fie.

"She's not doing well. Not at all," Tina said.

Cecilie told her the bad news, but also added that they would do everything they could to get Ulrik Østergård remanded as soon as possible.

"So he's . . . at large?"

"Yes. But hopefully not for long."

Tina told Cecilie in unequivocal terms what she thought of the Danish justice system, and Cecilie let her vent.

"As I said, I'll do everything in my power."

Tina began to cry. "She's just not the same anymore. Doesn't eat. Doesn't sleep. Doesn't talk. That bastard stole her life. Stole her smile. Do you get what I'm saying? I want her smile back again. Do you get it?!"

Cecilie got it. She promised to get back in touch as soon as she had any news.

That evening, Cecilie stood on her terrace gazing at the city. The flat was on the top floor of one of the run-down high-rises in Bellahøj. It had been an award-winning building in the 1950s, but it was now threatened with demolition, while the surrounding neighbourhood held the distinction of being just two steps from the national ghetto list. But there was nothing wrong with the view from up here.

Her roof terrace afforded 180-degree views of Copenhagen and its environs. From the Svanemølle Power Station in the north, the towers of the cityscape directly ahead of her, to Avedøre Power Station in the south-east. At her feet lay the Nordvest district with its depressing blocks of flats and the Bispeengbuen motorway, its six lanes winding through the neighbourhood like a concrete snake. She leaned against the narrow railing and looked down at Rødkilde Park some six hundred metres ahead of her. The dogs had spent all afternoon looking for a scent without any joy. The likelihood that the weapon or any other traces of the rape would turn up was minimal. But as things stood, they couldn't afford to let even the slightest of chances slip through their grasp. Cecilie felt cold, so she went back inside.

The roof terrace was very much the biggest asset of her home. The rest of the worn-out two-bed flat felt abandoned. The sparse furnishings and the lack of any personal touches testified to the fact that she wasn't one for home decor and she was rarely at home.

She went into the kitchen and made a cup of Nescafé. The neighbours in the flat next door were quarrelling loudly. It wasn't the first time and it was unlikely to be the last. She took her mug with her and checked that the three bolts on her front door were all secured before she returned to the living room. She was tempted to call Lasse and go over the case yet again, but she knew that his working day ended the very moment he left the Division.

She lay down on the sofa with the case files within reach. She wanted to go over the three previously reported rapes and compare them with Fie's. She considered whether she ought to take new witness statements from the other victims. While the perpetrator in all three cases had covered his face with a scarf, now that Ulrik was a suspect they might still be able to tie something to him. Perhaps the other girls had caught a glimpse of the dragon tattoo, a piece of jewellery, or something else that might surface in their memory now. There had to be something for her to find. Something that could stop him. Something that prevented him from striking again.

She sat there working until her eyes became heavy and the case files slipped from her grip. She disappeared into a dream that she hadn't had in a long time. It took place in a backyard, under a lean-to that the rain was drumming against very hard. The smell of refuse wafted from the dumpsters around her. She could make out the metallic taste of anxiety. The blow to her stomach had made her gasp for air. The blow that now struck her jaw paralysed her. She felt her legs give way. She sensed the pain in her scalp as he dragged her by her hair through the shed. He positioned her in front of him. He bent down and thrust his tongue into her mouth. First the tongue, then . . . In the dream, it all came back. The smell of urine emanating from him, mixing with the stench of the dumpsters. His limpness. The many slaps to her face that he delivered, slowly making him hard and ready. "No!!" she cried out, waking up. *For fuck's sake. Not again.*

Cecilie got up quickly in an attempt to rid herself of the dream. She grabbed her phone from the table and checked the time—it was half past midnight. The only cure for her nightmares that she knew of was to head out. In the old days, she'd roved around Copenhagen by night. First by bicycle, later by car. Her very own patrol. Not so much of the city as of her own mind. It was an approach that until now had prevented her from doing serious harm to herself.

7

Cecilie crossed the dark car park between the looming high-rises. The street was deserted, and not even the ever-present local yobs were anywhere to be seen. She unlocked her old Fiat Panda. The car was a rusty old banger whose only plus point was that no one could be bothered to steal it. Once she had got the engine running, she drove down the street between the blocks of flats. She passed the building that Fie lived in and pulled over. Through the window, she could see that the lights were still on up in her flat. She sat there for a while before trundling on towards the junction with the main road, Frederikssundsvej. She made for the crossroads at Borups Allé and then turned towards the city centre and the Bispeengbuen motorway, stopping for a red light. Beyond the raised arches supporting the motorway lay the neighbourhood where Ulrik lived. Cecilie wondered whether he had told Vinnie about his arrest, but she doubted it. The light changed to green and she continued parallel to Bispeengbuen before passing underneath it to the other side, heading for the next set of lights. Instead of continuing on towards to the city centre, she turned down onto Lundtoftegade. When she reached the series of blocks of flats on the left-hand side, she stopped in the car park outside Ulrik's door. She looked up towards the flat—the lights were on. Was he in there boozing it up with Vinnie? Or was he knocking her about because she'd had the audacity to ask where he'd been the night before?

Cecilie directed her gaze at the parked cars. She remembered that Ulrik owned a BMW, but she couldn't recall the registration. A stupid plan began to take shape in her head: find the car. See whether it was unlocked. Search for the knife. Search for the health insurance cards. Most definitely a stupid plan. But before she knew it, she'd found the registration number in her notes on her phone and she was getting out of the Fiat to search for the car. Five minutes later, she'd checked every row of vehicles without any joy.

On her way back to the Panda, it occurred to her that Ulrik might have driven to the Klovnens Bodega. She checked her watch—it was ten past one—and then set a course for Rantzausgade.

A few minutes later, outside the pub, she looked for the BMW among the nearby parked cars. It was nowhere to be seen, and she began to regret her enterprise. Now that the discomfort from the dream had dissipated, it was high time she went home and got some sleep.

At that very moment, the door of the Klovnens Bodega opened and Ulrik appeared on the steps. He swayed uncertainly, taking a drag from his cigarette before throwing it away. Then he meandered across the street and continued towards a black BMW at the far end of a row of vehicles. He unlocked the car with some difficulty, while Cecilie weighed up whether or not to detain him. It would put Ulrik in custody while providing her with an opportunity to search his car. The only problem was that if she didn't find anything, it might backfire. She was certain that the Terrier would be able to turn the arrest into a case of baseless police surveillance and harassment. That would hardly assist the Prosecution Service's case in court.

Ulrik pulled away from the kerb and drove down Rantzausgade. Cecilie followed. Shortly after, they reached the residential area in which he lived, but instead of pulling in, Ulrik continued towards Bellahøj. All of a sudden, she was concerned that he might be on the way to Fie's flat to harass her. Maybe he was going to threaten her to make her keep her mouth shut? When he pulled onto Frederikssundsvej, she was right behind him. If he entered the neighbourhood, she would stop him before he reached Fie's building. But when they got to the crossroads a minute later, Ulrik carried on past the high-rises and along Frederikssundsvej. Only on the outskirts of Husum did he pull off onto Åkandevej.

Cecilie followed him at a distance through Utterslev Mose, its large lakes and islets shrouded in darkness to their right. After they had gone a couple of kilometres down this road, the BMW swerved onto the other side of the road before quickly straightening up again. The rapid correction caused the back end to slide, and the red taillights meandered across her field of vision in the darkness. The car disappeared off the road on a direct course for the boggy lake before it hit a tree head-on, coming to a stop in some large bushes.

Cecilie approached the scene of the accident and pulled over to the verge. She retrieved her torch and got out of the car. Ahead of her, the grass had been carved up by two dark tyre tracks that led her towards the crashed BMW. The front of the car had crumpled around a tree, and a pillar of steam was rising from the smashed radiator. She walked over to the passenger side and looked in through the open door, across the passenger compartment. Ulrik was trapped behind the wheel, and he was bleeding profusely from a wound to his forehead. He was gasping awkwardly for breath, and his lungs were squeaking. She shone her torch inside the car and saw that the open glove box was empty. She played the beam of light across the floor, which was covered in litter and a couple of empty beer bottles.

"Help me, you cow . . ." Ulrik said, slurring his words. "Pull your fucking finger out . . . Vinnie."

Cecilie looked at Ulrik, who looked back at her in a daze. The blood from the wound had dyed the whole of one side of his face a shade of scarlet. "You're . . . you're not Vinnie." He shook his head. "But . . . know you . . . still . . . don't I?"

Cecilie turned the torch on the back seat and saw that it was empty.

"I know you . . . I do. Wait until I get out." Ulrik coughed a bloody mist onto the inside of the windscreen. He tried to move but was stuck helplessly behind the wheel.

Cecilie walked around the car and stopped at the rear. She pulled her sleeve down over her hand and opened the boot. Apart from a spare tyre and a few shattered beer bottles, the boot was empty. She closed it again.

"You're that bitch-cop . . . fucking dyke. Get me out of here," Ulrik shouted.

She went to the open door on the driver's side. One of Ulrik's legs was hanging out. He had lost his trainer, which was lying in the grass, and his white sock was soaked with blood. Cecilie shone her torch in his face. "Are you armed? Do you have anything sharp that might injure me?"

"Yes . . . my cock."

She leaned in and searched his pockets. She found his wallet in the inside pocket of his windbreaker. Apart from a couple of two hundred kroner notes, there was a debit card, a health insurance card, and a fuel card. All issued in his name. She chucked the wallet and its contents back into his lap.

"You thought you were . . . lucky."

She saw the grin on his lips. "What do you mean, Ulrik?"

"The cards . . . You thought . . . you'd found them."

"What cards are you talking about?"

He tried to say something, but all that came out was a gurgle.

He slowly raised his left arm and gestured at her with his bloody finger to come closer. Cecilie leaned in. "The health cards . . . Christina's . . . Helle's . . . Amalie's, and . . . Fiiiiiie's." He laughed quietly.

She felt how dry her mouth was. "Where are they, Ulrik?"

"Oh . . . wouldn't you like to know . . ."

"Very much."

"Makes your . . . cunt tingle?"

"Hardly."

At that moment, his hand shot up and grabbed her by the throat. Using both her hands, she tore at his arm to free herself. She saw that reptilian gaze. Cold and dead. She gasped for breath as he squeezed. He snarled: "I saw it . . . when you were in the pub playing it cool. I saw it in your stupid face . . . in your limp shoulders. You're just someone's bitch!"

"Let go of me!" She tried to pull free of him, but her feet slipped on the wet grass and she fell towards him.

"You were already broken . . . Was Daddy your first?" The carotid artery appeared, bringing the tattooed dragon to life. "Or was it one of the big boys?"

It felt as if she was being sent back to the lean-to. Hands around her neck. Sweat and saliva dripping on to her face. Him inside, throbbing.

She couldn't breathe. Her body was paralysed with terror. She wanted to go home. Home. Cecilie raised her leg and hammered her knee into his side. Ulrik let go, and she toppled backwards into the grass. She stared back towards the car, where he had slumped over the wheel. There was a bloody garland of saliva dripping from his mouth. It was impossible to tell whether he was still alive. She quickly crawled away from the car. She could hardly breathe. When she got to her feet, she turned around and ran back to her own car. She started up the Panda and drove off down Åkandevej at top speed. She drove along the dark roads at random, and only when she reached the bridge that crossed Hareskovvejen did she come to a halt. She had to report this. She leaned over the wheel, trying to marshal her thoughts. Fucking hell—what had she done? No matter how much he disgusted her, she couldn't just leave him like that. In fact, she had fled from the scene of an accident. She pulled out her phone but then she thought about the way he had contemptuously named his victims. Knowing full well there was nothing she could do. She thought about the way he had seen straight through her and targeted her greatest fear. She thought about the fact that if he ever recovered, he would just strike again . . . and again. In the end, she put her phone down on the passenger seat. Shortly after that, she turned the car around and set off home towards Bellahøj.

8

The morning rush hour traffic snaked along Åboulevard, and several impatient motorists were honking their horns. Cecilie was behind the wheel of her Panda on the way to the office. She texted Lasse to tell him she'd be late. The brake lights on the cars ahead of her lit up in the traffic jam, reminding her of Ulrik's erratic course towards the fatal tree. She hadn't got much sleep. Thoughts about the accident had kept her awake until daybreak. First thing that morning she had checked the news sites and 24-hour news reports online. But there was no mention of the accident.

Twenty minutes later, she arrived at Teglholm Allé and went in through the main entrance. On her way to the office, she passed the meeting room and saw Lasse through the large window in conversation with Andreas. When Lasse caught sight of her, he waved at her energetically, indicating that she should join them.

"Have you heard?" said Lasse, the second she poked her head around the door.

"Heard what?"

"The karma police have been out and about overnight," Andreas said, smiling.

"I'm drawing a blank," she replied.

"Ulrik Østergård has departed this life," Lasse said. Cecilie stepped into the room and closed the glass door behind her.

"How?"

"He wrapped his beemer around a tree. Happened out at Utterslev Mose last night."

"Any witnesses?"

"No one's come forward. He was found at around five o'clock by a jogger."

"Do we know how the accident happened?"

"Single car. According to the station in Bellahøj, alcohol was involved. But we're waiting for an autopsy."

"Did he die instantly?"

Lasse looked at her in surprise. "No, though he was seriously the worse for wear."

"But what makes them think he didn't?"

"Our colleagues found him with his wallet in his lap, all his credit cards out."

"Maybe a passerby went through his pockets?" Andreas suggested. "Was there any cash in the wallet?"

Lasse nodded. "Yes. That's why they're assuming that Ulrik pulled the wallet out himself. Perhaps he was looking for his phone but was in too much of a state."

Andreas wrinkled his brow in a grimace that indicated he didn't entirely buy that explanation.

"Did they find anything else in the car?" Cecilie interjected, although she knew the answer.

"Afraid we didn't get that lucky," Lasse replied. "No sign of a weapon or the girls' health cards."

"So what are you going to do about the case now?" Andreas asked. Lasse looked at Cecilie, as if searching for an answer.

"I suppose it's over, what with the perpetrator being dead," Cecilie said, sighing heavily. "There's not much else we can do except what we've already set in motion."

"That's good enough for me," Andreas said. "I've got plenty of living perps to deal with."

"Obviously, we'll have to square it with Karstensen."

"I'm sure you'll have no trouble persuading the chief of homicide." Andreas headed to the door and opened it. "Funny how justice sometimes takes its own course. Have a good day."

Lasse and Cecilie went to the Division, heading through the open-plan office. "Maybe we should talk to Vinnie again?" said Lasse.

"Why?"

"Maybe Ulrik's death will get her to reveal something."

"No," Cecilie said, sitting down at her desk. "Vinnie is the last person on earth that Ulrik would have confided in."

A couple of minutes later, Cecilie entered Poul Karstensen's office, which was at the far end of the divisional open-plan office. The office smelled faintly of tobacco. It was an open secret that Karstensen enjoyed a crafty smoke out of the window. She curtly informed him of the development in the case and recommended its closure. Karstensen, who was close to retirement, looked at her wearily. His sharp hunter instincts had ebbed away over the years as the number of grandchildren had increased. He coughed loudly as if attempting to clear his throat.

"Well, it would appear that the good Lord has helped out by liberating the world of yet another sinner. The kind of offer of assistance that investigators should jump at."

"So we can put this one onto the back burner, yes?"

"Yes, yes," he said, clearing his throat again. It sounded as if he had finally dislodged the phlegm. "I'm quite confident you can make that decision."

Late that afternoon, Cecilie returned to Bellahøj. She continued through the neighbourhood, passing the basketball court where the lads hung out, and made her way to Fie's building. A little later, she pressed the buzzer and Tina let her in. Cecilie took the lift up to the seventh floor where Fie's mother was waiting for her on the landing.

"How are things?" Cecilie asked.

"Not good. Not good at all," Tina replied, ushering her inside.

The flat was just as run-down as Cecilie's, but the living room was more cosily decorated. Tina went into Fie's room, and a moment later the two of them appeared in the doorway.

"Hi, Fie," Cecilie said, smiling cautiously.

Fie returned her greeting timidly and sat down on the armrest of the leather sofa.

"I've got something to tell you both."

"What?" Tina asked, looking as if she feared the worst.

"The man that Fie identified, Ulrik Østergård, was involved in a fatal car crash last night."

They both looked at Cecilie in surprise.

"Seriously?" Tina asked. "He's dead now?"

"Yes," Cecilie replied. "It also means that we're closing the case."

Tina wrapped her arms around Fie and drew her close.

"Then the bastard got what he deserved."

Fie quickly wriggled free from her mother's embrace. "So . . . so I don't have to go to court? I don't have to see him again?"

"It all ends here, Fie," Cecilie said.

"That the best news we've had in ages, isn't it, sweetie? Now we can move on."

Fie didn't reply.

"I'm going to put some coffee on." Tina went to the kitchen before Cecilie could decline. At that moment, her phone buzzed in her pocket to notify her of an incoming text message.

"Aren't you going to see what that is?" Fie asked.

"No, it'll keep. Are you back at high school?"

"Not really. Is he really dead?"

"Yes. You don't have to worry about him anymore."

Fie shook her head quietly. "So he's off the hook . . ."

Cecilie scrutinised Fie, who had lost weight and looked hollow-cheeked. "Do you have anyone you can talk to, Fie? I mean, apart from your mother?"

Fie looked down at the floor. "I don't want to talk to anyone about it."

"Sometimes it can help."

Fie snorted. "You think I don't know what they all think about me?"

"No. What is it you think they think?"

"That it was all my own fault. That I should have done something. That I'm a fucking loser . . ."

"Fie, no one thinks that."

"You don't have any idea what it's like. It's the same with the lads down there," she said, nodding towards the window. "They call me a whore."

"They're morons." Cecilie smiled at her. "Let me know if there's anything I can do."

"Can't you just go? Leave us alone?"

"Yes, of course, but . . ."

"Please?"

"Of course. You've got my number. Call me. Any time. Even if you just want to talk."

Cecilie popped her head into the kitchen to tell Tina she had to go. Tina offered her a mug, but then thanked her.

Once Cecilie was back in her own flat, she went out onto the terrace. The city was cloaked in a stale yellowish smog that only permitted a hint of the many towers and spires on the horizon. Even though it was chilly, it was as if she could feel the approach of spring. She pulled out her phone and saw that she had received an anonymous message with a video file attachment. She clicked on the file, which proved to be a grainy night vision recording from the scene of the accident at Utterslev Mose. The video, taken through the windscreen of a car, showed her violently kneeing Ulrik in the side and then her flight from the scene.

Cecilie felt as if she was going to be sick.

9

It was as if the windows of the surrounding high-rises were staring back at her. She quickly left the terrace and returned inside. She locked the door and tugged at the cord on the blinds to lower them. She dashed through the living room and rapidly drew the curtains across every window. Then she headed into the hallway to check that all the bolts were secured and that the front door was definitely locked. Finally, she curled up on the sofa and stared at her phone. It was over. They would find out that her kick had been the actual cause of death. She would be prosecuted and sent straight to jail. Ulrik would be smirking at her from beyond the grave. She picked up her phone and called Lasse. It went to voice mail and she hung up. What the hell would Lasse be able to do? Andreas maybe? Andreas might be able to do something? As a lawyer? As a prosecutor? She found his number and called.

When it was answered, she heard a child's voice: "Hi, this is Emma . . ." In the background, she could hear Andreas asking who it was.

Cecilie hung up. The scars on her wrist were horribly itchy, and she scratched at them. She tried to control her breathing, while the questions piled up. Who had sent this? How had said individual found her? Why had it been sent? The last question was easy. This was most definitely blackmail. She was aware of various instances of weak police officers, prison staff, and defence lawyers being extorted into committing illegal acts. In the case of the police officers, the pressure had been applied by powerful criminals who wanted illegal acts carried out or to gain access to police records. If that were the case in this instance, then the sender of the video had stumbled on a veritable gold mine. As a police inspector, she had expanded powers and enhanced access to records and other IT systems. She contemplated how long she might have been under observation. Then she reflected on what the person expected to get out of their surveillance. Ulrik's accident had been just that—no one could have predicted it.

Cecilie opened the file and watched the video again. Judging by the angle and the distance from the crash, the person had been parked on the other side of the road some sixty metres away. She paused the video and searched for something that might indicate what car it had been filmed from, but she was none the wiser. It was also impossible to tell whether there were other people in the car. However, it appeared to have been shot from the driver's seat, which might indicate that the blackmailer was acting alone. She grasped her arm, which had begun to burn, and looked at the old scars that she had inflamed.

Cecilie pulled the blanket up to her chin and curled into a ball. Might the video be from a stalker? Maybe it was from someone who lived locally? Or an old acquaintance of hers? She'd always had poor judgment when it came to men. Self-effacingly poor. In the last few years, she'd been on far too many dates. Most of them with people she would have done well to avoid. The same was true of her relationship with Andreas. If it was a stalker who by pure chance had bagged the video recording of their life, then she knew full well what kind of extortion would follow. It would be all about the power trip.

The next morning, Cecilie approached the main entrance. Once again, she hadn't got much sleep overnight, as evidenced by the dark circles under her eyes. In the car, she had been constantly checking the rearview mirror to see whether anyone was following her, but she hadn't spotted anything suspicious. She'd already considered contacting the IT investigators in NC3 to see whether they could trace the anonymous sender. But even if she removed the video from the message, NC3 would automatically report the inquiry to the top brass. She also didn't know whether it was possible to delete the file sufficiently well that the geeks at NC3 wouldn't somehow be able to reconstruct it. Ultimately, she risked incriminating herself just to find out that the sender had used an anonymous pay-as-you-go that was untraceable.

"Cecilie," said a voice behind her as she reached the Division. She turned around to see Andreas approaching her with a big smile on his face. He quickly looked around and then lowered his voice. "You called last night. That was a little . . . unexpected."

She tried to smile. "Yes. Your daughter answered, so I hung up. It was stupid of me. Sorry," she said.

"That's okay, although you know evening calls are a little tricky. You know how it is," he said.

"Personally, not really. So . . ."

He smiled wryly. "No. It's all a bit of a mess . . . soon be over. I'm in the process of moving out of the house, so . . ." He cleared his throat. "But what did you want?"

She searched for an answer. "I . . . I just wanted . . . to hear your voice."

"My voice?" he said in surprise.

"Yes, that was it." She looked towards Lasse's vacant desk. "Have you seen Lasse?"

"No, not today," Andreas replied, leaning in towards her. She could smell his aftershave, which brought back pleasant memories. "So see you soon?"

"Yes . . . Definitely." She made for her own desk.

"I'll call," she said with a smile. "Just not in the evenings."

Cecilie put her bag down on the desk and watched Andreas disappear out of the office. She turned on the computer and while it booted, she checked her phone for new messages. At that very moment, the door of Karstensen's office opened. Cecilie half rotated on her desk chair and saw, to her surprise, that Lasse was standing in the doorway. "Got a moment?" he said, avoiding looking her in the eye.

They know flew through her head. She stood up mechanically and headed into the office of the homicide chief.

10

Karstensen was sitting behind his desk, hands clasped in front of his chest. Cecilie tried to read his body language, which had always been more or less impossible. Karstensen had been in the exact same pose when he'd promoted her, and he'd been like that when giving her a royal bollocking. Henrik was standing by the window looking like an undertaker. He nodded curtly at her.

"What's this about?"

"Early this morning we received an inquiry about Ulrik Østergård," said Karstensen.

Cecilie felt her legs giving way, but she managed to remain upright. "From . . . who?"

"Vinnie," Lasse said behind her. "She had something she was eager to show us."

"Pretty incriminating stuff," Henrik added.

"You've spoken to Vinnie?" she said, looking around.

"Karstensen asked us to go and see her," Lasse replied, almost apologetically.

"Okay," she said briskly. "So what was it she wanted to show you?"

Karstensen picked up the small plastic bag in front of him and threw it towards her. Cecilie grabbed it and saw that it contained four health insurance cards. Fie's was on top.

"He'd stashed them away in a kitchen cupboard," Henrik said, smiling. "In a box of porridge oats."

"They fell out into Vinnie's bowl," Lasse said with a laugh.

Karstensen smiled, which forced Cecilie to do likewise. "I take it that we can definitely consider this case closed?" she said.

"I think we can conclude that Ulrik Østergård has collared himself from beyond the grave," Karstensen replied. "Good work, boys." He nodded appreciatively towards Henrik and Lasse. "Porridge," he repeated, chuckling.

When they emerged from Karstensen's office, Cecilie gave Lasse a look. "You might have called."

He held his arms out apologetically. "Karstensen wanted us down here right away. It all went so fast, Guppy."

"Of course," she said without really meaning it. "I assume you'll handle the last of the paperwork?"

"Naturally," he said, sighing deeply.

She reflected that Lasse's two-finger approach to typing would mean he'd spend most of the rest of the day getting through it. Which was a fitting punishment for not letting her in on developments right away.

She sat down at her computer and checked her inbox. The most recent message hit her like a club hammer. The subject line read: Congratulations on your first kill. The email was from an automatically generated address. She clicked on it and began to read.

Dear Inspector Cecilie Mars,

May I begin by congratulating you on your first kill? At the same time, I quite understand if you still find yourself shaken by the episode. Similarly, I quite understand that you may find my correspondence unsettling.

But fear not! What you did to that brute Ulrik Østergård was an act of heroism and you may rely on my utmost discretion. I would prefer that the video recording of your killing remain our secret.

I am writing this to reassure you that you are in the company of a like-minded individual. A citizen, who—like you—has had enough of seeing injustice reign supreme. A citizen who seeks change and who knows that change of that kind calls for extreme methods. YOU have led by example! You have demonstrated the only path through this godforsaken world where crimes are committed with impunity.

As you know, we find ourselves in a lawless age—some 30,000 violent assaults against women and children are carried out each year. The majority of those perpetrators remain unpunished and at large, or they are sentenced to receive treatment instead of time in a regular prison.

This is why I am glad to have made your acquaintance, Cecilie Mars. Above all, because I have a matter of the utmost importance that requires immediate intervention. I therefore urge you to contact me at this email address today before 13:00.

Lazarus

Cecilie slid back on her chair. It frightened her that the sender knew her name, rank, phone number, and email address. The right thing to do would have been to go straight to Karstensen's office and tell him the truth. But instead, she turned to Lasse. "What about the autopsy report?"

"What about what?" he replied, without lifting his eyes from his screen.

"The autopsy report for Ulrik Østergård. Has it come in yet?"

Lasse picked up the top folder off the stack beside him and passed it to her with an outstretched arm. Cecilie detached herself from her desk and rolled over to him, snatching it from his hand.

"It says that Ulrik was splattered onto his steering wheel more thoroughly than the insects on his windscreen," he said.

"Really?" she answered, trundling back to her desk.

"Yes. As if an elephant had planted its foot in his chest," Lasse said as he continued to type.

She began to read the report that detailed how Ulrik Østergård had sustained thirty-two rib fractures. Several of the ribs on his left-hand side had been broken in multiple locations. According to the medical examiner, the cause of death was a combination of the many fractures, the collapse of both lungs which had prevented breathing, and bleeding in the abdominal cavity. She flipped through the pages to the diagram showing all the injuries and stared dully at the pathologist's red crosses dotted across the left-hand side of the torso. That was where she had kicked Ulrik—just below the heart. She felt how dry her mouth was. It had been her bloody kick that had finished him off. If Lazarus's video came to light, she'd go to prison. At best for manslaughter, at worst for premeditated murder. Neither outcome appealed to her. If she followed her instincts and went to confess to Karstensen, it would mean with complete certainty that she'd be immediately escorted to the cells.

Cecilie looked at the clock on her computer desktop. There were ten minutes left until Lazarus's deadline. She found herself thinking about him as a *him*. But was it necessarily a man behind the alias, or might it be a woman? A woman who had at some point been abused herself? Cecilie reread the email. Regardless of the sender's gender, the language of the email demonstrated a certain level of education. She considered whether the person might have professional expertise in relation to crime statistics. On the other hand, the email didn't say anything beyond what most people could turn up by themselves using Google. Then there was the religious undertone to the email, such as the reference to a godforsaken world and the use of the alias "Lazarus."

She wondered whether a relative of one Ulrik's most recent victims might be hiding behind the moniker. On the other hand, Fie was the only one who had picked him out. It would be a surprise to the other three women when they were notified of Ulrik's death later that day and informed that he had been the one who had raped them. Cecilie didn't know much about Fie's family except that Fie had always lived in Bellahøj with her mother and little sister. The girls' fathers were as good as nonexistent, and Cecilie was sure that it wasn't Tina who was behind the email. The content of the message and the style were a little too advanced for her.

"Guppy . . . ? Guppy?"

She looked up at Lasse in horror. He was standing by her desk. "Yes," she said, closing the email.

"I asked whether you wanted to come for lunch?"

She shook her head dismissively. "Thanks, but no thanks. I've got a couple of emails to do."

Once Lasse was gone, she reopened the email. She had to reply, to play for time if nothing else. Perhaps she might be able to talk some sense into the sender. When she began to write, she weighed up her words, knowing full well that one misplaced sentence might result in the video ending up with the top brass or on YouTube.

In her reply, she explained that she was surprised to receive the message, but that after watching the video she very much understood how the situation might have been misunderstood. However, she had most certainly not caused anyone's death; all she had done was to pacify a wanted criminal. The case had subsequently been fully resolved and closed. She acknowledged Lazarus's concerns about the high numbers of crimes in Denmark. Writing in the same soothing tone, she asked whether the email to her had been triggered by a personal tragedy. Perhaps an *injustice* had been committed against him or a loved one. If that were the case, she was keen to hear more about it and meet with him.

When she was done, she read the email again and added a couple more courtesies before hitting send.

Other than the officer manning the phones and a couple of detectives, most of the Division was out to lunch. Personally, she had no appetite. Instead, she remained glued to her screen waiting for Lazarus's response, and she didn't have to wait long.

The subject line on the email that arrived read: LIES!

11

Cecilie looked around furtively before opening the email with the incendiary subject line.

Inspector Cecilie Mars,
I despise liars just as much as I detest criminals. We are both aware of the course of events that led to Ulrik Østergård's death.

Desist from treating me like an idiot. Your erroneous assumption will have far-reaching consequences for your future. You killed him, and you fled! That is what everyone will see if this video is brought to the public's attention.

Perhaps I was mistaken about you? Maybe you are not cut out for this partnership? I will give you one chance to apologise for your lies and convince me that you are still worthy to deal with this matter. I look forward to your IMMEDIATE reply.

Lazarus

The sudden change in tone and the fierceness of the email shook her. She stared blankly at the display. The scar tissue on her left wrist began to itch again, and she scratched the small wounds. More than anything, she was tempted to throw herself at the keyboard and apologise to him, but something held her back. *Neediness* had crept into Lazarus's email. A need for attention. Something that might be to her advantage.

At that moment, Lasse returned from lunch. He had brought a sandwich which he placed on her desk. "We can't have you wasting away, Guppy."

"Thanks."

"You're bleeding—what have you done to your arm?" he asked, pointing.

She tugged her sleeve down over her wrist. "It was just a cat that scratched me."

"You've got a kitty?"

She forced a smile in response to his question.

"You don't really strike me as a cat person."

"It's the neighbour's."

"Make sure you don't scratch it. It might get infected." Lasse sat down at his desk and heaved a loud sigh as he looked at the computer. A little while later, he was back to work with his two-finger approach.

Cecilie reread the email. Lazarus *needed* her. This was a power struggle that she *had* to win if she was going to have any hope of bringing him to his senses. Lazarus might very well have the video to threaten her with, but if he chose to make it public then his game was up before it had even begun. And she was certain that this was much bigger for him than getting some insignificant police inspector fired and imprisoned. Even if it was playing high stakes, she had to be patient and let him come back to her.

She spent the rest of the afternoon awaiting Lazarus's next move. When it was almost four o'clock and he still hadn't written to her, she wondered whether he would try again the next day. She was about to pack up her things when another email arrived.

Inspector Cecilie Mars,

Or perhaps I ought to call you Former Inspector? I sense that your career has come to an end. I cannot begin to describe my disappointment at your failure to reply. I must interpret this silence to mean that you wish to decline my offer to make a difference. It is the silence that indicates that you accept the status quo. Your complicity in the crimes perpetuated by these beasts is clear to see, and

I shall look elsewhere for an esquire. First, however, I shall notify your corpulent partner and see to it that he ensures you meet your fate and that an appropriate punishment is meted out.

Lazarus

Cecilie turned her head towards Lasse, who was stretching and yawning in his chair. From her own chair, she could see the email client open on his screen. She feared that at any moment she would hear that ominous chiming sound. Just then, Lasse stood up and pushed the chair under his desk.

"You on your way home?" she asked casually.

"Yes, unless you need me?"

She shook her head dismissively. "No, no. Run along."

"You'll have to forgive me, Guppy, for not calling you right away when Karstensen told us to head out."

"Forget about it. Now off to home with you."

"I really mean it, I swear. It won't happen again."

"I'm glad to hear it. See you tomorrow."

He grabbed his windbreaker and shrugged it on. "I've promised Martin we'll go to IKEA." He rolled his eyes. "The only mitigating circumstances are that at least it's not a Saturday when all the little kids are there."

"Happy shopping. And send him my best," Cecilie said, attempting a smile.

Just then, Lasse's computer chimed. Lasse sighed loudly and turned towards the display.

"Get out of here," she said hastily. "Work won't go anywhere."

"Unfortunately, nor will IKEA." Lasse leaned over the desk and grabbed hold of the mouse.

"Lasse . . ."

He clicked on the screen and she saw the email client close. Then he switched off the computer. "See you, Guppy," he said, turning around.

When Lasse had gone, she hurried to his desk. She looked around the almost deserted Division before she switched the computer back on. She knew that Lasse was too lazy to change passwords, and she logged in using the name of his childhood basketball team: Bakken Bears. The last email to arrive made her heart skip a beat. Lazarus was apparently not the bluffing type. With a single click, she deleted the email and video attachment. She shut down the computer again and returned to her own. She had averted disaster, but clearly lost the power struggle.

She pulled up Lazarus's first email on the screen and reread it. What exactly did he envision them working together on? She already feared the worst. But perhaps whatever it was Lazarus wanted resolved would in fact bring her closer to finding out who he was. Eventually, she wrote back to him:

Just what kind of matter is it that you want me to look at?

12

It was gone nine when Cecilie bade farewell to the security guard in reception. She had waited for Lazarus's reply, but he had never responded. When she crossed the street, she looked around but the dark road was deserted. With Radiohead's "Creep" playing on the stereo, she drove through the city centre heading northwest. The old song led her along Bispeengbuen and in among the concrete blocks of Bellahøj. She parked close to the basketball court where a group of lads were loitering. The scooter lads, as she'd dubbed them, since they spent all their time racing around on the footpaths on their souped-up scooters. She'd seen most of them grow up in the neighbourhood. The place hadn't done them much good. The boys had gone from being problem children to borderline criminal teenagers, and it was only a matter of time before a number of them became part of her workload. She passed the basketball court on her way to the stairwell. The lads' eyes followed her and terms of address such as *pig* and *whore* slipped effortlessly through the wire netting.

As she let herself in through the main door, she caught sight of a brown envelope protruding from her mailbox. She gently prised it free from the slot using two fingers. The padded envelope measured twenty by thirty centimetres and was a couple of centimetres thick. On it, written in neat handwriting, were the words: To Inspector Cecilie Mars. There was no sender noted, but she had an idea of who it might be from.

A few minutes later, she was standing in her kitchen. She laid the envelope on the table before her. She put on a pair of disposable gloves from the cupboard and found a small kitchen knife that she used to open the envelope. She carefully removed the contents and looked at the folded slip of paper that was at the top of the bundle. She unfolded the note and read the typewritten message:

> Dear Inspector Cecilie Mars,
>
> I am grateful that you have decided to cooperate. I must apologise if my tone seemed harsh, but you must understand that I am dedicated to this calling. As I have mentioned, I do not tolerate lies or betrayal. I dare say you are considering examining the enclosed materials for DNA, but you should spare yourself the inconvenience. Precision is crucial to me. Furthermore, I am not in your records. Instead, concentrate on the task that I present to you. It requires immediate action.
>
> The enclosed clippings describe the case against the beast Emil Kam. This case began in 2007 when his misdeeds were exposed. Despite Emil Kam's serious crimes against 18 victims, ages 6 to 11 years old, he received just one custodial sentence. Some 9 months ago, the decision was taken to release Emil Kam, who is now hiding under the name of Thomas Hempler. I have tracked down this beast, who has moved to Copenhagen where he has resumed his perversions. Not far from you, as it happens! As you can see from the enclosed, it is of the utmost importance that we eliminate him. At the time of writing, he is once again abusing innocent children. Contact me at 692hf@gmail.com as soon as you have reviewed the materials enclosed.
>
> Lazarus

Cecilie put the letter aside. She remembered Emil Kam and the "Hjem-IS case," as it had been known, very well. Who didn't? It had shaken all of Denmark when it had been uncovered. The sound of the ice cream company's distinctive jingle from its vans had lured children and adults alike to them for generations, but it had latterly come to be associated with the paedophile Emil Kam's abuse perpetrated in his role as an ice cream van driver.

She had only just joined the Division at the time, but the case had involved more or less every single detective. It had been Karstensen's big case—the one that had finally seen him promoted and bagged him the chief's office. Cecilie looked down at the bundle of yellowing newspaper cuttings which demonstrated with succinct clarity how closely Lazarus had been following Emil Kam. She wondered whether Lazarus was related to one of Emil Kam's victims. Was that how he had received his "calling"?

She flipped through the old clippings, skimming the articles. Even though she'd only been peripherally involved in the investigation, it still brought back unpleasant memories. Before he'd been unmasked, Emil Kam had been well liked by everyone in his local area. His job selling ice cream had made him popular with the neighbourhood kids, who had visited his home with their parents' permission. As well as driving the ice cream van, Emil Kam had also been a scout leader, tasked with organising countless weekend trips with the kids. None of his colleagues in the scout troop and none of the parents had harboured even the slightest of suspicions about a man who was always kind and funny. But that illusion had been shattered as the first reports of abuse had surfaced. The old clippings described a pair of siblings, ages seven and eight years old, who had initiated the case against him. At first, no one had believed them, but when more children from Emil Kam's district concurrently described Emil's *cuddle parties*, the police had intervened. Luckily for the detectives, he'd filmed much of the abuse. Several of his assaults were so serious that not even the tabloids had repeated the details. But for Cecilie, it had been the countless unbearable pictures that had burned themselves indelibly into her retinas. The case had also garnered international attention since Emil Kam had run a secret portal for paedophiles. This had allowed members to exchange child pornography that they had produced themselves. A total of 358 men from 29 different countries had been apprehended.

Cecilie remembered how everyone involved in the case had expected Emil Kam to get a life sentence. But the Medico-Legal Council had questioned his mental state and thus his suitability for a long spell in prison, which was why he'd instead been given a single custodial sentence.

She could certainly see why Emil Kam had changed his name and moved away from his old haunts. There were probably a lot of people who hadn't forgotten what he'd done. People like Lazarus, who wanted revenge. The question was whether Lazarus was right about the fact that Emil Kam was back at it. She set aside the bundle of old newspaper cuttings and looked at the stack of recently taken photographs. They all showed Emil Kam out and about in the city. Other than the extra pounds he'd put on and the receding hairline, his appearance hadn't changed significantly. At the bottom of the pile were a couple of photos taken in a large indoor swimming pool. She could tell that it was the Bellahøj Swimming Stadium based on the large foyer. The photographer must have taken their shots through the large windows overlooking the pools. Emil Kam was sitting on the edge of the smallest pool in a pair of tight swimming trunks. In the photos, it looked like he was interacting with a couple of the children in the pool in front of him. The scene itself was innocent enough, but given her knowledge of Emil Kam's past, the sight of it terrified her. On a Post-it note, Lazarus had written: The beast is here daily from 10 until 12 to look for new victims.

Lazarus had also enclosed one of Emil Kam's homemade posters. On it, he offered free private tuition in Danish to bilingual children from reception to third grade. The most disturbing thing was that a number of the strips at the bottom with Emil Kam's phone number on them had already been torn off. It was impossible to tell how old the poster was, and Lazarus hadn't noted where it had been put up or whether there were others like it around the neighbourhood.

While Emil Kam might have served his sentence, she was certain that he was still prohibited from working with children. A poster like this would most definitely be regarded as a violation of that, although she was unsure of what the punishment might be.

Cecilie pulled her laptop from her bag and opened the email client. She typed in Lazarus's new email address and wrote a reply to him. She thanked him for the materials he'd sent and praised him for his detailed research. She also noted that she would be happy to continue

the investigation into Emil Kam so that together they might acquire suffi-
cient evidence to secure a conviction against him. She went on to suggest
to Lazarus that they meet so that he could brief her further.

Cecilie doubted that Lazarus would accept the invitation or that her
reply would be satisfactory to him, but she hoped that it might be the
start of a dialogue and that it might remove the sting from his thirst for
revenge. Just a quarter of an hour later, she received proof that the latter
was not the case.

Inspector Cecilie Mars,
If it were a charge against Emil Kam that I sought, I would have
approached the police directly: quite possibly the Head of Homicide himself, so that he could finish what he started. But that is by
no means the case. I wish to remove Emil Kam from this earth
and send him straight to Hell. All with your help. I have attached a
detailed plan for his extermination. You have 48 hours to execute
it.
    Lazarus

Cecilie opened the attached PDF and skimmed Lazarus's plan for
murder. It made for disturbing reading, given the level of detail and
detachment, which demonstrated just how disturbed he was. But whatever she might think of Lazarus and his plan, she was at any rate compelled to consider whether the accusations against Emil Kam stood up
to scrutiny.

13

Cecilie was standing in the foyer of Bellahøj Swimming Stadium by the large sections of glass that faced in towards the pools. Below her lay the diving pool with its tall stack of diving boards, and behind that was the competition pool marked out with eight lanes. Light streamed through the huge glass façades, making the water in the pools sparkle. Early that morning, she had gone to the office to check Emil Kam's record. She had discovered that he'd been released on July 2nd the year before and that his new address and name change matched the details that Lazarus had included in the envelope. She had checked whether any fresh suspicions against him had been reported since his release, but they hadn't.

It was now a little after ten o'clock, and there was a surprising number of swimmers in the water. Most were either pensioners or parents with young children. Additionally, there was a group of elite swimmers lane training. She searched for Emil Kam among the swimmers without catching sight of him. However, she was certain that Lazarus was on top of his research and that Emil would be somewhere or other on the premises. She looked down towards the shallow pool to her left where a couple of women and a handful of youngsters were splashing about. That was where Lazarus had photographed Emil most recently—from the same position that she was now in. She glanced around the foyer, but apart from the ageing attendant behind the counter, she was alone. She went to buy a day ticket and then headed down the stairs to the changing rooms. Despite the spotless modern design, she felt thrown back to the PE lessons of her school days. She had always found it hard to undress in the company of others, even before the assault. She hurried into a shower cubicle and quickly pulled on the black swimsuit that she had found at the bottom of her wardrobe.

As she entered the main hall, she heard loud shouts from a group of youths clustered around the diving tower. The lifeguard's whistle cut through the air: Two of the lads wanted to jump off the five-metre board at the same time. Cecilie made her way between the edge of the pool and the grandstand seats. She looked for Emil among the swimmers and caught sight of a corpulent middle-aged man. She made for the nearest ladder and let the cool water close around her. With one leg outstretched, she checked whether she could touch the bottom. She couldn't. She clung on to the edge. The middle-aged man swam another couple of lengths, then he got out on the far side of the pool. He removed his goggles and brushed back his thinning hair. Cecilie recognised Emil Kam.

Emil grabbed his towel from a peg and dried himself off. He carefully dabbed at the waterproof plaster that attached an ostomy bag to his side. The lifeguard stopped next to him and the two men fell into conversation, although Cecilie was unable to hear what they were talking about. A little while later, Emil grinned and patted the lifeguard on the shoulder, then grabbed his sports bag and made for the shallow pool. He greeted one of the two women with a group of younger children, and then he sat down on the edge of the pool with his feet in the water. Cecilie struggled to see from her position what was going on, so she made her way to the ladder and climbed out of the water. She took her towel and settled down on the second row from the top of the grandstand, which afforded an uninterrupted view of the shallow pool. Emil was sitting on the edge while the kids played in the water in front of him. After around ten minutes, one of the two women left with her little boy. Shortly after that, the other woman left the pool together with her two girls. Emil waved to them, but the woman didn't respond in kind.

There were now four young boys and a girl wearing inflatable arm bands splashing about in the pool; their parents nowhere to be seen. Emil initiated contact with the children. The pool was too distant for Cecilie to hear what he said to them, but she could see him clowning about with big gestures. It was remarkable how quickly he was able to gain the trust of the children. Shortly after that, they were bouncing around him and allowing themselves to be tickled when he reached out for them. Not long after that, he looked around the hall furtively before slipping down into the pool with the kids. They continued to play as he lifted the children in turn and then dropped them back in the water. Given Cecilie's familiarity with Emil Kam's history as a rapist, the mere sight of this was nauseating, and she had to force herself not to intervene. But as yet, he hadn't done anything illegal. Emil's game with the children continued for another twenty minutes until he got out of the pool. The children continued to play while Emil retrieved his bag and towel. When he had dried off, he removed his phone from a holder on the outside of his sports bag and discreetly dropped it into the bag. It occurred to Cecilie that he might have been using it to film himself playing with the children.

"See you soon, kids!" Emil called out, waving goodbye to the children in the pool, who waved back at him. Then he vanished into the men's changing rooms. She wanted to follow him and make sure that he wasn't making overtures to the kids in there. Most of all, she wanted to wring his neck. But Lazarus had a plan for that, too, she thought to herself ironically.

Ten minutes later, Cecilie was outside the building waiting for Emil Kam to appear. She had rushed to put on her clothes in order to get out quickly and she hadn't had time to dry her hair, which now stank of chlorine. If Emil emerged in the company of one of the kids, she would intervene on the spot. She leaned against the balustrade and kept an eye on the entrance some twenty metres away. Behind her, the traffic on Borups Allé thundered past, and it was only because the phone in her pocket was vibrating that she realised it was ringing. When she answered, Lasse was on the line. She pressed a finger into her ear to hear him better.

"Where are you? It sounds like you're standing in the middle of a motorway."

"That's the sound of Nordvest for you. What's up?"

"I can see from your log in that you've already stopped by this morning. Will you be in again today?"

"I don't think so. Why?"

"I just wanted you to go over my report on the Ulrik Østergård case before it gets consigned to the archives."

"I'm fully confident that you're on top of it."

"Okay . . . Was there something in the autopsy report that bothered you?"

She felt her heart pounding. "What? What do you mean?"

"Since you asked for it? I saw it was still on your desk."

"No, no. Absolutely not . . . Everything is fine."

"Okay, so I'll archive the lot."

"You do that." Finally.

She waited another forty-five minutes for Emil Kam to exit the building but he never appeared. Either he had been faster to emerge than she had, or he knew a back way out and had slipped away unseen. She thought she had been discreet, but perhaps a man like Emil Kam, who was used to operating covertly, had a special ability to detect whether he was being watched.

She felt an urge to visit the address in Dyssegårdskvarteret where he lived. The fact that it had also been identified by Lazarus as the scene of his planned murder only made it more interesting. Especially in light of Lazarus seeming to have an intimate knowledge of both the area and Emil Kam's home. Perhaps something there might point her in the direction of Lazarus?

She retrieved the car and half an hour later she was out at Fruevej, just a couple of houses down from Emil Kam's home. Cecilie gazed down the street. Stringy hedges framed each garden. It was quiet and the whole neighbourhood reminded her of Assistens Cemetery. A little earlier when she had passed Emil Kam's house, she had spotted the car on the driveway and speculated that he might be at home. She got out of the Panda and headed for the front door. Further down the street, three girls came cycling around the corner, laughing loudly. Cecilie continued on her way and passed a driveway on which a couple of tricycles were languishing. She reflected that with all these families within arm's reach, Emil Kam had found the perfect hunting ground.

She stopped outside the unkempt garden in front of his house. The tall, unruly hedge made it almost impossible to see anything beyond. According to Lazarus, Emil had returned to his old childhood neighbourhood following his release from prison. He now lived there alone in a rented house. She doubted that Lazarus lived around here himself, but the richness in detail found in the murder plan demonstrated that he must have spent a considerable amount of time in the area over an extended period.

Cecilie went to the neighbouring house. The driveway was empty. Lazarus's plan identified the neighbouring garden as the easiest way to access Emil Kam's garden without being seen. She looked up at the dark windows. It didn't seem as if anyone was at home. She made her way into the back garden and found the gap in the hedge that Lazarus had mentioned. She squeezed her way through.

Standing there in Emil Kam's garden, she looked up at the dilapidated, yellow-painted house. A couple of broken windows had been covered in newspapers, and the place seemed almost unusable as a dwelling. Behind a frosted pane of glass that probably belonged to the bathroom, a yellowish light was on. She continued through the small garden, past rusty garden furniture that had toppled over, making for the house. Lazarus's plan said that the basement window would be open.

. . . it is from here that the attack on the beast must be initiated.

14

The branches on the trees in the garden were swaying in the wind, and it looked like rain. When the first drops fell, Cecilie turned up the collar on her windbreaker. She squatted by the basement window, which was covered in a thick layer of grime. On one side of the window frame, she noticed fresh indentations in the woodwork that indicated the window had recently been broken open. She carefully grasped the frame and opened the window. The warm, moist air from the boiler room rose towards her like rancid breath. Cecilie leaned forward and peered into the semidarkness. At the far end, she could make out the pipes and the white cabinet enclosing the gas boiler. A Vaillant Pro 24. Not that she knew anything about that kind of thing, but Lazarus had written what it was in his notes. In addition to the sketch of the basement and the location of the boiler room, he had enclosed a technical diagram of the boiler itself. The plan was as simple as it was deadly. To transform the boiler into a lethal weapon, she had to block the ventilation system at the top of the cabinet. The easiest way to do this was to dismantle the cabinet hatch and use some of the insulation that she would find on the inside. Clogging it up would impair the combustion process and increase the levels of carbon monoxide, which would rapidly spread to the rest of the house. Old gas boilers were renowned for these blockages, and they had cost lives in the past. According to Lazarus, it was the perfect crime. No one would ever know. His sole complaint was that it was almost too gracious a death for a paedophile and rapist.

She surveyed the bare basement expanse for footprints left by Lazarus, but she found none. She wondered why he hadn't carried out his own murderous plan. Why wasn't he satisfied with performing the killing himself, choosing instead to get her to do it? He had even written that if she suddenly found herself wanting for courage, all she had to do was think about the fate of the children: Pia, Marlene, Mia, Christian, Tor . . . It was a long list, and Lazarus had endeavoured to include all the names of Emil Kam's victims.

She looked back at the boiler. It would be the easiest thing in the world to follow Lazarus's instructions, and she would probably get away with it, too. But no matter what she thought about Emil Kam, or how much she feared for her own future, she was by no means going to execute this plan.

At that moment, she heard the gate to the front garden open, followed by crunching up the gravel path to the house. Cecilie stood up and carefully tiptoed to the corner. Hiding behind the ivy, she stared into the front garden. Over by the front door, there was a boy of around ten years of age, looking down at the ground. He was slenderly built, had a crew cut, and was of Middle Eastern descent. The boy blinked his eyes nervously. He plucked up his courage and knocked on the door. Some time passed before it was opened.

"Well blow me down. Little Alibaba's come back to the robber's cave," said Emil Kam's voice.

"Er, what?" said the boy, his mouth open.

Cecilie craned her neck, but she was unable to lay eyes on Emil in the doorway.

"You're too late . . . Ali . . . bali . . . bi . . ." Emil said.

"I was only free now," said Ali.

"'I was only free now,'" Emil mimicked. "You've got to be punctual. Understood?"

"I'm . . . sorry."

"See, that's better. In you come."

Ali hesitated and stuck his hands in his pockets.

"Well, what are you waiting for?"

"Give me the pictures. You promised . . . last time."

"Yes, yes. But come in. You thirsty? I've got coke."

"Pictures, now. Understand?"

"I do understand. It wouldn't be very good for you if they turned up online, would it? What would your mother say? Or your brothers and sisters? Or your friends? Do they know about the kind of mess you make?"

"I've got to have the pictures!"

"Then come inside with me," Emil hissed. "I don't have them out here, do I? Then we can see whether we can find a solution."

Ali was breathing heavily through his nostrils. He disappeared inside the house with Emil.

Cecilie could feel how dry her throat was. That swine. Bloody swine. No matter what he was blackmailing the boy with, he wouldn't get away with it. She withdrew from the ivy and went over to the windows, which were obscured by blinds. Emil Kam's voice was audible from inside, but she couldn't see him. She continued around the corner of the house and reached the bedroom window. Through the filthy window, she could see the unmade bed in the middle of the rest of the mess. The door to the living room was half open, and Cecilie saw Emil in there wearing a burgundy dressing gown and jogging bottoms. She continued to the front door and pulled out her police badge so that it was visible on the outside of her sweatshirt. She was about to knock, but then she hesitated. Emil Kam was most definitely not going to open up and would instead start destroying anything compromising inside. In the worst case, he might take Ali hostage. The alternative would be for her to sneak inside and secure anything that could be used against him. That wouldn't satisfy Lazarus, who would without doubt make good on his promise to unmask her. But fuck Lazarus! Right now, all that mattered was Ali's safety and securing evidence against Emil Kam so that he would never be at liberty again.

Cecilie returned to the basement window and she slid through. She landed heavily on the cement floor and lay there listening. She could hear footsteps and low voices from the living room above. She stood up and made her way through the semidarkness towards the stairs. She climbed up to the door, which she carefully opened before emerging into the dark kitchen. It smelled rancid, and there was rubbish and dirty crockery all over the place. She took care not to stumble over anything on the floor as she headed for the next room. She could hear Ali whimpering behind it.

"Don't whine now, Ali. It doesn't hurt one bit," said Emil.

Cecilie drew her service weapon and removed the safety. She pushed open the door and positioned herself in the doorway. The living room was a pigsty—just like the rest of the house. At the far end of the room, Emil Kam was sitting on a dining chair with Ali lying on his stomach across his lap. The boy's trousers were down around his knees and his buttocks were exposed. Cecilie raised her pistol. "Police!" she called out, taking aim at Emil Kam.

Ali started and slid off Emil Kam's lap. Cecilie moved closer while Emil Kam lazily raised his hands into the air. If he was surprised, then he was hiding it well.

"Are you okay?" Cecilie cast a sidelong glance at Ali who was pulling up his trousers. The boy nodded, wiping tears from his cheeks.

"The time is 14:18 and you're under arrest," Cecilie said to Emil Kam.

"What for?" he said with an arrogant shake of his head.

"Indecency with a minor. Is there anyone else in the house?"

"Indecent? I haven't done anything. You should put that gun down. You're scaring the poor boy."

"I said, is there anyone else in the house?" She looked towards the back room, which was empty.

"No, no. It's just me. Look, are you even allowed to burst in like this?"

"Lie down on the floor!" she shouted.

"You're shouting a lot. What's this all about?"

"I said lie down!" She raised the pistol.

Emil Kam took a deep breath and then lay down flat on his stomach.

Cecilie was on top of him immediately. She settled down on him heavily. "Hands on your back," she said, pulling the handcuffs from her belt.

Emil obeyed orders and she snapped the cuffs around his wrists. "Bloody hell," he groaned.

That second, Ali grabbed his backpack from the table and ran through the room. Before Cecilie had time to react, he was out of the front door. "Shit!" she said loudly.

"Yes, he's a speedy little guy," Emil said with a smile.

"Shut your mouth," she said, standing up. She scanned the room. "Where's your phone?"

"Look, sweetheart. You just told me to shut my mouth."

She put her foot on top of his head and mashed his face into the floor. Emil groaned loudly. "I'm not your sweetheart. Where's. The. Phone?"

"My jacket . . . on the chair."

Cecilie removed her foot and went to his jacket. She searched the pockets and found it. "Pin?"

"One-two-one-two," he groaned. "This is police brutality!"

"We haven't even got started," she said, unlocking the mobile. She searched his recordings and found the video. The sound of the swimming pool echoed through the living room as she watched the film. It showed Emil Kam playing with the kids in the shallow pool. She stopped the video and searched the handful of photos stored on the phone. There were pictures of children playing in the street, pictures of the neighbours' houses, pictures of gardens with trampolines and climbing frames. But none of the pictures were inherently criminal. "You doing research?"

"I don't know what you're talking about."

"What were you up to with Ali? And don't try telling me it was 'nothing.'" She stood very close, right in his face.

Emil Kam groaned in resignation. "The boy had a fever so I was taking his temperature. There's nothing illegal about that."

"We'll see about that," she said, turning towards the desktop PC standing on a desk in the corner of the room. There was a camera connected to the computer. "Filming much?"

"What are you talking about?"

"I think NC3 is going to have a party with that thing," she said, pointing. "Started a new group online, have you? What was it you called the last one? CandyCum?"

Emil snorted. "I still don't know what you're on about."

Cecilie went into the bedroom. She saw the two sets of handcuffs hanging at the head of the wrought-iron bed. Saw the stained mattress where there was a large dildo and a black butt plug. "How many have you had visit?" She felt the lump in her throat. "How many kids have been here?"

"I demand a lawyer. That's . . . that's my right!"

She turned and looked down at him. She felt the gun, which reminded her of its presence with its weight on her belt. Emil Kam the beast. That was exactly what he was. She thought about the gas boiler in the basement and how easy it would be to kill him. *Make it look like an accident,* she found herself thinking.

"That's . . . my right . . ." he whimpered again.

She knew that Emil Kam would never stop his abuse.

"A lawyer . . . I demand . . ."

"Shut your mouth," she said, exhausted. She pulled out her phone and called Lasse.

15

Emil Kam was sitting on a dining chair in handcuffs. Cecilie and Lasse were standing in front of him, staring down at him. At that moment, one of the Forensics team emerged from the bedroom with a couple of sealed plastic bags. Emil Kam caught sight of him. "That's . . . you're not allowed to . . . that's private, that is. You've no right to take my stuff."

"Easy now, Emil," Cecilie said.

Lasse carefully pushed the stacks of paper on the dining table out of the way and perched on the edge. "You'll get it all back when they're done examining it. Now tell us where we can find this lad."

"I'm not saying anything until I've got my lawyer here," Emil replied. He wriggled on the chair, watching another couple of officers pass through the living room.

"Why not?" Cecilie asked. "If you haven't done anything to the boy, then you've got nothing to worry about. We just need to make sure that he's okay."

Emil Kam looked at her incredulously. "You don't think I know how you guys work?"

Cecilie shook her head and went over to the officer who was at Emil's computer. She pulled the PC's plug out of the wall socket and helped him to pick up the monitor so that they could access the hard drive underneath it. "Make sure you get it all." She pointed in the direction of a couple of cardboard boxes with keyboards, cables, and other old computer kit spilling out of them. "Check whether there is any external storage lying around."

Emil Kam gawped at the officer walking past clutching the hard drive. "Hey, stop! You can't take that. There's confidential data on it . . . my patents and my inventions." He tried to stand up, but Lasse planted his big hands on his shoulders.

"We'll be sure to be careful, Emil. Now tell me about this boy. Ali, that was his name, right? You must have his phone number."

Emil did not reply, and his gaze dropped to the floor.

"Why are you making things worse for yourself?" Cecilie said, nudging Emil. "We'll find him with or without your help."

Emil closed his eyes, as if he were trying to shut them all out. At that moment, one of the officers in the bedroom shouted for them. Cecilie stepped past Emil and went over to the officer, who had appeared in the doorway. "We've found blood," he said in a low voice, pointing towards the sheets. Cecilie looked at the dried out brown spots. "Take it with you," she said.

She turned around and stared gloomily at Emil Kam. "Get him out of here. Now!"

Lasse heaved Emil up from the chair. "You heard the boss," he said to the two uniformed officers who stepped into the room.

"I demand a lawyer!" Emil Kam shouted. "A lawyer! This is going to go badly for you!" he yelled as he was led out of the room.

"We need the NC3 boys to get into that computer as quickly as possible," Cecilie said to Lasse. "If there's any dirt on it, Andreas needs to be able to show it to the judge in the preliminary hearing. That sick bastard isn't getting out again."

"I'll get the geek squad onto this," Lasse said.

"And we need to track down the boy," she said, troubled. "He must be scared shitless right now. Of us, of Emil. Worrying that his whole world is about to come falling down around his ears."

"Should we canvas the area?"

"Yeah, get uniform to knock on doors, although I don't think Ali comes from this neighbourhood."

"Then how did Emil make contact with him?"

Cecilie looked away. She couldn't tell Lasse about the posters that she knew Emil Kam had posted around town offering language tuition. Nevertheless, she tried to direct the investigation in that direction. "He spoke broken Danish, didn't look like he came from this neck of the woods. More likely from Nordvest."

"Your neighbourhood? Maybe he met him at the swimming baths?"

"Yes, my neighbourhood. But I'm not so sure about the swimming baths. Maybe they met online?"

"He was groomed?"

"At any rate, I overheard them talking about something to do with pictures that Emil Kam was using to blackmail him."

Lasse took a deep breath through his nostrils. "Fuck me, Guppy, you stink of chlorine. Tell me again how it was you got onto Emil Kam's trail. It's going to go down in police history."

"Nonsense," she said in an attempt to brush it aside. They left the living room. "Like I said, I was at the swimming pool and spotted Emil behaving inappropriately."

"I never saw you as a girl who went swimming."

"I'm like a duck to water," she replied, heading out of the front door with Lasse on her heels. "When I saw him filming the kids, I decided to follow him."

"This is completely fucking insane," Lasse said. "But why didn't you arrest him at the pool?" he said, opening the garden gate for her.

She shrugged. "I had the feeling that I'd seen him before—like an old acquaintance. Turns out I was right."

Lasse stopped by the patrol car. "I can't wait to pass this story on. You're beyond cool, Guppy."

"Let's just concentrate on making this stick to Emil for the time being. See you there," she said, making for her Panda.

It was almost six o'clock when Cecilie and Lasse were escorted by Kurt Osbourne through the elongated office. Osbourne was Head of the National Cybercrime Centre based in Glostrup, but with his gaudy waistcoat and impressive moustache, he was more reminiscent of an old-school singer on the Danish popular music circuit. The office hummed with the sound of thirty computers at which NC3 technicians were working. The air in here was dry and cold like a frosty morning. It seemed that the indoor climate was more suited to the needs of the machines than those who served them.

"Don't you guys ever knock off?" Lasse asked.

"This is the night shift. NC3 never sleeps," Osbourne said without a hint of irony.

"How far have you got?" Cecilie asked as they continued past the rows of desks.

"We've managed to open Pandora's box. That much I know."

A moment later, they had reached the final computer, where a swarthy technician in his mid-thirties was working away. On the trolley beside him was one of the hard drives taken from Emil Kam's house. The top of the computer had been removed and the motherboard was connected to the technician's own computer via a series of cables.

"What about the second hard drive? And the diskettes and SD cards?" Cecilie asked.

"We've got three people checking it all out. Last I heard, the diskettes and SD cards had all been formatted."

"So nothing?"

"Nothing ever disappears completely," Osbourne said, twirling the tip of his moustache between two of his fingers. "We just have to dig deeper."

"So when?"

"Before the end of the week."

She pointed to the open hard drive. "And that one?"

"How far have you got, Ismail?" Osbourne asked.

"I've managed to get in through a back door. It wasn't that hard," Ismail said cheerfully, without lifting his gaze from the screen. His fingers swept across the keyboard as green figures and symbols created a coding language that neither Cecilie nor Lasse understood.

"So what now?" Cecilie asked Ismail.

"I'm trying to reconstruct his history so that we can see where he's been. The only problem is that his Tor browser has hidden it."

"Is that something you can re-create?"

"I'm trying to, but it won't be easy. This guy knew just what to do to cover his tracks."

"Surveillance is always easier than re-creation," Osbourne added.

"What about the files on the computer?"

"Encrypted. Pretty well, in fact," Ismail said, nodding with an impressed expression. "There's a whole terabyte hiding on there. Given that size, I should think it's video files."

"Anything you can open?" Cecilie asked.

"It's going to be tricky, but not impossible. It'll take time, and it might entail some outside support from colleagues abroad," he added without elaborating further.

Lasse's phone rang, and he pulled it from his pocket. A moment later, he turned to Cecilie. "Emil Kam's lawyer has shown up at the station. You'll never guess who it is."

"The Terrier?"

"Spot on. Should we head back?"

Cecilie looked at Osbourne. "You going to get any further tonight?"

Osbourne shook his head dismissively. "Not likely. Expect us to be able to document his online behaviour by the end of the week. As for the files, both these ones and the external media, that's going to take rather longer. *If* it can be done at all, that is."

"It can be done," Ismail said, defending his pride. "I just need time."

"Which we won't have much of, but thanks all the same," Cecilie said. She turned to Lasse. "Let's leave Emil to sweat."

"And what about the Terrier?"

"He can sweat, too. Call in an hour to cancel."

"So no questioning before the preliminary hearing tomorrow?"

She shook her head. "We're not going to get anything out of him anyway."

Once they were outside again, Lasse looked at her. "I can see there's something bothering you."

"Yes. Ali."

"Maybe he'll turn up in the course of the investigation," Lasse said, smiling. "Just as long as Emil can't get to him, it'll be fine, surely?"

Cecilie smiled again, but her concern did not go away.

16

Despite the early hour, the court gallery at Stutterigade was half full for Emil Kam's preliminary hearing. Cecilie and Lasse had taken their seats in the front row on the prosecutor's bench beside Andreas. Across the room, Phillip Vang the defence lawyer was sitting with his arms crossed. Emil Kam was in the centre of the room, looking like someone who had been dragged out of bed. The hearing had been going for forty-five minutes and during Andreas's presentation of the charges against Emil Kam, Judge Mogensen had repeatedly suppressed a yawn.

When Andreas had concluded his request for four weeks' remand, Phillip Vang immediately took over the floor. "I'm going to try and exercise a little more concision than my honourable friend," he said, holding out his hands. "Over the past *hour*, my client has been on the receiving end of the Prosecution Service's suspicions, simply on the grounds of past behaviour for which he has *already* served his sentence. For the Prosecution Service to attempt to create a case on such flimsy grounds is frankly offensive. The defence thus requests that the petition for remand be dismissed and that all items belonging to my client that have been seized by the police without justification be returned posthaste. I may add that the defence finds the conduct of the police in this case to be both shocking and an affront to the rule of law."

Lasse leaned in towards Cecilie. "Is the Terrier really telling us that Emil wants all his dildos back?"

Cecilie hushed him.

Andreas once again addressed Judge Mogensen. "The rule of law is doing just fine. The intervention of the police is solely related to the fact that the accused, Emil Kam, was illegally filming minors in a public swimming pool."

Phillip Vang perched on the edge of his seat. "If that is the case, the defence raises the question of why an arrest was not carried out when the insinuated situation took place. Instead, the police resorted to unsanctioned surveillance and illegal trespass on private property."

Andreas was about to object, but Phillip Vang raised his arms into the air before continuing: "My client acknowledges using his mobile phone to make a recording at the swimming baths, but this was the result of a regrettable error for which he apologises. Had it not been for the police seizure of my client's phone, the recording would already have been deleted."

"We're talking about children being filmed in secret," Andreas said, looking gravely at Judge Mogensen.

"No," Phillip Vang said, interrupting. "We're talking about conduct that would in most cases result in a reprimand from the swimming pool attendant."

This comment precipitated laughter in the courtroom and the hint of a smile on Judge Mogensen's lips.

Phillip Vang clearly noticed that he had a tailwind as he continued: "The conduct of the police in this matter has been wholly disproportionate."

"It amazes me that the defence is attempting to make light of such a serious case," Andreas said. "The intervention of the police prevented an assault on a minor."

"Yet another distortion of the events that took place. My client was drinking a coke with the boy in question. At least, until the police turned up and scared him away."

Cecilie shook her head. She'd had just about enough of the Terrier. "Shut your dumb mouth," she muttered to Lasse.

"If the defendant would like to provide the name and address of the boy, we will be able to shed light on the circumstances. But apparently the defendant is unwilling to do so," Andreas said, looking up at the judge. "On the other hand, we have the arresting officer's statement that the boy was undressed and being held over the lap of the accused."

Phillip Vang shook his hands dismissively. "There was no nudity. It doesn't amount to anything."

"Well, what *was* the boy doing then?" Judge Mogensen asked.

Phillip Vang cleared his throat while he searched for the right words. "They were talking . . . and having a nice time. Drinking a coke."

Andreas opened his briefcase and removed a transparent folder from it, which he held up. "While searching the home of the defendant, the police found this poster on which the accused offers home tuition to minors."

Phillip Vang's face turned bright red. "That . . . the Prosecution Service should have disclosed that to the defence," he said, pointing at the folder with a stiff finger. "We haven't been told anything about this," he said, looking to Judge Mogensen.

Andreas lazily held out his hand. "This is just a preliminary hearing. We are simply informing the court of matters we perceive as relevant in relation to our petition for remand."

Judge Mogensen nodded. "What response does the defendant have in relation to this discovery?"

Phillip Vang approached Emil Kam and the two began to whisper in conference.

Lasse leaned in to Cecilie. "What the hell is that? We didn't give it to him, did we?"

Cecilie whispered into his ear: "It was one of the first things I found at Emil's."

"Why didn't you say anything? This is big!"

She put a finger to her lips and turned her gaze towards Emil Kam and the Terrier. The truth was that earlier that morning she had taken Emil Kam's poster with her from home and entered it into formal evidence along with the rest of the stuff they had found. When she had gone through the case with Andreas, she had drawn his attention to the poster, which he was now using as a trump card.

"The court is still waiting for a response," said Judge Mogensen.

Phillip Vang appeared to swallow. "My client was keen to assist bilingual children in the local area by offering them free tuition in the Danish language."

"Does he have any qualifications to do so?"

"A big heart and . . ." Phillip Vang had run out of words, a rarity in itself.

"This is a clear violation of the prohibition that remains in place as a result of his previous conviction on the defendant working with minors," Andreas said.

"That only relates to paid employment," Phillip Vang said hastily.

"No, it doesn't."

"Furthermore, only the boy in question has accepted my client's offer. And he has only been there on one . . ."

"So the boy was there to receive tuition?" Andreas said, now fishing.

Phillip Vang blinked. "The defence acknowledges that this is a grey area in which misunderstandings may arise. As such, the posters will be removed from those locations in which they have been posted as soon as this preliminary hearing is brought to a close." He attempted a smile at Judge Mogensen, who did not return it.

Andreas cleared his throat. "It is not just these posters which form the basis for the Prosecution Service's petition. Allow me to draw the court's attention to the fact that the police found various sex toys and video recording equipment during their search of the home of the accused. Furthermore, a large number of encrypted files have been found on one of the seized hard drives. We are led to assume that the accused has returned to his old ways and must be regarded as dangerous to those around him."

"And may *I* draw the court's attention to the fact that the Prosecution Service is yet again seeking to sully my client's reputation. As far as I am aware, the prosecutor is no psychologist," Vang added snidely.

Andreas smiled slowly, as if that were the opening that he had been waiting for all along. "No, not personally, but I have brought with me a previous psychological assessment of Emil Kam which sets out in detail his psychopathic traits and the dangers he poses." He picked up a folder to make it visible to all. "Incidentally, the psychologist involved in the preparation of this assessment just so happens to be in attendance and would be happy to elaborate on it for the court." Andreas turned towards the gallery and pointed to Steen Holz, who was sitting in the second row.

"This is . . . unprecedented!" Phillip Vang managed to splutter.

"I think we'll bring the submissions to a close at this juncture." Judge Mogensen straightened up in his seat and sighed deeply. He brushed his white hair back and turned towards Andreas. "I assume that the police have seized anything that may be of relevance to the Prosecution Service from the defendant's residence?"

"That is correct. NC3 is currently in the process of decrypting the files in question. Likewise, a number of technical leads are being investigated."

Judge Mogensen surveyed the courtroom. "In light of what has been submitted to the court, I do not find that the minor violations as outlined give rise, in themselves, for pretrial detention . . ."

Andreas moved forward on his chair. "But the defendant is most decidedly dang—"

Judge Mogensen stopped him with a hand gesture. "Even though I have full understanding for the fact that the Prosecution Service wishes to investigate the accusations against the defendant in further detail." Mogensen cleared his throat. "It is my clear impression that we will all meet again soon. Court dismissed."

Cecilie shook her head quietly. "Fuck me," she muttered.

Lasse stared angrily at Emil Kam, who had stood up and was being led away from his seat. Phillip Vang, on the other hand, was taking his time, gathering his papers.

Cecilie and Lasse emerged out onto Stutterigade where drizzle was falling, forming a greyish shroud. "We'll get him," said Lasse. "This doesn't mean a damn thing."

A moment later, Phillip Vang came out of the entrance. Cecilie could usually hold her tongue, but not this time. "How do you sleep at night?"

Phillip Vang craned his neck. "Very well, as it happens. But then again, I have just bought a bed from Hästens for a hundred and twenty thousand kroner. It has an incredible mattress. Two metres wide."

"I'm happy for you. We found blood in your client's bed. Just like we did back in 2007. That means there are new victims."

"Well, it's up to you to prove that," said Phillip Vang, striding off down the street.

"I could wring the Terrier's neck," Cecilie said.

"That makes two of us," said a voice behind them.

Cecilie and Lasse turned to face Andreas, who was accompanied by Steen Holz and a young clerk. "The Terrier got bloody lucky today," Andreas said, sighing deeply.

"Yes, yet again," she said.

"They should have castrated him," Steen Holz said.

"The Terrier?" Cecilie said, surprised at the psychologist. Steen Holz smiled. "No. I meant Emil Kam. Medical castration is the only thing that works on one hundred per cent of paedophiles."

"Yes, but unfortunately there's no basis in law to force them to undergo treatment," Andreas said, biting his lip.

"Which is a damn shame," Cecilie said, also sighing deeply. "I hope to have a response from NC3 before the end of the week so that we can bring Emil Kam back in."

"Sounds good. We'll get him sent down," Andreas said, smiling. "That's one hell of a killer instinct you have." He patted her on the shoulder and headed off down the street with the others.

17

It was after two o'clock in the morning and the house-lined streets in Dyssegårdskvarteret were deserted. The sound of pouring rain resounded along Fruevej, where the residents had long since gone to bed. Only at Emil Kam's were any lights on, and the bluish tinge of the TV illuminated the newspapers affixed to the windows. At that moment, the rusty garden gate opened and a figure in blue coveralls, their cap pulled down over their ears, stepped into the garden. The figure made its way up to the front door and pulled a set of lock picks from their pocket with a gloved hand. It took less than a minute to open the door, and then the figure vanished noiselessly inside.

In the living room, Emil was precariously swirling a glass of vodka in one hand and clutching the remote in his other. He was wearing an open dressing gown and a pair of threadbare boxers, his ostomy bag emerging from the waistband. From one corner of his mouth there hung a lit cigarette with a long ash tip. Emil tried to change the TV channel from the current entertainment show, but eventually he gave up and chucked away the remote. "Stupid piece of shit . . ."

He removed the fag from between his lips, raised the glass to his mouth, and began to drink, the vodka dribbling down his chin. The sound of the floorboards creaking behind him made him stop short. He listened attentively through the noise of the TV, and when there was another creak, he turned around slowly. His eyes widened and he lowered his glass. "The fuck . . ."

Standing in the doorway was the figure in the coverall, their face obscured by a dust mask and dark-tinted protective goggles. In one hand it held a torch which was directed at Emil, while in the other there was a long-bladed chef's knife.

Emil Kam dropped his glass. "Who are you? What do you want?"

There was no reply. Instead, the figure stepped closer and raised the knife, so that the blade flashed in the light.

18

Cecilie pummelled the boxing pad that Julie was holding up in front of her. It was obviously difficult for the slender girl to maintain her balance, and Cecilie continued to deliver her lightning-fast slashes, forcing her yet farther back. Cecilie put her foot behind Julie's, making her fall backwards. Then she sat down on top of Julie and shadow boxed a couple of rapid blows to the girl's face before getting back to her feet. Her sweaty T-shirt clung to her, and she pushed her damp fringe out of her eyes as she caught her breath. Around her in the small workout space were a group of girls ages 12 to 18 years old.

"Get into pairs and practice the combination I've just demonstrated for you," Cecilie said, resting her hands on her hips. "It's important that you make use of your speed. Speed is more important than strength. Get cracking!"

The girls quickly gathered up the pads spread across the floor and began to practise. Cecilie watched them closely, constantly increasing the tempo. Over the last couple of years, she had been giving self-defence classes once a week at the martial arts academy based at the old Grøndal sports centre. The session had gradually become a draw for local girls, and there was now a waiting list. When the class was over and the girls were on their way out, Cecilie stopped a couple of the oldest. "I haven't seen Fie in a long time."

Julie looked at her sadly. "Nor have we. Not after . . . what happened."

"So she's not back at school yet?"

The girls looked at one another and shook their heads. "No, it's been ages since she came in."

"Have you called her?"

"Not lately, no. But then she doesn't call back either," Julie said.

"Okay. See you next week."

The girls disappeared out of the door and Cecilie promised herself that she would stop by and see Fie soon. She went to her sports bag and retrieved a towel from it. As she wiped her sweaty face, she checked her phone for any missed calls or emails, but there was nothing important.

While the arrest of Emil Kam had only been subject to limited press coverage without his name being mentioned, she reckoned it was enough for Lazarus to be sure of what had happened. But he still hadn't replied to her or otherwise made good on his threat to publicise the video featuring her. She pulled her hoodie over the sweaty T-shirt and bade farewell to a couple of the trainers behind the counter.

She made her way across the site, passing the bowling alley and squash courts. Just then, her phoned buzzed and she checked the display before answering.

"S'up Lasse, you heard anything from NC3?"

"Sorry, not yet. But it may not matter much any longer."

"What do you mean?"

"Emil Kam was found dead at home this morning."

She stopped and took a deep breath. "How?" she asked, thinking about the gas boiler in his basement.

"I think we can rule out the idea that it was an accident or suicide. They say it was violent."

"Okay, see you there," she said, hanging up.

The fleet of patrol cars at Fruevej had drawn attention from the locals, who were standing by the cordon blocking access to Emil Kam's garden. Cecilie had parked her Panda farther down the street. She greeted the two officers standing on guard at the garden gate. At that moment, Lasse came down the garden path towards her. His face was ashen. "Jesus, Guppy. It's not a pretty sight."

"Who found him?"

"Guy flyering the neighbourhood. He spotted that the door was wide open and there was blood in the hallway."

"How did the killer get in?" she asked bluntly.

Lasse consulted his notebook in his hand. "Through the front door."

"So Emil let his own killer in?" she said, coming to a halt in the doorway. She put on the disposable gloves proffered to her by Lasse.

"No, Forensics reckon the lock was picked." He pointed at the lock in question. "The cylinder's been scrambled. They'll confirm later on."

She saw that Forensics had already brushed the door in their hunt for fingerprints.

They entered the living room where a whole pack of forensic specialists in blue coveralls and masks were busy securing evidence and thoroughly documenting the scene with cameras.

"I don't remember the dining table being overturned on our last visit," she said.

As she said that, Ole Madsen the forensic pathologist emerged from the bedroom in his white coverall. "Blimey Cecilie, you come straight from the gym or something?" he said in his cheery mid-Zealand drawl.

"A plus for observation, Ole. Doing okay?"

"Fine, thanks." Ole was in his mid-thirties and fit. The large Suunto sports watch that he always wore indicated just how serious Ole was about his workouts.

"So what have you got for me?" Cecilie asked.

"One very dead man in the bedroom. Fancy a gander?" He gestured invitingly.

Cecilie entered the bedroom, which was permeated by the stench of the perforated ostomy bag lying on the floor. Then she saw Emil Kam's yellowing corpse, clotted blood extending like a bib from his throat down his chest and stomach. "What time are we thinking?"

"I reckon it happened last night. I'll let you know as soon as we've got him back to base and taken a closer look."

"Cause of death?"

"An artery's been cut." Ole bent down and pointed to the large incision that had ripped open Emil's neck. "You don't survive that kind of thing. But he's also been stabbed repeatedly. Some of those stabs could have been fatal in themselves. We'll know more after the autopsy."

"Weapon?"

"We haven't found anything as yet," Lasse said. "We've called in the dog team."

"Any sense of what we're looking for, Ole?"

"Hunting knife or perhaps a big kitchen knife. Something sharp as hell," Ole said.

"Did it all happen in here?"

"No, no. We've also found blood in the living room. My best guess is that it kicked off in there and ended in here."

Lasse nodded from his position in the doorway. His gaze was fixed to his notebook. "We've found signs of a struggle in the living room: broken glass, toppled furniture, a smashed up mobile phone."

"Maybe we'll get lucky and find that some of that blood is from our killer?" Cecilie suggested.

"Maybe," Ole replied. "But judging by the defensive wounds on the victim's arms and hands, I should think it's all his own."

Cecilie looked around. "So the killer gained access to the house, surprised Emil in the living room, they fought, then Emil fled in here, where he was killed. Is that what we're saying happened?"

"That's where I'd put my money, at any rate," Ole said. "But I'm inclined to think that the killer hunted the victim down rather than them having an all-out fight. The stab wounds to the buttocks and crotch indicate he was pursued around the living room."

"You think he might have been tortured first?"

"Maybe. It's probably no coincidence that a large concentration of the stab wounds are around his genitals."

Lasse appeared to swallow. "Sounds like the murderer is almost more of a psychopath than Emil was."

"Do you need some air?" Cecilie asked.

"No, no," he replied quickly.

"So what kind of killer are we dealing with?" Cecilie asked, looking at them both.

"The way he gained access to the house seems professional," said Lasse. Cecilie nodded. "He definitely wanted the element of surprise in his attack. Did it require physical strength to kill him? I mean . . . Emil was a big, heavy guy."

Ole shrugged. "A sharp knife and the victim's own fears can be enough to accomplish that, if you ask me."

"Judging by the empty bottles around the house, Emil was thirsty by nature," Lasse said. "Perhaps he was drunk when the killer struck?"

"Again, we'll only know *how* thirsty he was once we've got him on the slab," Ole replied.

"Okay," Cecilie said. "So let's assume that Emil is drinking alone in the middle of the night when all of a sudden the killer is there in his living room with a large knife. He tries to escape, but he's stabbed repeatedly with the knife. Possibly in a torture-like scenario. So does that mean we're dealing with a crime of passion? Did it all happen in a blood rush?"

Ole shook his head. "My guess is that it was all relatively controlled."

"So we're talking about a pretty cool customer?"

"Yes. At any rate, it takes a great deal of willpower to cut someone else's throat," Ole said.

"Good. That means we can discount the idea that this was a crime of passion?"

"I would describe this as nothing less than an execution," Ole said.

"I . . . need to get . . . some air," Lasse said, disappearing from the bedroom.

Cecilie looked down at the corpse, scrutinising Emil Kam intently. It felt unreal that just two days ago she had caught him abusing Ali, only for him to be miraculously released following the preliminary hearing before ending up with his throat cut. She had to admit she wouldn't mourn his passing.

Ten minutes later, Cecilie found Lasse in the front garden. "Are you okay?" she asked, smiling at him. "Too much blood in there?"

"No, no. Course not," Lasse said, clearly attempting to look fine.

Out in the street, more curious onlookers had appeared—they were trying to peer over the hedge. "Do you think any of them noticed anything?" she said, looking back towards the bystanders again.

"Doubt it. I grew up in a neighbourhood just like this one. Everyone always has stories to tell, but no one ever knows anything for sure. Those privet hedges might as well be iron curtains."

Just then, a flash went off in the street—a sure sign that the press had also found the scene.

"It might be worth our while delaying the door-to-door inquiries for a bit," Cecilie said. "So that we don't have the vultures all over us."

19

The meeting room was permeated by the bitter smell of stewed pump-flask coffee. Cecilie and Lasse were sitting opposite NC3's Ismail, Nils from Forensics, and Andreas, who had sneaked into the meeting. Looming at the head of the table was Karstensen, who was drumming his fingers on the stack of newspapers in front of him. "Everyone's eyes are on us," he said, looking around at them as if to emphasise his point. "And I don't just mean the papers—the top brass are also following this with great interest. Which is never a good thing. And why shouldn't they?" he asked rhetorically. "Because the next second it all ends up political, and before you know it, heads start to roll. So I would urge you all to get to the bottom of this case as quickly as possible and find the killer."

Andreas adjusted his tie. "The killer has, however, spared the tax-payer the expense of prosecuting Emil Kam. That ought to cheer up politicians of any stripe."

Karstensen looked at him sharply. "If you had successfully remanded Kam, this would never have happened."

Andreas held out his hands. "And I'm the first to regret that outcome, but Judge Mogensen is unpredictable in those kinds of cases. On the other hand, if we look at the bigger picture pragmatically, the case hasn't become any less sensational with Kam's demise. This may end up being a case that makes all our names."

"Yes, or the one that sees us straight out the door if we don't solve it." Karstensen turned his gaze to the autopsy report which was next to the newspapers. He didn't open it, looking instead to Cecilie. "Has Ole left us any the wiser?"

Cecilie straightened up in her chair, picked up her copy, and flipped through it. "Death occurred between one and three o'clock in the morning. We've confirmed that the ultimate cause of death was the cutthroat which damaged the main artery, as well as injuring the victim's windpipe. None of the twenty-three stab wounds inflicted on him were deep enough to injure his internal organs. The cuts to his arms are described as defensive wounds. These weren't fatal either. Kam's blood alcohol level was two point one per cent. In other words, he was pretty squiffy."

"An easy victim, then," Karstensen interrupted. "What else?"

"He may have been hampered by his ostomy bag, not to mention the butt plug that the pathologist found in his rectum."

"He had a sex toy up his rear end?" Karstensen asked in astonishment.

Cecilie nodded. "There were no signs of any fresh damage to the rectum, so Ole reckons it was self-inserted prior to the killing."

"Was he gay?"

She shrugged. "Emil Kam's sexual assaults had previously encompassed both underage girls and boys. His sexual preferences probably inclined him towards both sexes."

"Played in every position, as they say," Lasse added.

Karstensen rolled his eyes. "Well, what else? Any DNA from the killer?"

"No."

"That seems bloody incredible," Karstensen said brusquely. "Kam was slaughtered and the killer didn't leave a single trace? No saliva, no blood, not even a hair?"

"Nothing that we've found," Cecilie replied.

"Standards slipping with Ole? Or should we be blaming Forensics?" Karstensen directed his x-ray vision at Nils. "You're being very quiet, matey. You sure you don't have anything to share with us?"

"Hmm, well . . ." Nils said hesitantly. He was in his late thirties, blond, and with facial hair that would never be more than a sprinkling of down.

"We've found traces of talcum powder, including on the front door lock, on the dining table, and on the floor by the body. We're therefore pretty certain that the murderer wore rubber gloves. Which is consistent with the fact that we haven't found any fingerprints."

"Talcum powder? So you haven't found anything that we can use?"

Nils nervously scratched his left cheek.

"What about the weapon?"

"We've had the dog teams out searching the whole neighbourhood," said Cecilie. She felt her phone in her pocket vibrate as a text message arrived.

Karstensen threw himself back in his chair. "For the love of Christ! This is the flimsiest investigation I've seen in ages. A killer who stabs their victim in a bloody knife attack without leaving a trace?"

"He might have taken precautions," Lasse interjected.

"What do you mean by that?" Karstensen asked.

"Well, covered himself properly, used a hairnet, maybe a face mask . . . and those gloves that Nils mentioned."

Karstensen looked at Lasse as if he were a moron. "Do you seriously think the killer strolled down the street in *that* neighbourhood in that getup without anyone noticing?"

"It was the middle of the night," Cecilie said. "He could have parked close to Emil Kam's house and waited until it was safe to come out. Or perhaps he changed into his *getup* in the garden." She felt her phone vibrate again.

"Yes, maybe," Karstensen acknowledged. "What do the neighbours have to say?"

"The same thing neighbours always say," Lasse said. "Kam always said hello. Kept himself to himself. They're all shocked to discover what a monster he was. They're all appalled that such a terrible crime could take place in their little slice of heaven. Although several of them were pretty satisfied with the outcome. Said it was justified."

"But do we have any witnesses?"

"No; no one saw or heard anything at the time of the crime," Lasse said.

"Well, that's just bloody great, isn't it," Karstensen said sarcastically.

Cecilie discreetly pulled her phone from her trouser pocket and checked her messages under the table. Nice to see you, beautiful, said the first message sent by Andreas, followed by, See you soon at *our* hotel?

She glanced over at Andreas, who was smiling. Cecilie gave him a cool look and put her phone back in her pocket.

"So in other words, we've got sweet fuck all to go on," Karstensen grumbled.

No one said anything.

Ismail cautiously raised his hand. Karstensen looked at him with a gaze that showed no signs of recognition.

"Ismail, from NC3," Ismail said, pointing to himself.

"Where's Osbourne? Have you managed to crack those computers?"

"We're working on it, and I'm afraid Osbourne is off sick."

"And?"

Ismail opened his folder. "We still haven't managed to decrypt the files we found on the hard drives, and we haven't made any progress with the three SD cards either."

Karstensen leaned forward across the table. "Tell me about something that you *have* succeeded with, Isam."

"Ismail," he said, smiling cautiously. "We've been able to re-create Emil Kam's online activities. I—we—managed to find his log in and password for the Tor browser that he used when he was participating in open groups, as well as on the dark web."

"Nice work, Ismail," Cecilie said.

"Wicked," Lasse chimed in.

"Yeah, yeah. Wicked, whatever. But what does this bring to the investigation?" Karstensen asked. "Have we got any closer to finding Kam's killer?"

"It tells us who he was mixing with in the virtual world. It may have been one of them who killed him," Ismail said.

"Perhaps. What else?"

"Emil Kam created the paedophile forum called CandyCum. He was the administrator. We've got around seventy IP addresses for new members who we'll open investigations into. Judging by the volume of encrypted files being swapped between members, the group seems active."

"Have you been able to see what they're sending?" Andreas asked, interested for the first time.

"Not yet. We're working on it. But judging by the chat logs that we've been able to read, it's the rape of children as young as two years old. Emil wrote that he fantasised about killing a kid that he had just met. He called the boy Alibaba."

Andreas leaned back in his chair. "If we'd had that information at the preliminary hearing, things would have gone very differently."

"Anything else?" Karstensen asked.

Ismail looked around at the group. "We've been able to track Emil Kam's movements on regular social media. He had multiple profiles. He was most active on Arto, where he passed himself off as a minor using four different avatars. He's been in contact with around fifty users whom he tried to groom. We're in the process of identifying them using images and videos that were exchanged."

Karstensen snapped his fingers enthusiastically. "Perhaps that's where he met this boy you saw, Cecilie?"

"Ali? Yeah, maybe."

"It wouldn't surprise me one bit if our killer is to be found in the immigrant community."

They all looked at Karstensen in disbelief.

Karstensen leaned back in his chair and smiled smugly. "That throat slashing might well indicate the killer has Muslim roots."

"Erm . . . isn't that grasping at straws?" said Lasse.

"And why would that be?" Karstensen asked.

"Firstly, it would require the boy to have told his nearest and dearest about the abuse. Thus far, it seems as if he's done everything in his power to cover it up."

"So? Perhaps he was exposed or had a breakdown."

"But wouldn't his relatives have contacted the police if that were the case?"

"Well, Lasse, you might well ask yourself that. Would they?" said Karstensen, screwing his eyes shut. "I'm not receiving any better ideas . . . Cecilie?"

Lasse looked at her. Cecilie took a deep breath. "As soon as NC3 is done identifying the kids that Emil Kam was in contact with, we'll look into all of them. Then we'll see what that turns up."

"Ali!" Karstensen said, pointing to Ismail, his arm outstretched. "He's our top priority. When we find him, we need to give his family a proper going over. A brother, a father, an uncle—any one of them could be our killer." He drummed his fingers expectantly on the newspapers and looked at Andreas. "It may very well be that you're right on this one, Andreas. This case might well turn out to be valuable . . . for the unit."

It was half past six in the evening and Cecilie was on her own in the office. The other detectives had gone home long ago and even Andreas, who had been floating around, had finally departed. No more enticing text messages had arrived from him, and she took that to mean that he'd got her silent message. No matter how tempting he was, she knew full well that a relationship with Andreas was doomed to failure in every respect. What was more, she didn't appreciate his cocky manner, and she had made up her mind that it was over between them.

Now that she was alone, she pulled up Lazarus's documents with the information about Emil Kam. If, as she suspected, Lazarus was responsible for the killing, she was surprised that he hadn't used his own murder plan. That would have been the easiest and most discreet thing to do. So why had he instead carried out this macabre, sensational killing? The only answer she could think of was that Lazarus wanted to prove that he could get away with it. He was exhibiting his power to her.

She wondered whether she could somehow involve Lasse in her inquiries. But no matter how loyal Lasse was, and how much esteem he held her in, he would still have to take it to Karstensen. Just then, the mobile on her desk buzzed and she assumed Andreas hadn't got the memo after all. But she was wrong. Instead, it said Unknown number on the display, and she wondered who it might be.

"Cecilie Mars."

"Just the person I was hoping to speak to." The voice was deep and masculine, but it was also digitally distorted, giving it a metallic sound.

"Who am I talking to?"

"Lazarus."

20

Cecilie could feel her heart pounding in her ribcage like a runaway piston.

"Cat got your tongue?" said the metallic voice on the line.

She took a deep breath. "Who am I talking to?"

"We've already established that: Lazarus. You seem surprised by my call."

"Yes," she managed to blurt out.

"Why? Were you expecting something else from me? Perhaps a video sent to the Independent Police Complaints Authority?"

"I . . . had no expectations." She took a pencil from the tub and wrote on the notepad on her desk: Male. Articulate. Voice electronically masked. Middle-aged? She added a note to herself: Keep your fucking cool.

"I had high expectations of you. I imagined there to be untapped potential waiting to be set free."

"Is that right? And how do we know each other?"

He let out a small laugh. "I know you better than you know yourself, Cecilie Mars. So much better. And right now, you're not only a disappointment to me, but to yourself."

"You seem pretty confident in your analysis of me—where do you get your insights from?"

There was a deep sigh on the other end of the line. "You're asking

questions like some wet-behind-the-ears newbie detective unhelpfully trying to fish for information from the accused. That seems rather beneath
the dignity of an inspector. Perhaps they allowed you to rise too quickly
through the ranks?"

Familiar with my career, she wrote rapidly. "Sorry . . . I was just
curious."

Her apology seemed to satisfy him. "Let's talk instead about why you
failed to follow my instructions. Why did you have such difficulty doing
so, Cecilie? Do you mind if I call you Cecilie?"

"That's fine. Because you see, it's as you say, I'm a police inspector. I
don't kill people. I arrest them and bring them to justice."

"That wasn't the fate that you intended for Ulrik Østergård. You
killed him in cold blood. Just as your silence killed that pervert Emil
Kam."

She drummed her pencil on the notepad while searching for the
right words to humour him with. "That's rather different to following a
detailed murder plan. Don't you agree?"

"Certainly. I must say, your poor decision had macabre consequences
for Emil Kam. Not that I mourn his death. No one does. But when I
think of all the resources his death has drawn upon, it seems like an
unparalleled waste of police time and taxpayers' money. Had you instead
followed the plan, Emil Kam would have been put down like the sick dog
he was. Entirely without the knowledge of the press or the police."

"Doesn't everyone deserve a fair trial?"

"There's no such thing."

"What about his victims? What about their legal rights?"

"If you were worried about his victims, then you should have followed
the plan. Don't forget that they must now go through a painful process.
Now they have to wait for you to come blundering in to remind the poor
sods about his atrocities again."

Is he a victim, too? she wrote.

"If you had followed the plan, we would all have been able to sleep
soundly. You could have been at home in your flat right now, instead of
sitting alone in the office." At that moment, she heard the noise of traffic
in the street outside and she heard it on the phone, too.

Cecilie got up from her chair. "I would go so far as to say that your plan was pretty clever given its simplicity." She made her way around the desk and headed to the large windows overlooking Teglholm Allé.

"Clever?" he exclaimed. "It was flawless! All it needed was a trivial intervention on your part instead of this mess."

"May I ask you something?"

"If it's relevant."

"Why did you need me to carry out your plan?"

She stood by the wall beside the front window. Although the office was in semidarkness, she debated whether she should step forward to look down into the street.

"Because we had a deal."

"We didn't have a deal. You tried to blackmail me."

"Motivate you. Create justice where there is no justice," he said.

Cecilie stuck her head out. Down below in the square, there were some ten or twelve cars parked up in the bays. She leaned back against the wall. He was down there somewhere. She was certain of it. "It seems personal for you. Like a mission. A calling, perhaps?"

"Now you're on the right track."

"Did you know Østergård and Kam?" she asked, quickly returning to her desk.

"What on earth does that have to do with anything?"

"I'm just trying to understand what is driving you." She unlocked her drawer and pulled out her service weapon.

"That ought to be clear. Even to you. I've already described that in my first communiqué to you. The law is no longer capable of curbing crime. Thus, a special effort is called for. Our effort."

She hurried through the office and then down the corridor. "Emil Kam would have been found out in due course."

"Is that right?" he said incredulously. "And how many victims would it have taken? Five, ten, fifteen?"

"I understand what you're saying, but that doesn't justify his liquidation."

"That's the police officer in you speaking. But you're capable of so much more, Cecilie. You can't help but feel that Ulrik Østergård and Emil Kam got what they deserved. Isn't that right?"

"Maybe," she said, opening the door. Right now, she was going to tell him whatever he said was right. "I assume it was you who killed Emil Kam," she said, running down the stairs heading for the lobby.

"Hold your horses, Inspector Mars," he said gleefully. "What in the world do you base that on?"

"The fact that you sent me a detailed murder plan."

"Well, you can't accuse me of anything other than having a lively imagination."

"And wanting Emil Kam dead."

"Again. There's no actual proof. Especially not when we consider how Emil Kam was killed."

Cecilie carefully opened the main door and looked towards the parked cars.

"Have you found any traces of the killer?"

"Yes, we've found all sorts of interesting things." She bent low and ran across the street towards the parked cars. When she reached the first one, she crouched beside it and took the safety off her gun.

"Sorry, but I find that unlikely. Cecilie, are you lying to me?"

She half stood up and peered over the car's radiator. Her view was only able to take in the nearest cars, which were all empty. "Why would I do that?"

"I can think of several good reasons why. But given all the evidence that you apparently have, what's your theory?" he asked, his voice dripping with irony. "Was it a crime of passion? A vengeful citizen? Perhaps it was a disgruntled parent who couldn't handle the truth that their little pride and joy had been desecrated?"

"We're working on a slightly different theory." She moved carefully towards the rear end of the car to get a better view.

"Is that right? Doesn't it bother you that you can't brief your colleagues on what you know? Does it bother you that you have to *lie* to Lasse?"

She didn't allow herself to be provoked, instead scanning the cars. In one of them, parked farthest away, she caught sight of a figure. The individual in question had their back to the side door and was on the phone. "Who says he hasn't already been briefed?" Cecilie said.

"Oh, Cecilie, now I know you're bluffing. Lasse wouldn't be able to keep a secret like that, would he?"

She aimed her pistol at the figure while moving along the row of cars.

"You're also much too jealous of your honour, aren't you? You've got far too much to lose. You've fought your way to the top, overtaking all your male colleagues. You know that they're already whispering behind your back: saying you're not good enough, saying you must have slept your way up the ranks, saying that you're weak. Not that it affects you. I should imagine you're indifferent because in the end it's you who is their boss. You're just a few short steps from bagging the homicide chief's office."

"Ah, you know me so well," she said ironically.

"But all that might come to an end. All your ambitions. Everything you have struggled to achieve. All that could end with a single email to the Independent Police Complaints Authority. A short video of you and Ulrik Østergård, and you'll be done. Done for good."

"I think that video might fade into insignificance if it helps to apprehend the killer in the Emil Kam case." She was almost at the car. The figure with its back to her had an incipient bald patch in the middle of its greying hair, and it wore a dark coat.

"Perhaps you're right," Lazarus replied. "But you might be surprised by what you find . . ."

She yanked the door handle and the figure fell backwards towards her. "This is the police!" Cecilie shouted.

With her free hand, she pulled the man half out of the car.

"What the hell . . . ?" he shouted, looking up at her in horror.

She aimed her gun at him while taking a step back. "Out of the car and get down on your stomach. NOW!"

The man crawled the last bit out of the car and lay down flat on the ground. "What's . . . what's going on here?" he stuttered. At that moment, there was a cry from inside the car and Cecilie looked in through the open door. Sitting in a child seat on the passenger side was a little boy of some two or three years old, tears pouring down his cheeks. She lowered her gun and looked at the man before her. "Sorry, there's been a . . . misunderstanding."

He got up from the ground. "Are you out of your mind?!" he shouted, getting back into the car. "Crazy bitch."

"Sorry," she said, turning around.

The man slammed the door and started his engine. Cecilie put her phone back to her ear as she watched him driving off.

"I think we still need to build the necessary trust between us," Lazarus said coldly.

She glanced around, but there was no one to be seen.

"On the other hand, I think you may be right," he said.

"In relation to what?"

"That my video of you might very well get you charged, but it would probably pale into insignificance in comparison to the police arresting Emil Kam's killer. I read that you still don't have a weapon."

"And?"

"I think if it was found and it had the killer's DNA and fingerprints on it, it would represent a breakthrough for the investigation."

"If you're in possession of it, then feel free to send it in," she replied casually.

"Be careful what you wish for, Cecilie Mars. Have a pleasant evening," he said, cutting the connection. A moment later, she heard a car accelerate away in one of the side streets. Cecilie crossed the street and made her way back to the main entrance. Her phone buzzed, and she saw another anonymous message had arrived. It contained a photograph of a bloody kitchen knife in a transparent plastic bag. The message said: Recognise this, Cecilie?

It felt as if her legs were going to give way.

21

Cecilie took the final step up to the landing outside her front door. She kept her service weapon at her side as she dug into her pocket for her keys. She stooped and noticed the small, fresh scratches on the bottom of the lock cylinder. Something indicated that it had been forced using either a lock pick gun or a skeleton key. She carefully inserted her key into the lock and pushed the door open. With her gun raised, she made her way into the hallway and then into the darkened living room. She searched the rest of the flat and concluded that it was empty. Back in the kitchen, she opened the top drawer, where she kept the few kitchen utensils that she owned. Among them she found a couple of kitchen knives, but not the big Global knife that Lazarus had photographed. She quickly searched the other drawers and the rest of the kitchen without finding it. At this moment in time, the fact that Lazarus had broken into the flat felt worse than the fact that he had used her knife as the murder weapon. She went into the hallway and checked that all three bolts were secured.

The memories of the rape in the backyard returned. It hadn't happened by chance. He had been building up to it for months. It had begun with his visits to her childhood home and had continued when he'd sought her out in the street. Each time, she had rejected him and thought that he would eventually get the message. She had learned better on that point in the backyard. In the backyard, he'd taken revenge for all those rejections. He had taken plenty of time. Now he was getting under her skin again. Drilling into her brain and taking control. Just like Lazarus was trying to.

She went to the bathroom and splashed some water on her face. She had tablets in the cabinet that could fix this. Tablets that she hadn't taken in a long time, but which would suppress the panicked anxiety. The fact that they also turned her into a babbling zombie was another matter. She opened the cabinet and found the bottle at the back between some toiletries. The expiration date on the label had long since passed. She wondered whether that mattered, and then dropped two tablets onto the palm of her hand. It was as if they were staring back at her. Eventually, she dropped them into the running water. Panic attacks were the least of her problems. She needed to think clearly. She turned off the water and went back to the living room to find her bag. She got out her notepad with her jottings and sat down at the dining table to reread them. It dawned on her that the only reason Lazarus had called was to toy with her. The call had been a prelude to his real plan to send her a picture of the knife. Lazarus liked being the centre of attention. Attention and control were what drove him. The fact that she had tried in vain to catch him had probably given him even more of a kick. What else did she know about him? Lazarus was good at operating covertly. He was both strategically and tactically adept. He was a man who had experience of surveillance, gathering information, planning, intrusion . . . not to mention murder. When she put all this together, he seemed downright professional. As a result, she thought that his experience must have been from a criminal past, or perhaps a military background. She opened the file containing the picture of the knife. Lazarus would definitely have planted her DNA on it. A hair taken from her hairbrush in the bathroom or some skin cells from a worn T-shirt would be enough to bring her down. She leaned back in the chair. At least she had now clarified why Lazarus hadn't used his own murder plan. It was all about taking control over her and tightening his grip. She had to contain his power before he made his next move.

A little after nine the next morning, the locksmith arrived. His name was Claus. He was in his mid-thirties and wore a dark jacket like a uniform that stretched across his potbelly. He looked at the three bolts on the inside of Cecilie's front door in surprise. "Did you fit these yourself?"

"Yes," she replied. "And the latch."

"Then it should be plenty safe already."

"Yes. When I'm in the flat, but not when I'm out at work."

"Have you had a break-in?"

She looked at her watch without answering his question. "How long will this take?"

"For this thing?" he said, proffering the new lock cylinder. "I'll be done in ten minutes. This unit is a simple plug-and-play job."

"Well, don't drag your heels," she said, pointing at the lock. "And is it unpickable?"

Claus shook his head as he unscrewed the old cylinder. "Nothing ever is. It's a constant struggle against the burglars who are always trying to outdo us."

"Okay," she replied, disappointed.

"An electronic lock like the X19 here goes a long way to doing what you want. Bank keys and whatever else the villains try using won't work."

She smiled. It had been a long time since she'd heard anyone use the word *villains*. "What if the villains have got hold of a lock pick gun?"

"No use either. This is good stuff. Of course, they can always kick the door down. Have you ever considered fitting an alarm?"

She had and had then rejected the idea. "I doubt anyone in the neighbourhood would come running if they heard an alarm going off."

"The security company comes by though."

"Usually too late, right?"

"Yes," he admitted. "But at least you get a message on your mobile if someone breaks in. And if you have a motion-sensitive camera inside, then you'll also get pictures of the villains."

"A camera, huh?"

"As many as you want. I can also set one up by the front door. It can all be run through an app."

"I see you're a bit of a salesman, Claus."

Claus's plump cheeks blushed. "Well, I could make you a good offer. And install it right away. Plug-and-play, like I said."

"Okay," she said, checking her watch. There was only a small chance that Lazarus would come back, but it was still worth it. "Get it all set up."

The locksmith's visit had given her an idea.

22

An hour later, Cecilie arrived out of breath at the office and dropped her bag onto her desk. Lasse half-turned in his chair and threw her a hasty glance. "Guppy, you look like shit."

"Thanks, Lasse. You're not exactly looking beautiful yourself."

"Do you ever sleep?"

She shrugged. "You've spilled something," she said, pointing to the dried stain on the front of his shirt. Lasse looked down at the stain and rubbed the fabric. "Bloody yoghurt," he muttered. "Martin's put me on a diet. He says I'm too fat." Lasse gave up on the stain and looked back at her. "By the way, we've got the results back on the talcum powder found at Emil's."

"What do they say?"

"That it contains the same type of plastic fibres that are found in the gloves used by medical staff and the emergency services." He smiled. "*And* by our own Forensics team."

She raised her eyebrows. "So it could be Forensics that contaminated the crime scene?"

"You're unlikely to get Nils to admit to that, but yes. Or it means that our killer is a doctor, paramedic, or copper," he said cheerfully. "I've always suspected those guys in Forensics were borderline psychopaths," he added with a chuckle.

She perched herself on the edge of her desk. "On my way here, I stopped by the swimming baths in Bellahøj."

"You don't smell of chlorine today."

"I didn't get in the water. But it occurred to me that they might have CCTV in the pool or by the entrance."

"And?"

"Out of luck. According to the manager, the proposal was voted down by the council. They didn't want to make the local area any more Big Brother than it already is."

"What were you hoping to find out?"

She took a deep breath. "Whether anyone was watching Emil Kam."

"Interesting," Lasse replied, leaning forward in his seat. "What are you thinking? That Emil was under surveillance for a period of time?"

She looked down at the floor. "It's a possibility, isn't it?"

"Most definitely."

"That's why we need to know where he's been. We should check out whether any of the places where he put up his posters have CCTV. Let's start by concentrating on the days immediately prior to his death. We should be able to use his phone data."

"Still sounds like a lot of work."

"Yes," she said. "What about NC3? How far have they got in identifying the members of Emil Kam's online group?"

"CandyCum? Good question. I haven't heard back from Ismail yet. But do you think the killer was one of them?"

"Yes, perhaps."

"What would the motive have been?"

"That's what I'd very much like to know." Karstensen was standing in the doorway with his arms crossed.

Cecilie felt her cheeks redden. "Well, you see . . . If the killer had been watching Emil Kam for a longer period of time, then it might well have been online as well as in the street. Perhaps he managed to gain access to the group?"

"Waste of time," said Karstensen.

"And why's that?"

He looked sternly at Cecilie. "Because I've asked you to search for the killer among the families of Emil Kam's victims. That Ali boy . . . you remember?"

"NC3 is right on top of that," Lasse said. "They're working through all the online portals for kids that Emil Kam visited."

"So what have they found out? Have they found Ali?"

"Maybe. Maybe not."

"What's that supposed to mean, Lasse?" Karstensen made an impatient gesture.

"That the kids all use different avatars and that they mostly remain anonymous in those groups. Some of them even used Tor browsers. They're not completely stupid," said Lasse, smiling slightly.

"And where does that leave the investigation?"

"NC3 are pulling together all the IP addresses for people that Emil Kam spoke to."

"Still?"

Lasse nodded. "Hopefully, we'll soon have some names and addresses to move forward with."

"That needs to be today," Karstensen said, wagging his finger. He turned on his heel and vanished into his office.

Lasse leaned back in his chair and lowered his voice. "Whatever happened to our 'multipronged model of investigation'?"

Cecilie shrugged. "I'm not sure Karstensen's ever heard of it."

"Cecilie Mars?" said a voice behind her. She turned around.

A young female bike messenger with pigtails was smiling broadly at her. She handed Cecilie a large bouquet of red roses. "Seems to be someone's lucky day. Have a good one," she said, before leaving.

Cecilie gaped at the large bunch of flowers. Lasse whistled and clapped loudly. Before long, he had the whole Division joining in.

Cecilie slumped down into her chair.

"I didn't know you were dating someone. I demand to be informed of that kind of information," Lasse chortled. "Is this the explanation for those bleary eyes, Guppy?"

"Shut your face."

"Are they from a certain lawyer?" Lasse asked, pointing curiously at the white card nestled between the carnations.

"I've no idea who you're referring to," she said.

"I'm not a complete moron," Lasse said, tapping his nose with his index finger. "I don't think I've seen hide nor hair of him this morning. So what does he say?" It was apparent that Lasse wasn't going to drop it until she'd read the card. Cecilie removed it using her thumb and forefinger and then laid the bouquet down on the desk.

Sorry I had to rush off so abruptly yesterday. I hope you didn't take offence at my message. It was only intended as a friendly reminder. Remember: The righteous shall prevail. All the best for today. L.

She felt like everyone was staring at her. Her hands were trembling, and she quickly pocketed the card.

"So who's it from?" Lasse asked.

"Wouldn't you like to know?" she said, attempting a smile. She spotted the shiny flash drive attached to one of the stems with an elastic band.

"You're so mean," he said, chuckling. "Shouldn't they go in a vase? I think there might be one in the cupboard in the corridor."

"Good idea," Cecilie replied, taking the bouquet with her.

23

Cecilie walked down the corridor towards the meeting room at the far end, closest to the exit. She stuck her head around the open door and saw that the room was empty. At the other end was a computer. She went over to it and switched it on. She wrenched the flash drive off the stem and put the flowers down on the table. She inserted the USB into the computer, and a window containing a text file opened. Cecilie hesitated before opening the document.

Dear Inspector Cecilie Mars,

Your next target refers to himself as the "Serpent." At present, I am aware that he is responsible for the rape and murder of three women. All these killings occurred within the last year and represent the Serpent's sacrifices to Odin.

The Serpent is a believer in Asatro, and his hope is that the gods will look favourably upon him and pave his way to Valhalla. These ritualistic killings take place at the new moon and he commits his acts in secluded outdoor locations. Acts that are no different to those of the Vikings of old. The Serpent's three victims were all raped and then ritually dismembered into nine parts. The Serpent keeps the victims' breasts as his trophies, and I know that he transports them in a cool box. He disposes of the other body parts at the Vestforbrænding incineration plant where he works.

The Serpent's civilian name is Morten Pier Nielsen. According to his beliefs, he must bring the gods nine sacrifices in order for his Blót to be fulfilled. It is therefore of the utmost importance that we neutralise him before he strikes again. Need I mention that there will be personal consequences for you if you make anyone else privy to this knowledge? Contact me immediately on the phone number provided for further instructions.

Lazarus

Cecilie felt nauseous. If she hadn't known what Lazarus was capable of, she would have taken the letter for a psychotic fantasy. Just another in line with the many messages that the Division received on a weekly basis from the mentally ill seeking attention. It puzzled her that Lazarus could have such detailed knowledge of both the killer and the killings that had apparently already been carried out.

Cecilie reread the letter while trying to ignore her sense of horror, focusing instead on the facts. He wrote that three women had already been murdered within the last year, and she thought about the unsolved homicides the unit was dealing with. There was nobody who immediately sprang to mind. But the Serpent's victims might be concealed among the missing persons cases, and there were hundreds of those every year. Most missing people usually resurfaced, but there were always a handful who were never found. It was not inconceivable that three women had succumbed to a killer who had managed to remain in the shadows.

She looked up the phone number that Lazarus had provided, without getting any hits. She assumed that he was once again using a fresh, unregistered pay-as-you-go SIM. Just like all the biker gangs. That would make it impossible to track his whereabouts. Cecilie had no intention of calling him. Instead, she logged in to the population register. She found Morten Pier Nielsen and saw that he had a rap sheet as long as it was frightening. As she read the details of his many criminal offences, which were drug- or violence-related, it began to dawn on her. She hadn't been directly involved in any cases against him, but she knew that Morten Pier Nielsen and his nomadic brethren had kept the force's biker gang task force occupied for years. As a consummate gang member, Morten had been mixed up in the vast majority of their cases. She skimmed the report of the most recent one and read that he and three others had been charged with the abduction and torture of a young man who had owed them money. This abuse had lasted for days, and as part of his punishment the man had been forced to cut his own thumb off using a pair of shears. Even though Morten had been the ringleader, he'd got off lightly with a two-year treatment sentence. And Cecilie knew why. Morten had secretly flipped on some of his brethren. His information had led to countless arrests and the seizure of a huge consignment of cocaine. At the same time, the cases against Morten had been quietly dropped and the Prosecution Service had applied leniency in the kidnapping case. As far as Cecilie could remember, it had been a cakewalk for the Terrier at the city court.

In the files, she found a couple of photos of Morten, whose wild eyes and huge beard made him resemble a bloodthirsty Viking. She found an address for him on Rådmandsgade in Nørrebro. If it were true that Morten was transporting his trophies in a coolbox, that might mean he still had them at home. Possibly mummified, she reflected, shuddering at the thought. And if Morten worked at the incineration plant, there was a chance that his place might be empty right now.

Cecilie logged off the computer and headed back to the office for her things. When she reached the end of the corridor, she found that Lasse's chair was empty. She turned towards Henrik, who was engrossed in his own computer. "Henrik, do you know where Lasse's gone?"

He squinted at his wristwatch. "Lunch, I should think. I seem to remember him saying something about rissoles. You know what he's like."

She nodded. "I'm just going to run an errand."

"Okay, Boss."

Just how long is that going to last, she thought to herself as she retrieved her service weapon from the drawer.

24

Cecilie drove down Rådmandsgade in her Panda while keeping an eye out for number 6C, which was where Morten Pier Nielsen lived. In the middle of the day, the neighbourhood seemed quiet and the street ahead of her was deserted. Once she had passed the high-rise blocks of flats, she spotted a low workshop building with boarded-up display windows. Spray-painted onto the gable end was 6A. She continued down the alley that led to the building behind and a garage. She stopped the Panda and got out. When she emerged into the small courtyard at the end of the alley, she made for the entrance to the rear building. She tried the front door—it was locked. On the sign by the door, it said there was a yoga centre on the ground floor and an auditor above that. She surveyed the dark windows. It looked as if it had been some time since anyone had sat in the lotus position or had their accounts reviewed.

She headed to the nearest basement window and peered through the filthy glass. Other than a couple of rims without tyres and an overturned sofa, the space was empty. She speculated that Morten might be using the address as a front. She considered whether to head over to the Vestforbrænding incineration plant to check whether he still worked for them, and to find out if they had an alternative address for him. As she returned to her car, her phone rang. She could see that the number was the same as the one Lazarus had asked her to call.

"Cecilie Mars," he said coolly on the other end of the line. "I thought one of the first things they taught at the police academy was to obey orders. The one I issued to you was, frankly, quite simple."

"Who am I talking to?"

"Do not try my patience."

She inhaled sharply and leaned against the Panda.

"How did you become aware of Morten Pier Nielsen?"

"That is immaterial to the matter at hand."

"Not if this conversation is going to continue."

He let out a mocking laugh. "In light of the incriminating material that I have on you, you are hardly in a position to make demands. Your impertinence surprises me."

"As I see it, it's you who wants something from me, not the other way around."

"Good God—of course you want something; you want to remain in the Homicide Unit."

"You apparently still think you know me."

"Tut, Cecilie," he said, laughing again. "I take it you're at Rådmands-gade and have just established that the Serpent is not at that address? You're most probably considering whether you can track him down with-out the assistance of your Division. So how well would you say I know you?"

She peered up and down the street, looking for Lazarus. It was deserted.

"I shall interpret your silence as tacit approval. But before you rush off to the incineration plant, allow me to reveal to you that you will not find him there. Nor will they be able to provide you with any further details of where he lives. By the way, do you know what day it is today?"

"Wednesday," she replied dryly.

"Not just that. Tonight is the new moon. While we are talking, the Serpent is making himself ready. Sharpening his knives. Sharpening his axes. He's got his little blue coolbox ready for his trophy. Let me send you a picture, Cecilie, so that you understand the gravity of the situation."

She prepared for the worst while waiting for his message. But the photograph that arrived from Lazarus was quite ordinary. It depicted a young woman, African in appearance, of around twenty years of age. She wore a low-cut top and striking red lipstick. The photo had been taken through a car windscreen.

"She calls herself Sugar. She's been in the country for a month."

"A sex worker?"

"Good guess, Inspector. The Serpent selects his victims from among foreign prostitutes. Those who are constantly on the move around Europe. Those whom no one will miss if they disappear. Those that the police don't even bother to write a report on."

The last statement wasn't altogether true, but she didn't contradict him. The fact was that regardless of what working girls were subjected to, they were rarely inclined to talk to the police. "How do you know that Morten . . . that the Serpent has chosen her?"

"Because I'm thorough," he replied bluntly. "That's also why I'm familiar with his modus operandi. The Serpent has been in contact with the girl for a while now. He has won her confidence so that he can take her away from the neighbourhood to his *sacrificial ground*."

"Why haven't you stopped him? Why did you let him kill three women?"

Lazarus sighed deeply. "I can't save the world. But I can punish the sinners I encounter."

Cecilie snorted. "You're more interested in the perpetrators than the victims. Have I got that right?"

"What you have is a very busy day ahead of you."

"So how do I find the Serpent?"

"Start by driving to his hunting ground. See whether you can find poor little Sugar before it's too late."

"And where can I find her?"

Lazarus groaned. "If you can't figure that out for yourself, then you're not much of a detective," he replied, cutting the call.

She got into the Panda. The biggest cluster of foreign sex workers was found on and around Istedgade. As far as she knew, the Eastern European girls opted for Skelbækgade, while the Africans working the streets preferred to be round the back of the central railway station. But she doubted that Lazarus would make it that easy for her to find

Sugar. For that matter, the girl could just as well be installed in one of the brothels down there. This was Lazarus's way of moving the pieces around before the new moon arrived and the hunt really began. She started the engine.

25

It was gone midnight and Cecilie had spent the whole evening driving around the blocks near Istedgade looking for Sugar. Yet despite the many streetwalkers loitering in the area, she hadn't spotted the girl. It had otherwise been a busy evening with lots of girls out on the streets, and new punters constantly pulling up in their cars. Judging by the turnout of estates and four-wheel drives, there were plenty of family men among their number.

Earlier that evening, Lasse had called her. NC3 had finally turned up Ali Khan and six other children that Emil Kam had been in contact with. Social services had been notified, and Lasse already had details about Ali and his family. The boy lived with his mother, who was on sickness benefit, and his three older sisters, which suggested that Karstensen's theory of a patriarchy thirsty for revenge didn't hold true.

Cecilie stopped on Istedgade right outside Kebab-Ministeren, where she picked up her dinner. She was almost all the way through her durum wrap when her phone rang. "Cecilie Mars," she said, answering it with her mouth full.

"Have you found Sugar?" Lazarus asked.

Disturbed, she put down her food. "No, but something tells me that was never what you intended me to do."

"You were provided with the information you needed to find her. The rest was up to you."

"Just tell me where she is so that we can avert whatever it is you think is going to happen."

"Firstly, there's nothing to be averted. That's not what you use a decoy for. Quite the contrary. Secondly, it's not about what I think. It is about what I *know* will happen."

"Okay. I can tell you with absolute certainty that Sugar isn't here, and I haven't seen the Serpent or the Dodge Ram registered to Morten."

Lazarus chuckled. "So you have done something then. Good move to check on the car, even if it didn't turn anything up."

"Where is he?"

"If the Serpent is following his usual approach, I should think he's on his way to pick up little Sugar."

"Where?"

"At Turisthotellet. But you'll have to hurry before he gets away again," Lazarus said, hanging up.

Cecilie tossed away the rest of her food and got into the Panda. Lazarus had to be nearby to orchestrate his play. She drove down Istedgade heading towards the central railway station: Turisthotellet was on one of the adjacent side streets. Calling the place a hotel was an exaggeration. More than anything, it was a silo in which sex workers—especially those in Denmark illegally—could pay hand over fist to rent a mattress on one of the overfilled floors. Some years ago, she had been involved in a police raid there, and she still remembered the stench.

Five minutes later, she turned onto Reverdilsgade and drove along it until she reached the hotel, where she pulled over. Sugar was already standing on the front step wearing a thigh-length skirt and green satin jacket. The girl was shivering and looked like someone who was either freezing or needed a fix. At that moment, she caught sight of someone farther up the street and she jumped off the step. Cecilie watched the girl run across the street in front of her towards a black pickup that was parked by the kerb. Morten Pier Nielsen had his arm hanging out of the open window, and he was smiling. His hair was tied in a ponytail, and his beard was better trimmed than it had been in the photo in the police file. On four of his fingers, he wore massive silver rings that combined to form a fearsome knuckle-duster. Morten tilted his head to indicate to Sugar that she should get into the passenger seat. As the girl walked around the front of the truck, he gently patted the driver-side door and then withdrew his tattooed arm. A moment later, the V8 engine roared and he drove off down the street.

Cecilie followed right behind him. She already hated him, and was tempted to pull him over, even if that wouldn't lead to the right outcome. Regardless of whether he had any weapons in the vehicle, it wouldn't offer any proof in terms of his plans for Sugar. Morten would be back on the street within twenty-four hours. She would have to catch him red-handed.

As they drove up Skelbækgade, her phone rang. "Congratulations, you made it," said Lazarus.

"Where's he taking her?"

"All will soon become clear. But don't tail him too closely—you might be spotted."

"This isn't my first time following someone." She checked in the rear-view mirror to see whether Lazarus was following her, but there were no cars in immediate proximity.

"I have every confidence in your abilities, Cecilie. In fact, I'd like to compliment you if I may."

"For what?" she said, keeping one eye on the mirror. At the far end of Skelbækgade, a car appeared, but it was too far away to make out what brand it was, or to catch a glimpse of the driver.

"For keeping a cool head. For not calling for backup or trying to arrest the Serpent. This demonstrates to me that you have understood your task. I'm pleased. Truly."

"Good," she replied. She slowed down to allow the car behind to get closer.

"While I may not be an Asatro believer, I still think that this evening with its new moon may serve as a watershed for us all," Lazarus said enthusiastically.

"Is that right?"

When they turned on to Vasbygade, Morten put his foot down, and she had to accelerate, too, to keep up. "Then why don't we meet up?"

Lazarus chuckled. "Cecilie, I'm sure that will come to pass. Don't you worry! Now concentrate on the task at hand. Not too close to him. We really don't want to alarm the Serpent."

She looked in the rearview mirror—she now had several cars behind her. "He doesn't seem like the type to get alarmed," she replied.

They passed the Scandic hotel and then crossed the Sjællandsbroen bridge. When they reached the crossroads at Bådehavnsgade, Morten turned off.

"Where are we going?" she asked.

"To his sacrifice site. Where else? This is where blood must be shed."

"Has he used the same place before?"

"This is his place. Sacred soil. I have no idea why. Perhaps the Vikings landed here?" Lazarus added wryly.

The Dodge Ram's lights went out, and a moment later the truck vanished like a shadow around the corner onto Speditørvej. Cecilie checked her own rearview mirror again and saw that she was alone on the dark road. Just like Morten, she switched off her lights and turned around the corner. Speditørvej extended some three hundred metres ahead of her before ending in a turning circle. She pulled into the side and surveyed the dozen or so vehicles at the end of the street. In the darkness, most of them resembled abandoned wrecks. If this place was Morten's sacrificial site, then it could only be described as the scrapyard's answer to Stonehenge. She looked for Morten's Dodge without spotting it. "So is this the place?" she asked.

Lazarus didn't reply.

"Hello?" she said. She could hear his heavy breathing, but he still wasn't answering.

Cecilie made her way down the road past the squat buildings to the end. She swept her gaze across the wrecked cars, but the Dodge Ram seemed to have been swallowed up by the earth. The turning circle itself was surrounded by the greenery of the Sydhavn peninsula, with a car mechanic's on the other side. She stared at the deserted workshop, which was hidden behind a huge lattice gate. "He's disappeared. For fuck's sake, Morten's disappeared," she said loudly. She thought about Sugar and the fate that awaited her if she didn't find her.

"Calm down, Cecilie," Lazarus said breathlessly on the phone. "Get out of the car and head past the last row of cars."

Cecilie followed his instructions. When she got there, she saw that there was a whole section of the wire fence missing. In the rutted grass she saw a fresh set of tyre tracks. "Follow him on foot. But be careful. You're close to him now."

She hesitated briefly and then stepped through the gap in the wire fence.

26

Cecilie pulled her Maglite out of her pocket and shone it ahead of her. Fifty hectares of the Sydhavn peninsula's grassy parkland lay before her. The moonlight forced its way through the cloud cover, revealing the many low trees and shrubs that were scattered across the landscape like dark shadows. She followed the tyre tracks towards the meadow, where they disappeared.

"Follow the meadow until you reach a small gravel path," Lazarus said.

She shone her torch around. "Where's he taken her?"

"Just follow my instructions. Otherwise you'll never find him."

"Wouldn't it just be easier if you told me?"

"No. And if you don't find him, then little Sugar will soon be sharing the fate of Brandy, Joy, and Lulu. Nine parts, no breasts, and at the incineration plant."

It was the first time Lazarus had named Morten's victims. "Did you know them?" Cecilie asked. She strode through the tall wet grass, her trouser legs already soaked.

"When you see someone get dismembered, you always feel a certain degree of attachment to them afterwards. But apart from that, no. Have you reached the path?"

"No," she said. "But I think I see it."

"You're doing very well, Cecilie. Hurry, so we can stop this beast before he starts cutting her."

Cecilie stepped onto the path. "Now what?"

"Bear left and head down the path until you reach the bench farther on."

She began to run, her footsteps echoing into the night. Soon after, she reached the bench, which was built on top of a couple of tree trunks. "Where do I go now?" she asked breathlessly.

"Crouch down and look under the bench."

She squatted and shone the light of her torch in an arc under the bench. Towards the very back there was a white tote bag. She pulled the bag out. It felt heavy. When she opened it, she found herself staring at a sawn-off shotgun and a box of cartridges. "What . . . what is this?"

"A double-barrelled Browning, that I've shortened for you. You'll also find ammunition there."

"I've brought my own service weapon. Where's Morten?"

Lazarus sighed deeply. "It's pointless liquidating the Serpent with your own gun. That would require an implausible explanation down the line, and it would leave far too many loose ends."

"I'm not going to . . ."

"Take the Browning and load both barrels. Next, I'm going to lead you towards him."

"This is insane."

"Not at all. We need to make it look like a biker gang execution."

"I'm . . . I'm not going to."

"Cecilie Mars! If I don't hear you load that weapon now, this all ends right here. Then it will be your fault that girl dies. Because you chose not to save her."

"Tell me where she is and I'll save her."

"Load the gun and cock it. Now!"

In the distance, a half-strangled scream was audible. Cecilie spun around and listened in the darkness. There was no saying where it had come from. "Where are they?"

"Cock it and I'll lead you to them. Sugar is already suffering. Perhaps you'll still be able to save her other breast."

"For Christ's sake, tell me!"

"For the last time, load the weapon."

"Okay." She returned the torch to her pocket and cracked the rifle open. Her fingers trembled as she dug into the box of cartridges and inserted one into each barrel. Then she snapped the rifle shut and cocked it. "Satisfied?"

"Very. Now hurry. I don't think Sugar has long left. It's high time the Serpent met his fate. Behind the bench there is a hill—you must go up it. Now run!" Lazarus commanded.

She ran up the steep hill and a couple of minutes later she reached the top, out of breath. From here, there was a clear view of the dark land-scape. Far across the waters of Kalveboderne, the red warning lights on the motorway bridge crossing the bay were visible. And below, the meadow ran down to the shoreline a couple of hundred metres away. She caught sight of the Dodge, right by the water. Lying on the back of the truck was a figure, and she saw Morten standing on the running board. Cecilie dropped the sawn-off shotgun in the grass and ran down the hill towards the vehicle. Morten was bare chested and had his face turned towards the sky as he chanted. His muscular upper torso was tattooed with mythical beasts and runes. In one hand he held a long knife, while in the other he had a double-bladed axe. He was leaning a little over Sugar, who was naked and had her wrists tied together, a dirty rag stuffed in her mouth. Cecilie slowed down and pulled out her service weapon. Fearing that Morten might hurt the girl, she didn't dare shout at him yet. Instead, she tried to bring her breathing back under control as she approached him from behind.

"You shall be my thrall in Valhalla!" Morten shouted, looking down at Sugar. Tears were pouring down her cheeks as she desperately attempted to free herself. "You must wait on me at the table of the gods. You must ensure it is set when your warrior returns home." He raised the axe above his head.

Cecilie stopped a couple of metres away from him. "Morten! Drop your weapon! NOW!"

Morten froze midmovement. Slowly, he turned his head and looked at her, his eyes dead. "How dare you interrupt my Blót?"

"Put down the knife and axe. Now!"

He smiled and lowered the axe to hip height. "Yes, of course, my thrall. Naturally. Happy?"

"I told you to drop it. The knife, too."

At that moment, Morten threw the axe, which spun through the air towards her head. Cecilie threw herself to one side and felt it whizz past, close to her face. Morten jumped off the running board, the knife held in his outstretched hand. Cecilie raised her gun, but before she could take aim, Morten kicked it out of her hand. She made to grab it again, but Morten trod on her hand, hard. She felt the bones in her fingers break and she shrieked with pain.

"Perhaps you're the chosen one? Instead of this black whore? The gods might appreciate some white meat!"

She withdrew her hand and scrambled away from him. The pain was radiating up through her arm.

"You look like a thrall, crawling around like that." He bent down to reach for her.

Cecilie kicked him in the chest. It felt as if she had hit a wall, and Morten smiled, unfazed. "You squirm well, thrall. I like that." He sheathed his knife and pulled down his trousers. "Come here. You must honour your ruler."

Cecilie leapt from the ground and aimed a circular kick at his head.

The kick made Morten falter. He reached out for her, but he was too slow. She followed up by kicking him in the balls. Morten fell to his knees, groaning. She swung her right leg towards him, aiming for his jaw. Morten parried and grabbed her ankle. His fist felt like a claw. He yanked hard on her leg and toppled her to the ground. Cecilie tried to kick with her left leg, managing to dispatch a barrage of rapid blows at him. None of them touched Morten, who lunged at her. His weight squeezed all the air out of her lungs. The next moment, she felt his hands at her throat. Morten returned to half standing as he continued to squeeze. She tried to release his grip with both her hands, but he was too strong.

Morten smiled at her. "I'll fuck you when you're dead," he said, squeezing harder until her vision went black. "I've done it before. It's okay," he said with a shrug. "Although I prefer the squirming."

Her left hand was searching the ground. She hoped to find the pistol but could feel nothing but wet grass between her fingers. Morten had become a shadow swaying indistinctly above her. Her head was throbbing and her eyes stung—it felt like they were about to pop out. Her mouth opened automatically in a silent death scream. She nudged him with her right hand. She felt his sweaty chest. The hair at his navel. His belt. The metal buckle. The hilt of the knife in the sheath. Her broken fingers grabbed the hilt and drew the knife out. Her arm outstretched, she swung blindly. Stabbed once. Twice. Three times. Then she let go and everything went black.

27

Cecilie was lying on her side in the damp grass. When she tried to swallow, it felt as if she'd eaten shards of glass. She opened her eyes and looked at Morten, who was lying beside her with a blank expression in his eyes. She instinctively pulled away from him and half sat up. Her right hand hurt, and she could see that it was swollen. Her ring finger and little finger were crooked, the outer joints broken. She looked at Morten again. And the knife sticking out of his throat. There was also a stab wound to his shoulder, and yet another had split his left ear in two. She put two fingers to his throat to check for a pulse. Nothing.

Cecilie got up from the grass and headed towards the Dodge, calling out to Sugar. When she reached the back of the truck, she looked up into the cargo space, which was empty save for a few pieces of gaffer tape. She pulled out her torch and shone it around. In the glow, she spotted a smear of dry blood in the corner, but whether that came from Sugar or one of Morten's other victims it was impossible to tell. She coughed and put a hand to her throat. There was nothing to do other than call this in. She wondered whether it would make any difference if she contacted Lasse first. Whether he would appreciate it or whether she would merely be putting him in a difficult position. At that moment, her phone rang. She reluctantly answered. "Yes?" she said hoarsely.

"Congratulations, Cecilie. You've liberated the world of another beast," Lazarus said. "Although it didn't go quite as elegantly for you as I had planned."

"Kiss my arse."

"There's no need for such crudeness. Not now that our partnership is finally bearing fruit. I'm proud of you. I knew you had it in you. The way that you showed such initiative when under pressure was exemplary."

She looked around in the darkness, thinking to herself that he must be nearby. "His death was an accident. I didn't know where I was stabbing."

"Now, now. Don't talk down your own performance. I think it was impressive to see how you turned an otherwise impossible situation to your advantage."

Cecilie returned to the corpse. "Why don't you come out so we can talk properly?" She found her gun lying in the grass not far from Morten and picked it up.

"Oh, I'm sure we shall meet when the time comes. May I suggest you concentrate on cleaning up and removing all traces that you were ever here? I fear that it would be most unfortunate to leave your fingerprints on the knife."

"There's no need for that," she replied, returning her pistol to her holster. "I'm about to call the police myself. I acted in self-defence, so if you filmed this, too, then you're welcome to send me the file."

"Don't talk nonsense. Of course, you shouldn't report this. Just think what the two of us could achieve."

"The two of us are going to do nothing."

"Don't you understand how important this is? We're the only ones who are willing and able to continue where the law will not step in. We are the bulwark against the beasts prevailing out in the wide world. Surely you of all people ought to understand that?"

"And why's that?"

Lazarus's voice changed to a hiss. "Aren't you haunted by your own past? Indeed, aren't you haunted by that night in the backyard? When he held you tight. When he forced his way into you . . ."

She could feel the tears coming. "Who . . . who the hell are you?"

"I'm Lazarus. The one restored to life from death. I hope that you will also be restored soon."

"You're sick. Absolutely fucking sick," she said, choking a sob.

"No, Cecilie. It's the world that's sick. The justice system."

"We'll see when they convict you."

"It'll never get that far. You would be better off worrying about your own situation. Don't you understand what the consequences will be? The police and the Prosecution Service will not look kindly upon your actions. Perhaps the victims' relatives will. But hardly the authorities. They will see a clear pattern running from Ulrik Østergård to Emil Kam and now on to Morten Pier Nielsen. They will see you as a vengeful woman with a clear motive rooted in an assault in her own past. They'll draw a straight line between them all. They'll cage you with all those beasts. And if you betray me, I won't be able to protect you. Better to remove the rotten fruit from the basket. Do you understand?"

She turned off the phone and put it back in her pocket. She looked at the corpse, at the knife protruding from the neck, and the axe in the grass. Once again, she felt Morten's iron grip and she couldn't cope. The backyard crept up on her. Drilled into her brain, groaning and reeking. She bent down and wiped her fingerprints off the knife. She had to get away now. Away from this madness. She sprinted up the hill she had come down. On her way to the top, she noticed her phone vibrating in her pocket, but she didn't answer. When she reached the top, she searched for the shotgun, but couldn't find it. Eventually, she made her way down to the bench and searched for the tote bag containing the ammunition, but it, too, was gone.

Lazarus wasn't going to let her go. The nightmare was going to go on forever. Or until they were both exposed.

28

When Cecilie unlocked the front door of her flat, the alarm system emitted a meek beep and she entered her code. She had yet to hear how loud it would be if activated. She went into the kitchen and rooted through the freezer for something cold to apply to her injured hand. In the bottom drawer, she found a bag of stir-fry that she had no memory of buying. She examined the broken digits, which forced her fingertips to point unnaturally upwards. As soon as the swelling to her hand had subsided a little, she would prepare a makeshift bandage to force the broken digits into place. A few years ago, she had broken the ring finger on her left hand while training. Even though she'd been to the doctor and got it plastered, the finger had never been quite the same since.

Cecilie put the bag of frozen stir-fry on her hand and wrapped a tea towel around it. She headed for the bathroom and examined her reflection in the mirror. The broken capillaries on her throat from Morten's stranglehold were like dark stains on either side of it. They showed very clearly how close to death she had come. She thought about Sugar. Had she seen anything, or had she been too busy getting out of there? Cecilie doubted that the girl would report the attack. Most likely, she'd beat a hasty retreat from Denmark, probably making for one of Europe's other red-light districts. Cecilie opened the bathroom cabinet and found the jar of zombie tablets. She knew they would stop the whirlwind of thoughts so that she could get some sleep. This time there was no hesitation. She downed two of them. How could Lazarus know about the attack in her own past? The newspapers had only mentioned the case superficially at the time, and none of them had named her. It would have required in-depth research. Had he seen the old story and read the police reports? Had he followed the trial? Who was he? She went into the bedroom and lay down on the bed. The bag of stir-fry was slowly thawing and moisture had soaked through the tea towel. She thought it might be best to change it. Thought she should have bandaged her fingers. Caught Lazarus. Reported the killing. Searched for Sugar. Died in peace. She heard herself snoring before she fell into a deep, nightmarish sleep.

Some hours later, she awoke to the sound of a text message arriving. She saw that the bedroom had grown light, but she had no idea how long she had been sleeping. When she sat up in bed, the room began to spin and she felt nauseous. When she tried to fish her phone out of her pocket, it slipped from her grasp and she remembered how smashed up her hand was. She looked down at it. The swelling had subsided a little, to be replaced by the dark purple of accumulated blood. The two broken fingers were still at a rather odd angle. Using her good left hand, she pulled the phone from her pocket and looked at the display. It was a text from Julie. It took a moment for Cecilie to associate the name with the slender girl from her self-defence class.

Just wanted to let you know:
Fie is in Bispebjerg hospital.
She tried to kill herself yesterday :-(
Apparently ok now.

Cecilie tried to dial the number, but Julie's phone went straight to voice mail. She didn't want to leave a message, so she hung up. She found the number for Fie's mother and called her but had no luck there either. Cecilie cursed herself for not having spoken to Fie before this happened. She got out of bed and felt her entire body aching. She checked the internet on her phone. Although it was already nine o'clock in the morning, there were no news reports of a body found at the park in Sydhavn. But she knew that it was only a matter of time before a jogger or a dog walker passed by and happened upon the macabre scene.

29

An hour later, Cecilie was walking down the narrow white corridor in the youth psychiatric ward at the Bispebjerg hospital. She wore a scarf around her neck to conceal the dark bruises there. Nevertheless, it felt as if they were visible to all, and she put her hands to her neck to make sure that the scarf hadn't slipped down. She had taped up the broken fingers using some plasters and a roll of surgical tape she'd found at the back of her bathroom cabinet. The result was respectable enough, at least taking the strain off the fingers.

A few moments before, when faced with the on-duty nurse in reception, her police ID had gained her access to both the ward and Fie's medical records. Fie had been admitted to casualty the day before, following an overdose of Cyclizine. According to the nurse, this medication to prevent travel sickness had become the hot new trend among the suicidal, now that they could no longer buy enough headache pills over the counter.

Cecilie tapped on the open door to the last room on the corridor. She entered the room, which was in semidarkness since the curtains were drawn. Fie was lying in the big hospital bed with a drip attached to her arm. She seemed frail, and Cecilie reflected that she had lost yet more weight since she had last seen her. When Fie spotted Cecilie, she turned onto her side, her face to the wall.

Cecilie pulled up a chair and sat by the bed. "Hey," she said, gently stroking Fie's shoulder. "How are you doing?"

She heard a quiet sob from Fie.

"I'm sorry to see you like this."

"Why don't you just go away?" Fie said, half choking on her sobs.

"Of course, in a bit."

"Please. I want to be left alone."

Cecilie withdrew her hand. "We've missed you at training."

Fie turned around. "Please. Just go."

"Yes, yes. We're just chatting. Are they treating you well?"

"I don't know . . . well, maybe. I guess. Okay?"

"Has your mother been to see you?"

Fie turned onto her back. "Yeah, but I was asleep . . . well, I was pretending to be."

"Sorry I've not been round to yours to visit you recently."

"Why would you?"

"Because I care about you."

Fie was clearly trying to hold back tears.

"Have you talked to anyone? Other than your mother?"

Fie shook her head. "I've kept myself to myself."

"That's not healthy."

"At least you avoid all the looks and the boys catcalling."

"The same ones as before?"

"Among others."

Cecilie took her hand. "You're better than them. You know that, right? The lot of them."

"It doesn't feel like it. I couldn't even figure out how to kill myself."

"Don't beat yourself up. You don't deserve it."

"And why not?"

Cecilie squeezed her hand until Fie turned her head and looked her in the eyes. "Because it's not your fault. It's his fault. He attacked you. There was nothing you could have done to prevent it. He's the one at fault. He's the one . . ." She let go. ". . . who got what he deserved." Cecilie looked down at the floor. "I really do understand what you've been through, Fie. Believe me."

Fie shook her head quietly. "Everyone says that, but you have to go through it yourself before you can understand."

"You're right about that," Cecilie said, taking a deep breath. "When I was your age, my parents were building a lean-to. They were the height of popularity in Vangede back then," she said, smiling slightly. "So my stepfather got hold of a carpenter called Bjarke. Bjarke was a bit of a piss head, but he was cheap. He spent that whole summer working at our house while my parents were at work. Bjarke was the kind of guy who always had a dirty joke to share. Generally, just after I'd got out of the bath. In fact, it happened so frequently that I ended up taking a change of clothes with me to the bathroom."

"Did . . . did he do something to you?"

Cecilie hesitated. "Bjarke finished that lean-to and then he left, taking his jokes with him. But not long after, I started bumping into him all the time. Coming home from school, when I was out at the shops, on my way home from training in the evening. At first, I thought it was just chance since he lived nearby, but in the end, I was seeing him every day. It started to dawn on me that he was following me."

"Creepy."

"Yes, very creepy. Not least because he was getting more and more brazen. He kept making all sorts of suggestions. Wanted to go to the cinema, out for a drive, invited me round to his. One day when he was really drunk, he ran into me on my way home from training. He threatened me and said that if I didn't go home with him, he'd tell my parents that I'd been walking around naked trying to seduce him all summer."

"What the fuck?!" Fie said, half sitting up in bed. "So what did you do?"

"Told him to go fuck himself. Called him all sorts until he scarpered."

"Did you tell anyone?"

"No, and that was a mistake. I didn't see him at all for a couple of weeks. I figured he'd finally got the message."

"Had he?"

Cecilie dismissively shook her head. "No. One night after I'd been to a party at the youth club, he attacked me on my way home. He dragged me into a backyard not far from where I lived. There, he . . . he . . . well, I think you can imagine what he did. So yes, I understand what you're going through, Fie."

"Did they catch him?"

"Yes. They sentenced him to treatment and he was out in a couple of years," Cecilie replied. Then she smiled again. "It's important for you to talk to someone about this. Professionals." She pointed towards the ward.

"I'm guessing you did?" said Fie.

"No, and that was another mistake I made."

"So what? You've got your shit together," Fie said, falling despondently back into bed. "I'm not like you." Tears were pouring down her cheeks again.

"Fie?" Cecilie pulled up her sleeve to reveal her scarred forearm to her. "I haven't had any of my shit together since that night. Not when I cut myself to push the thoughts away nor when I was popping pills like M&Ms. This is nothing but a façade. A fake," she said, feeling her own eyes tear up. "I don't even know who I am any longer. You can't let that happen to you. Do you understand me, Fie?"

"Yes." At that moment, she looked at Cecilie's neck. "What have you done to your neck?"

Cecilie quickly pulled the scarf up. "Oh, that's nothing."

"Have you been in a fight? Are you okay?"

She nodded. "At any rate, I'm feeling better than the other guy," she said, standing up. "See you again soon."

"Cecilie?" Fie said, smiling cautiously. "Thanks."

30

When Cecilie returned to the Homicide Unit, she looked for Lasse. She had tried without success to get hold of him earlier. In addition to the officer manning the phones, there were just three other detectives in the office. She passed between the empty desks and spotted that the door to Karstensen's office was open. At that moment, the man himself appeared in the doorway. "Cecilie, could you pop in for a moment?" he said.

"Yes, of course," she said, trying to seem unaffected.

She sat down on one of the chairs positioned in front of the desk, while Karstensen slumped back into his own. He looked at her for a long time before clasping his hands together. "You do know that I took a chance when I promoted you, don't you?"

Cecilie shook her head. "No. I didn't realise that, but I'm very grateful for the confidence."

"Several of the top brass thought you were too sensitive for a position as demanding as this. They thought it took more balls. Do you see where I'm going with this?"

"You're painting a pretty clear picture, yes. Is there anything specific about my work you'd like to discuss?"

He picked up his ballpoint pen from the desk and drummed it against the notepad in front of him. "I thought I was quite clear about the fact that the Emil Kam investigation ought to be concentrated on the search for Ali."

She nodded quickly. "I asked NC3 to follow that avenue of inquiry."

"Yes, yes. Alongside all sorts of other things they were supposed to look into on that case."

"It seemed natural that they handled it at the same . . ."

"No, instead it seems as if you disregarded my explicit order."

"I'm sorry if that's the way you took it."

"So am I," he said, pushing the pen away from himself.

Cecilie looked down at the floor. "But so far as I've understood it, the investigation into the family of the individual in question hasn't gone anywhere."

"That's not the point. As it happens, that chapter isn't yet closed." He leaned back in his chair, making it creak under his weight.

"So you'd like us to continue pursuing that line of inquiry?"

"I want my orders to be carried out without a hitch. Is that understood?"

"Yes, sir. I'll follow up on it right away."

"That won't be necessary," he said, sighing deeply.

"No?"

"The case has been passed to social services. We'll have to see what turns up as they work on it."

"Of course," said Cecilie. This was the closest Karstensen was going to come to acknowledging that he had been mistaken. "Well, then we'll wait."

Karstensen looked at her seriously. "Consider this conversation a verbal warning."

"Yes, sir."

"And there won't be any more."

"Understood." She sensed that the meeting was over and got up from her chair. "Where's everyone else?"

"Homicide in the park at Sydhavn," he said, yawning. "Came in this morning."

"Sydhavn?" She tried to sound surprised. In reality, she was unable to breathe. "Why wasn't I told?"

"Because you were missing in action this morning," he said reproachfully.

"I was at the hospital. I called in to let people know."

"With that?" he said, pointing to the bandage around her fingers.

"No . . . Something else." She shook her head dismissively. "But who's leading the investigation?"

"Lasse."

"Lasse?"

"Yes, I thought it might do him some good. He's got potential, don't you think? To rise through the ranks?"

"I don't know." She shrugged. "Maybe."

"Well, of course . . ." Karstensen said. He frowned. "But I suppose his private life is none of our business."

"That's *not* what I was getting at. Did you say the park in Sydhavn?"

"Yes."

Cecilie said goodbye and left.

Half an hour later, she was on the hilltop where she had dropped the sawn-off shotgun less than twelve hours earlier. She couldn't help looking for the weapon in the grass, even though she knew full well it had been removed. It was a windy day, and the falling rain was lashing against her face. Below her, the officers had cordoned off the crime scene around Morten's body and his black Dodge Ram by the shoreline. Among the forensic team in their blue coveralls, she spotted Lasse and a couple of other detectives. They looked like industrious ants as they all searched the crime scene for evidence. She took a deep breath and made her way down the slope.

31

Lasse was standing next to Ole Madsen as they surveyed Morten's body. Droplets from the intensifying rainfall were settling on the yellowish skin of the corpse like small beads. The blood around the stab wounds was like black crusts that merged into the many tattoos. At a little distance, two paramedics were preparing a body bag in which to transport him away. Cecilie ducked under the police tape and made her way over to Lasse and Ole. She kept her hands jammed deep in her pockets and had the hood of her jacket pulled tightly around her head.

"Ah, Guppy. There you are," said Lasse, smiling sheepishly.

"Here I am," Cecilie replied. "I've been trying to reach you."

"Oh, right. Coverage is bad out here," he said, looking away.

Cecilie looked at Ole. "Cause of death?"

"It's sticking out of his throat," Ole said, pointing to the knife. "But before things reached that stage, he was hit in the shoulder and around the ear." Ole looked impatiently at the paramedics, who were struggling to unfold the bag.

Cecilie recalled the situation and it felt once again as if Morten were squeezing the last of the air out of her. "When did it happen?"

Ole looked back at her. "During the night."

"The weapon may have been his," Lasse added.

"Really?" she said.

"At any rate, it matches the size of the empty sheath on his belt."

"What else?" she asked.

"Judging by all the soil that's been displaced, there was a violent struggle right here. He's a pretty muscular guy, so perhaps we should be looking for a killer of the same calibre?" Lasse bent down and pointed towards the small yellow flags left behind by Forensics. "There are a few distinct prints that weren't left by the victim's trainers. Forensics are going to take casts, then hopefully we'll be a step closer to the size and maybe the brand."

It felt to Cecilie as if both Lasse and Ole could see that the footprints matched the very shoes she was wearing. She squatted and turned her gaze towards the empty sheath on Morten's belt. "You haven't found any other weapons?"

"Oh, well, yes. There's a double-bladed axe. Looks like something out of a Viking museum. And a whole host of smaller knives," Lasse said.

"No shortage of weapons here," Ole added. "The question is whether they belong to the victim or the killer."

"Any idea who the victim is?" she said, standing up again.

"Yep," Lasse said as cheerfully as if he had already solved the case. "It's an old acquaintance of ours. Bit of a celebrity. According to his driving licence, we've provisionally identified him as Morten Pier Nielsen, also known as the Midgard Serpent or just the Serpent. He was in the Nomads biker gang until he ended up in bad standing with them."

"I remember that," Cecilie replied.

"Me too," Ole added. "I was summoned as an expert witness in the case about the guy who was tortured and had his finger cut off. Seems as if fate has finally caught up with the Serpent."

Cecilie nodded.

"So it's presumably gang related," Ole added, gesturing to the two paramedics with the body bag to approach. "We'll have to get him under cover before the rain washes away too much evidence. If they were fighting it out here, then the killer is highly likely to have left behind plenty of DNA."

Let go of it, Cecilie thought to herself. Instead, she said: "Maybe Ole's right?" She looked at Lasse speculatively. "Maybe this is a showdown or even a straight-up liquidation?"

"At first, I thought that, too."

"But?"

"There's something to suggest it wasn't. Come and see." He waved at her to follow him to the black Dodge Ram, which the Forensics team were scouring for evidence.

"What we found on the truck bed might put paid to your theory."

"How so?"

"I think that Morten had a woman with him out here, and that things turned violent. We've found traces of blood and semen in the back. The strips of gaffer tape here might indicate that said individual was restrained. There are also traces of lipstick on some of them, and we've found long black hair and glitter that might have come from makeup."

"Quite the date," she said dryly.

"That he may well have been paying for," he said.

"What do you mean?"

"There was no cash in his wallet. Just a driving licence and a debit card. And we found these." He picked up a transparent evidence bag. It contained a long garland of condoms. "They were in the back. Twelve in total."

"Are they Morten's own?"

"Maybe, but we still haven't found any that have been used. So why bring an arsenal of condoms only to end up having unprotected sex? What's more, the packaging is covered in the same powder we found in the back and on the passenger seat."

"So what are you thinking?"

"That Morten was with a prostitute whom he probably assaulted and had sex with before his own death. Either the woman was able to break free and kill Morten, or more likely there were one or more killers. Maybe it was a clumsy attempt at robbery gone wrong?"

"Okay. Interesting theory," Cecilie replied.

"We're also found something strange."

She cleared her throat. "And what would that be?"

He pointed to the small blue coolbox that was standing by one of the rear wheels in another evidence bag.

"A coolbox? Have you looked inside?"

"Yes. Empty except for some water at the bottom that is presumably from melted ice." Lasse looked at the box thoughtfully. "He was hardly having a bloody picnic."

She didn't reply, instead staring at the surrounding landscape. "Have you called in the dog teams?"

"Four patrols already out searching the terrain."

"Have they found anything?"

"Not yet. But who knows. She might be out there somewhere."

Cecilie nodded uneasily. She was convinced they wouldn't find Sugar, but there might be other clues.

Henrik came over to Cecilie clutching his phone and greeted her. "I've just pulled up Morten Pier Nielsen's registered address. It's on Rådmandsgade."

"Great, let's head over and see what's there to be found," said Lasse, looking at Cecilie. "What do you say, Guppy?"

"Of course," she replied hastily. "What about next of kin? Have they been notified?"

"We've yet to find them," he replied.

"There was some insurance paperwork and a couple of letters addressed to Willy Pier Nielsen in the glove box," said Henrik. "Might be a father or a brother."

"Might be," said Cecilie. "So where does Willy live?"

Henrik walked over to the open passenger door and looked inside, where the contents of the glove box were strewn across the passenger seat. "Boltonvej," he said, reading from the top letter. "Sounds like Amager."

"Okay. I'll drive out there to let him know the bad news," said Cecilie. It wasn't a visit she was looking forward to, but on the other hand it couldn't be ruled out that this was where Morten had hidden his trophies.

"I'll tag along," Lasse said. "Maybe they'll be able to tell us what Morten was doing out here."

"Maybe," she said.

"What about Rådmandsgade?" Henrik asked, looking at Cecilie.

"You can handle that one, Henrik," said Lasse. "Take Benny along."

Henrik nodded, apparently surprised that Lasse was the one now issuing orders.

* * *

Fifteen minutes later, Cecilie and Lasse were in her Panda en route for Sydhavnsgade. They crossed the Sjællandsbroen bridge and then passed by the Bella Sky Hotel, its uppermost floors hidden in a curtain of rain. As yet, neither of them had spoken. Lasse looked at her bandaged hand on the wheel. "What did you do to your fingers?"

"Hurt them at training. Hit a sandbag at a weird angle," she said, shrugging.

"I've always said you have to be careful with all that sport." He smiled gently.

"Hmm."

Lasse glanced at her again. "You know that it was Karstensen who sent me down there today?"

Cecilie nodded.

"It wasn't any sort of attempt to overtake on the inside or anything. You know that, right?"

Cecilie nodded again.

"I'm not going to lead a bloody thing." He shook his head. "Even if I think Karstensen has ambitions on my behalf in that respect."

"You'd make a good leader."

He looked at her in surprise. "You think so?"

"Yes. But you might have called me back. Coverage can't have been *that* bad."

He looked down at the floor. "Sorry, Guppy."

32

The house that Willy Pier Nielsen lived in was at the far end of a cul-de-sac. A wooden fence painted red and two metres tall bordered the garden and mounted to the gate was a sign with a picture of a Doberman and the caption: I'm on guard. Lasse put his hand on the handle but hesitated. He turned to Cecilie. "Do you think it's safe?"

"Of course," she said, giving him a look.

Lasse pressed down the handle and pushed the gate open. He was immediately greeted by a growling Doberman and a black mastiff. Lasse quickly slammed the gate shut again, and the dogs barked. "Bloody hell!" he said.

"I didn't know you were scared of dogs."

"Did you see how big they were?"

Cecilie slipped past him and hammered hard on the wooden gate. The dogs went crazy and began to claw violently against the other side.

"What are you playing at?" Lasse asked.

"Waking up the owner."

A moment later, someone on the other side of the fence shouted at the dogs. Shortly after that, it fell silent and the gate opened again. An elderly couple emerged and stared at Cecilie and Lasse. "Who bloody knocks on the door like that?" the man said with a voice like a welding torch.

The elderly couple were conspicuous proof that people who lived together long enough began to look alike. They had the same short haircut and the same number of tattoos. Both wore faded tank tops: the man's in faded blue, the woman's in faded purple.

"Who are you?" the old man asked. He shared Morten's wild eyes.

"Police," said Cecilie, pulling out her ID. "My name is Cecilie Mars and this is Lasse—"

"What are you here to accuse us of now?" he interrupted.

"Yeah, what are we going to get saddled with this time?" his wife asked, her voice almost identical.

"Are you Morten Pier Nielsen's next of kin?"

"We're his parents," the man replied, crossing his arms. "If you've got nothing else to do, then you can always do our son, isn't that right, Ina?" he said, glancing at his wife.

"We've got some sad news for you."

"And what, may I ask, is that?"

"Morten has been the victim of a crime. It's pretty serious."

"Ser . . . ious?" Ina faltered.

"Yes."

The light vanished from Willy's eyes and his jaw gaped slightly. "So . . . so they caught up with him in the end. Is that what you're here to tell us?"

"Is he . . . dead?" Ina asked.

"Yes. Morten passed away last night."

"How?"

"Maybe it'd be best if we went inside?" Cecilie asked. Willy looked at her suspiciously.

She smiled back at him empathetically. "It'll be easier for me to explain the circumstances to you, and what we know about the killing so far."

"You're sure that it's Morten . . . and that he's dead?" Ina asked.

"They wouldn't be bloody standing here if they weren't," Willy said through gritted teeth.

"Yes, we're sure. Sorry."

"Well, you'd better come inside," Ina said with a sniff.

Willy nodded. "Yes, you'd better come inside."

* * *

The living room inside the small house was full of clothing and other clutter so that it looked like a flea market. Hanging above the thread-bare sofa was a Confederate flag suspended between two Amager-style shelves. Cecilie explained with concision that Morten's body had been found in the parkland at the tip of the Sydhavn peninsula earlier that morning. They had already established that Morten had been stabbed several times, including in the neck, which had been fatal.

"So he was fighting for his life?" Willy asked.

Cecilie didn't reply. It disturbed her that she was the one telling the grieving parents about Morten's death.

"Yes. It looks like there was a fight at the scene," Lasse said. He was glancing anxiously towards the kitchen door, where the dogs were still audibly whimpering.

"Do you know how many people were involved?"

"Not yet, no," Lasse said, frowning thoughtfully. "Willy, just now you said that *they* had caught up with him. Did you have anyone particular in mind?"

Willy snorted. "The Nomads, of course. Those cowards have been after him ever since he got out of the nick. Since he ended up in bad standing."

"Yes, he was in bad standing. That's why he's been staying here," Ina added.

"What about the address at Rådmandsgade?" Lasse asked.

"Just a formality. Morten lived with us," Willy said.

"When did you last see him?" said Lasse.

"I'm honestly not sure. Yesterday sometime. We're not in each other's pockets."

"No, we don't get mixed up in other people's lives," Ina said, before adding: "Sometimes we eat together, and obviously I do his washing."

"Naturally," Lasse said, smiling kindly. "Do you know why Morten was out in the park at Sydhavn?"

"Not a clue."

"We've found evidence to suggest that Morten might not have been alone there. He may have been with a woman."

"I guess that's why he went out there then?" said Willy. "They must have been lying in wait for him, then nailed him. Is the girl dead, too?"

"Missing. Do either of you have any idea who she might be?" Lasse asked.

"Morten's always been popular with the ladies, but no, I don't have a clue who he's been sleeping and messing around with lately. He never brought them home."

"No, never. We didn't see any of them," said Ina.

"What about his friends? Did you see any of them?" Lasse asked.

"Morten mostly kept himself to himself."

"So you don't know who he had been mixing with lately?"

"No."

"Could we see where he was staying?" Cecilie asked. Willy looked at her with a strained expression. "His room? Why?"

"So that we can get to know Morten a bit better," she replied.

"We're not having the bloody rozzers going through his stuff. Especially not now that he's dead."

"We won't go through anything," Lasse said, looking at Ina placidly. "It's more about whether there's anything that might point us in the direction of his killer. If there is, it's vital for the investigation that we find it right away."

"It's this way," Ina said, pointing back towards the hallway. Willy held out his hands in resignation.

Cecilie and Lasse followed on Ina's heels as she descended the narrow stairs to the basement. It smelled of mould, and when they reached the dark narrow basement passage below, the air was heavy with mildew. Ina opened the door to Morten's room. Inside, it was just as messy as the rest of the house. Hanging on the walls were colossal posters showing Vikings in battle side-by-side with pictures of busty women without any clothes on. A couple of broad-bladed axes hung in a cross on the far wall. "Was Morten into the Vikings?" Cecilie asked innocently.

"It's . . . it was . . . his great passion. He couldn't talk about anything other than the Æsir and the Giants," Ina said, her eyes moist. On a low table there were countless mobile phones, some chillum hash pipes, and a bone pipe. "It would be a great help to the investigation if we could take the mobile phones away," said Lasse. "They may contain vital information."

Ina waved her hand to indicate that would be fine. Lasse found a bag in his jacket pocket and took the six mobile phones.

Lying in the bowl on the table were a couple of lighters and a quarter slab of hash. "I'm afraid we'll have to confiscate this, Ina."

She shrugged. "You guys done?"

"In a second," Cecilie said, looking around the tip of a room. She went to the wardrobe, which was open, and peered inside. The clothes were heaped on the shelves, and she searched them without finding anything out of the ordinary. Cecilie turned to the bed, which was unmade. She bent down to look under it and spotted a faded shoebox. She carefully pulled the box out and looked at Ina. "Do you have any idea what this contains?"

"I've never seen it before," she said, shoving her hands in the pockets of her denim skirt.

Lasse came over to Cecilie and looked at the box. Using two fingers, she prised open the lid. Lying inside the box were a small black pistol, a few bundles of thousand kroner notes, and a bag of white powder. "Ina, did Morten sell drugs?"

"What do I know? You said you wouldn't go through his stuff."

"Sure, but we'll have to take this with us, Ina," he said.

"Very well. Are you done?"

"For now." Cecilie put the lid back on the box.

As they left Morten's room, she turned around and looked down the passage, which ran to a door at the end that led outside.

"What's down there?"

"Nothing," said Ina.

Beside the door there was another doorway.

"Just a moment," said Cecilie to Lasse, heading to the doorway for a closer look. Beyond the door, there were some rusty garden tools and a couple of white plastic chairs—and a chest freezer buzzing away at the back wall.

"Where's she got to?" Ina called out from halfway up the basement stairs. In the kitchen above them, the dogs began to bark. Cecilie approached the freezer. With her free hand, she opened the lid. A puff of dry iciness rose towards her in a white mist. She looked down into the baskets, which were full-to-bursting with frozen ready meals. At the bottom was a yellow carrier bag from Netto folded over. Cecilie leaned in over the freezer and grabbed hold of the bag, pulling it out by the handles. She opened it and looked inside. The sight made her drop the shoebox.

"What's up, Guppy?" Lasse called out, appearing in the doorway. When she didn't reply, he came over to her and pointed at the bag. "What is it?"

Cecilie let him see for himself.

"Is that . . . ?" He was struggling for saliva.

In the bag lay six severed female breasts, each with a thin layer of ice crystals covering the skin. On one of the breasts there was a faded rose tattoo.

"Lasse . . . call . . . for . . . backup. Now."

33

Cecilie was perched on the edge of her desk surveying the office. It was a quarter past eleven and Karstensen had called a meeting ahead of his press conference. After three days of investigation, everyone in the Division looked done in, except Karstensen who was radiant. It was as if the sensational nature of the case and his daily contact with the press had cheered him up. Every day had brought a new press briefing with Karstensen in fine fettle and his shirt unbuttoned some way.

Despite the fact that the marks on Cecilie's neck had almost disappeared and her two broken fingers were on the mend, the encounter with Morten was still deeply embedded in her mind. Not like the rape, which had tormented her for decades. No, this dominated her mind in a different way. The last few days' investigation of Morten's violent past had brought about a sense of victory. A feeling that made adrenaline course through her and gave her self-confidence she didn't remember having experienced before. It was also something that had helped her through the interviews with Morten's parents. Both of them had seemed shocked by the discovery in their freezer. They were most definitely unaware of their son's crimes. Following Karstensen's orders, Cecilie and Lasse had gone to the incineration plant to speak to a couple of Morten's former colleagues. None of them had had a single good word to say about him, but they also hadn't seen him behaving in any way suspiciously. Cecilie had stopped by the area where the waste plant had its grinders and noted how easy it would have been for Morten to dispose of bodies there.

"Cecilie? Cecilie?"

She looked towards Karstensen, who was standing with his arms slack at his sides. "I beg your pardon?"

"The Nomads? The bikers? How far have we got looking into them?"

She blinked. "We're forming an overview of the club's members, and especially its hangers-on. We're doing this in partnership with Section Two, which has run several operations against the Nomads. We've also got NC3 looking into who Morten was in contact with digitally, and where he was before the killing."

"But . . ." Lasse began.

"But what?" Karstensen asked, looking at him.

"*If* it's biker-related, then we're looking for a bandit with very small feet. Forensics took casts of the footprints at the scene and have concluded that Morten's killer was wearing size fives."

There was scattered laughter around the room, which didn't seem to please Karstensen. He shifted his gaze to Cecilie to indicate that he wanted an answer. She smiled slightly. "We're also working in parallel on a slightly different theory."

"Which is?" he said impatiently, checking his watch.

"That Morten was killed by one of his victims."

Karstensen raised his eyebrows. "The press will bloody love that. Does it hold water?"

"When we searched the parental home, we found various drawings and texts prepared by Morten that might explain his motives," Cecilie said.

"Quite the Picasso," Lasse interjected, holding up a folder of Morten's illustrations. The drawings were childish, mostly focusing on the blood spurting from severed limbs. "Most of the drawings depict women being dismembered. We've also found some scribbles about honouring the Norse gods through blood sacrifice. So-called *Blodsblót*. A total of nine women needed to be killed."

Karstensen crossed his arms. "So what are you saying? You think the woman who was with him should be regarded as our killer? Was she an immigrant?"

Lasse put the folder down on the desk in front of him. "The trace DNA we've found on the back of the pickup truck suggests it was someone from a non-Danish background, but it doesn't match the DNA we found on Morten."

Cecilie looked down at the floor.

Karstensen sighed deeply. "So what are you saying, Cecilie? There were two people who killed him?"

Cecilie shook her head dismissively. "Our best guess is that Morten took two victims with him to the park. Then one of them managed to overpower him and kill him."

"Are either of them in the DNA database?"

"We haven't got any results back yet," said Lasse.

"But is it even plausible that a woman could have killed Morten? We're talking about a tooled-up biker weighing in at one hundred kilos. A true killing machine."

"The pathologist has found traces of cocaine and magic mushrooms in his blood," said Lasse. "Morten was pretty high when it happened. Our killer may have taken advantage of that fact."

"I still think it seems unlikely. Do we have a profile?"

"We think she's likely to come from one of the prostitution rings," said Cecilie.

"And likewise for the other woman who also got away, and Morten's previous victims for that matter," Lasse added.

"We've got a meeting with Task Force City later today to coordinate a joint operation in the area," said Cecilie. "Someone must have seen or heard something on the street."

Karstensen raised his finger in a warning. "Very well. But don't let those shits snaffle all the credit. I know them. No matter what's found in terms of evidence or witnesses, it all comes here." He pointed directly to the floor.

Just then, Commissioner Volmer Bangsgaard came through the door. The small, greying man was escorted by four officers in uniform, which was Volmer's own way of establishing some gravitas. "Ready?" he said with a glance at Karstensen. "The press awaits."

Karstensen tugged at his shirt neckline a little. "Cecilie, Lasse," he said as he headed towards Volmer by the door.

"You coming?" said Cecilie, looking at Lasse.

"Yes, sure," Lasse replied. He threw another glance at the transparent folders containing Morten's drawings before he returned them to the case file.

"What's on your mind?" she asked him on the way to the door.

"I'm wondering when something goes from being a sick fantasy to a physical act."

"Surely it's an individual thing from psychopath to psychopath?"

"Perhaps. Anyway, I'm just thinking that there must be a common tipping point. Something that changes it all."

"I've no idea."

In the company of around a dozen other officers, Cecilie joined the backdrop behind Karstensen and Volmer, who were both standing in front of a forest of microphones. Cecilie had been placed at one end of the flock, while Lasse had been pushed towards the centre, where he stood with his hands clasped along with the uniformed officers. It was obvious that he didn't care for the attention, and Cecilie couldn't help grinning.

"We never talk anymore," whispered a voice in her ear.

She half-turned her head to see Andreas, who was smiling.

"We talk every day, don't we?" she whispered.

He leaned in towards her. "You know what I mean. May I take you out sometime?"

"That sounds like the worst idea in the world."

"I haven't said where we're going . . ."

"And you don't have to."

"I miss you."

She didn't reply.

"I heard you received flowers the other day. Are you seeing someone else?"

"That's none of your business, Andreas," she said, turning her gaze to the audience.

Ten minutes later when the press conference was over, Volmer and Karstensen departed, while the reporters tried to lob final questions at them. Cecilie followed slowly on the heels of the entourage of officers.

"I mean it," Andreas said when he caught up with her. "I . . . I miss you. Why don't we have dinner together? I know the most wonderful place."

"And I still think it sounds like the worst idea in the world."

"I . . ." He looked down at the floor as they made their way towards the entrance. "I've moved out of Louise's, if that's why you're having misgivings."

"Misgivings?" She smiled. "No, I'm completely certain."

"I've got my own apartment in the city centre."

"Congratulations," she said ironically.

"If I can't take you out for dinner, then could we at least have a cup of coffee?"

She reached the door. "Thanks, but no thanks. I'm trying to cut back. Have a good day, Andreas." She was about to go back inside when he grabbed her gently by the shoulder. Cecilie spun around and pushed away his hand.

"Hey?" he exclaimed in surprise.

She stared at him coolly without saying anything.

Andreas held his hands out in front of him in an apologetic gesture. "Sorry," he said ironically before turning around. She could feel the anger simmering inside her as she watched him disappear across the square.

34

The pouring rain had sent a gaggle of sex workers on Colbjørnsens-
gade into the nearest doorway, where they were now standing and
shivering. Cecilie looked towards them as she rolled by in the unmarked
police car and stopped on the opposite side of the street. Together with
Lasse and Nikolaj from Task Force City, she had been driving around
the neighbourhood all evening. Nikolaj had spent the last fifteen years
working around Istedgade and he was one of the most seasoned officers
on the Task Force. At their briefing earlier that day, he had said that a
new group of sex workers had arrived in the area and that the girls on the
street would be unlikely to know much about the murder case. So far, his
prediction had held true.

"Perhaps we'll get lucky this time?" Nikolaj was in his mid-forties and
blond with a powerful eagle's nose. He jumped out of the car and hurried
across the street to some African girls. Judging by their body language, they
all seemed decidedly dismissive, and he was back a couple of minutes later.

"So? Did they know anything?" Cecilie asked, looking at him in the
rearview mirror.

The shoulders of his thin windbreaker and the thighs of his jeans were
soaked through. "Nothing except that it's three hundred kroner for a
blow job." Nikolaj wiped his wet face with his hand.

"Apparently, some things never change," said Cecilie, starting the
engine.

Lasse looked at her in surprise.

"That it?" Cecilie asked.

"Maybe we should stop by Turisthotellet."

Cecilie cleared her throat. "Is that . . . worth it? I mean, it's getting late and the girls must all be out on the street by now?"

He shrugged. "Given the weather, you wouldn't blame anyone who decided to take the night off. It's down there," he said, pointing at the crossroads.

A few minutes later, they stopped outside the tacky hotel.

"Should we come with you?" Lasse asked.

Nikolaj opened the door. "If you like."

Cecilie half-turned around in her seat. "Maybe it's best if you go inside on your own, Nikolaj? Just so that we don't scare anyone by sending in the entire cavalry."

"Okay," he replied quickly. "Back in five minutes."

At that moment, Cecilie's phone buzzed. She pulled it out of her pocket and looked at the display—it was an unknown number.

"Feel free to take that," said Lasse, leaning against the door and yawning.

"No, it's fine." She rejected the call and put the phone back in her pocket.

Lasse turned his head to look at Cecilie. "What was up with you and Andreas earlier today? It almost sounded like you were arguing."

She quickly shook her head. "It was nothing."

"I think . . ."

"Andreas is the kind of guy who struggles to take no for an answer."

Lasse grinned. "Was he hitting on you? Well, Guppy? Was he?"

She looked silently out of the window.

"He's married. It's a bit cheeky."

"Separated, apparently," she replied with a shrug.

"Bingo!" Lasse said, laughing. "That means the coast's clear. You guys going on a date?"

"No, Lasse, we are not."

"No need to be so precious."

"He's just not my type. Okay? And, Lasse?" She looked at him gravely. "Don't gossip about this with everyone in the Division."

"Of course not," he said, zipping his mouth with a hand gesture. He turned his gaze back to the street and smiled. "Although I can see you as the newly installed lawyer's wife," he said with a laugh.

She gave him the finger in response.

Ten minutes later, Nikolaj returned to the car. "Nothing new. The closest I got was someone who said she knew someone who might have known a girl who'd heard something. I think she was probably just seeing if she could profit from this information."

"What about the staff?" Lasse asked.

"There was only a half-with-it night watchman. He said that until last week there had been a black girl staying there, but he didn't know what had happened to her."

"Did she at least have a name?"

"Yes," Nikolaj said, smiling. "Sugar. But I think you'll find another ten girls with that name around here. Right, I've seen enough whores for one evening. Should we call it a night?"

Cecilie nodded.

"So this lead has gone cold?" Lasse asked as they made off down the street.

"Not at all. We'll try again tomorrow."

Cecilie drove them back to the station, where they parted ways. Half an hour later, she parked outside the high-rises in Bellahøj. From the darkness outside, she could hear the heavy pounding of hip-hop resonating between the buildings. She got out of the car and made her way down the long dark path that led to her stairwell. When she was some way along it, she spotted the lads by the fenced-off basketball court. The music was thumping out of the sound system on one of their scooters. Cecilie took a deep breath and carried on along the path towards the group. As she got closer, she recognised most of the faces. It was the same group of mini arseholes who had spent years making the neighbourhood an unsafe place.

"Mind if I just squeeze past?" she said briskly to the first of them blocking her way.

The lad, who was some seventeen or eighteen years old, didn't dignify her with a glance. "Sorry," he said loudly. He put a hand to his ear. "What?"

The others in the gang guffawed.

"You want to move?"

"The lady wants to get past," said his friend, who was clutching a joint.

"Suck me off!" he said, turning his back to Cecilie.

She quickly edged her way past him and made her way through the rest of the group. A chubby boy on a scooter revved up and pulled in front of her. She stopped and looked at him distantly. He turned down the music. "What's the rush, bitch?"

She looked around and saw that she had been surrounded. She counted seven, most of them with their hands buried in the pockets of their black tracksuit bottoms. They were scowling at her with the same dead eyes. The young guy to her right took a drag from his spliff and puffed out a large cloud of smoke in her direction. "Oops. You gonna arrest me, pig? For smoking dope?"

Cecilie turned to him. She'd seen him around the neighbourhood over the years. She knew he was called Hassan. "No. I just want to go home, but your friend is blocking my way. Maybe you could ask him to move his moped?"

"Bitch, that's a scooter," the lad said, revving it so hard that the customised exhaust crackled.

The other lads chuckled. She felt like they had moved closer, but it was probably just burgeoning anxiety deceiving her.

"Please move. Now!"

The boy laughed and looked at the others. "Bitch be mad now. Probably her time of the month, Hassan."

"Fucking cop-bitch got the painters in," one of them muttered behind her, shoving her in the back.

Hassan took a deep drag on the joint before throwing it away. "Is that it?" he said through a cloud of smoke. "Is it your time of the month?"

Cecilie didn't reply.

Hassan stood close to her and looked at her with unfocused eyes. "I don't care if it is. Doesn't mean. A. Thing. I also don't care if you're a pig or a wrinkly. All the same to me. I'm not picky, see?" He grabbed her by the cheek and forced her head up. "I'll fuck you either way. Hard and relentless. And in the ass. You like it up the ass?"

"Fuck her, Hassan," said someone behind her.

"Fuck the bitch-cop," said the boy on the scooter.

They moved in closer around her. She could feel their breath, like sharks seeing whether the prey was worth sinking their teeth into.

She met Hassan's gaze. "Thanks for the offer, Hassan. It's sweet of you to offer to fuck an old biddy at her time of the month, and in the ass at that, although I can't say I'm especially fond of it."

"I can teach you to appreciate it."

She flashed a wry smile at him. "I'm sure you can. There's just one small problem . . ."

"And what's that?"

"You'll have a hard time doing it without your cock." There was a click as she removed the safety on her pistol and then pressed it to his crotch.

"Fuck, she's . . . she's got a gun," the boy on the scooter said. Hassan looked down at the gun in alarm.

She grabbed his top and held him firmly while pressing the pistol hard against his genitals. "Buzz off!" she shouted.

The lads all backed away, looking around uncertainly.

"Buzz off, or I'll shoot his balls off!"

Hassan appeared to gulp. "You wouldn't dare. You're a . . . cop."

"No, Hassan, I'm not just a cop. I'm a goddamn inspector. Which means that if I shoot your bollocks off or put a slug through your thick head . . ." She moved the gun from his crotch and pressed the muzzle to his chin, ". . . then I'll get away with it. They might even give me a medal."

"She's. . . . sick," said the boy on the scooter. He twisted the throttle and disappeared down the path at top speed.

"I said buzz off!" She removed the gun from Hassan and waved it at the others. The lads began to run off in different directions. She shoved Hassan hard in the chest, making him take a few steps backwards.

"No witnesses, Hassan. Just you and me . . . What was it that you wanted?" She held the pistol with both her hands and took aim.

His lower lip was quivering. "No . . . nothing. S . . . s . . . sorry."

She shook her head. "It's a bit too late for that kind of thing now." She took a step towards him.

"Stop . . ." he said, closing his eyes.

"Look at me!" she shouted. "Fucking look at me!"

He slowly opened his eyes. "Stop . . . please stop."

A dark puddle on the ground was growing around one of his feet.

"You pissing your pants?"

"I'm begging you . . ."

"You and your shithead friends are going to stay a long way away from this basketball court. A long way away from this neighbourhood. Capeesh?"

"Y . . . yes."

"If I hear you've been shit-stirring. If I hear anything from any of the girls. If you so much as go near them. I will come after you. And only you. Is that understood?"

"Y . . . yes." He walked backwards down the path towards the car park.

"Is that understood?!" she shouted at him.

Hassan ran off.

When she could no longer see him, she secured her pistol and reholstered it. Her body was shaking uncontrollably. The sob stuck like a lump in her throat made it hard to breathe, and she tilted her head back, gasping for air. Above her, the clouds flitted quickly across the night sky visible between the looming blocks of flats. Then she began to cry.

35

Cecilie was standing naked in the morning light streaming through the kitchen window. She looked down at the empty basketball court at the base of the high-rises. The view was dizzying, and she swayed slightly. She hadn't got much sleep during the night. Only at around three o'clock when she'd got up and taken her zombie tablets had she finally managed to get a bit of sleep. She was in no doubt that the lads would be back—the only question was when they'd summon up the courage and what would happen when they did. She went back to the bedroom and found some clean clothes. The phone, which she had left on the bed, was buzzing and she could see that it was from an unknown number. Just like the six previous calls that morning. She sat down heavily on the edge of the bed and answered. "What do you want?"

"To bid you a blessed morning, Cecilie Mars," said Lazarus.

"It doesn't seem very blessed to me."

"It's merely a question of attitude. I think you can be quite satisfied both with the morning and yourself."

"Is that right?"

"The newspapers say that you and your colleagues are working on the theory that the Serpent's killer might be a prostitute. Nice angle you found there. That theory seems more plausible than my original idea of a biker killing. So far you've managed to misdirect everyone. Bravo."

"Yes, it's all just great."

"Truthfully, yes," said Lazarus, apparently picking up on her tone of voice. "I can also cheerfully state, based on the same media outlets, that we have the people on our side."

"The people?"

"A poll of Ekstrabladet readers shows that eighty-one per cent are more interested in stopping criminals like the Serpent than in punishing the person who got rid of him. There are several comments below the line that describe your actions as heroic."

"Hooray for opinion polls," she said, while putting one foot into a boot. "And now that we've established that, why are you calling?"

"To maintain momentum. I've got an urgent matter on standby. A matter that will see the removal of yet another beast from the face of the earth. But we have to work fast." Despite the digitised distortion of his voice, she could sense his manic state very clearly.

"Then let's meet," she said, fishing.

"I've already told you: when the time is right."

"I know you have, and it is," she replied.

"I alone shall determine that," he said.

"There are things I need to know."

"What things?"

"Well, to begin with: How do you know about my rape?" She got up too quickly and felt the room around her spinning.

"That is altogether unimportant. Now listen . . ."

"Not to me. How?"

There was a deep sigh. "I'm meticulous in my research, Cecilie. That should have become apparent by now."

"Okay, so where have you been looking?"

"In all sorts of places. It's a puzzle and the pieces have to be gathered up. That shouldn't come as a surprise to a detective like yourself."

"Where have you been looking?"

"The newspapers . . . the media . . ."

"Lies."

He gasped. "I really don't care for your tone, Cecilie. I have my sources. Perhaps we should leave it at that?"

"No. Not if we're going to continue this . . . collaboration."

"Very well. I'll explain it all, but only when . . ."

"When the time is right?"

"Right," he said impatiently. "For now, let's concen—"

"What about Ulrik Østergård, Emil Kam, and Morten Pier Nielsen? Tell me how you found them."

"As I've already told you, I'm meticulous in my research. Very meticulous."

"Why them in particular? It can't have been random. How did you know about them?"

"My dear Cecilie, you will gain nothing from these questions. As you yourself know, there are hundreds of these people at large. It's simply a matter of choosing between the beasts. Now let us concentrate on the task at hand."

"Of course. Just say where you'd like to meet."

"You're going round in circles now. I've already said that . . ."

"If you want us to collaborate, then we have to meet. End of."

"I'm warning you, Cecilie."

"About what? That you're going to expose me?"

"Yes. Your DNA is on the Serpent's body, just like it's on the knife that was used to kill Emil Kam. Have you forgotten? If I send that video of you and Ulrik together with the photo of the knife, you'll be placed under investigation. Step one will be to take a DNA sample, and that'll be the end of the line for you."

"Who's going round in circles now? You've threatened me with all this before."

"Then you should be more careful."

"In reality, you're nothing without me. Without me, you can't carry out your plans in real life. You need me for this, more than anything."

"Now you're putting yourself on a pedestal. A pedestal that's a little too high up," he snarled.

"Am I? Either we meet, or you can forget about your next matter."

"You do not make demands! You do not make demands of me!" he shouted.

"That's exactly what I've just done."

He was breathing heavily. "I cannot protect those who do not listen to what I say."

"That's your choice. Where are we meeting?"

"Goodbye, Cecilie. I held you in such high esteem. I had such grand plans for your future." There was a click as he hung up.

Cecilie still felt dizzy shortly afterwards when she set the alarm and closed the front door behind her. She had pushed Lazarus over the edge—there was no doubt about it. She had done it with a defiance and courage that she'd had no idea she even possessed. Perhaps the zombie tablets had seriously impaired her judgment? Hopefully, Lazarus would cool off and realise that he had no alternative but to return and agree to a meeting. Until then, she would have to try and find him herself, and she'd had an idea of where to start searching.

36

Cecilie headed down the long corridor towards the Homicide Unit. Two middle-aged officers passed her, going in the opposite direction. She thought one of them looked at her strangely, and she turned her head slightly. The two officers continued unconcernedly towards the stairs, where they disappeared from sight. The zombie tablets weren't helping with her paranoia, which was now on the rise following the manifestation of an idea: What if Lazarus was on the force?

Perhaps Lazarus was younger than the middle-aged man she had pictured. He had technical skills, otherwise he wouldn't be able to cover his electronic tracks. He also knew how to conduct an investigation and how to carry out street reconnaissance. And he could kill. The more she thought about it, the more she believed they shared the same experience and expertise. Cecilie opened the door into the Division office and made her way between the desks to her own. She greeted her colleagues distantly and looked at them as if she could determine from their aura alone whether one of them was Lazarus. She nodded to Lasse, who was on the phone. He flashed a brief smile at her before turning his back. Then she checked her own mobile phone for messages, noting that there was still nothing new from Lazarus. Cecilie sat down at her computer and stared at the dark display.

Lazarus's use of language seemed educated, but she couldn't make up her mind whether it seemed affected. Perhaps he was trying to conceal his identity by using it, in the same way that he did the digital voice distortion. However, there was one thing that did seem genuine: his temperament. Lazarus was a touchy bugger. He was irascible to an extent that bordered on choleric. Despite his altogether controlling nature, his ability to plan, his strategic sensibilities . . . he was at the mercy of his own emotions.

Cecilie found the case files for Emil Kam and Ulrik Østergård among the stacks on her desk. Then she logged on to the computer and looked up Morten Pier Nielsen's record. Lazarus hadn't wanted to explain about his prior knowledge of the three male victims. Instead, he had said that he could have chosen any one of the beasts at large. But she was now certain that the trio had not been selected at random. They all had previous convictions, which meant it was likely that Lazarus had a deeper awareness of their cases. If he was a cop, his name might feature somewhere in the reports. When the results of the talcum tests had been returned, Lasse had joked that the killer might be found on the Forensics team. Perhaps he'd been nearer the mark than he'd realised. In reality, there was no need to confine themselves to Forensics. The same type of glove was used throughout the Homicide Unit and by the pathologists. However, she struggled to imagine sweet Ole being Lazarus. Although it could be someone in his office. Or someone in her own.

To find Lazarus, she would have to review all the cases involving Morten, Emil, and Ulrik to see whether any of the detectives or other police employees cropped up in all the reports. Not that this would prove anything in itself, but it might point her in the right direction.

She embarked on the search for the names of those involved, and it quickly turned into a demanding task. Morten's record was—as she already knew—very lengthy, and in addition to the members of the Task Force who had been attached to the last slew of cases, there were some members of the Division who had also been involved over the years. By the time she had gone through all the interview transcripts in his file, she had a list of around fifty names, and that was just investigators. She still needed to note which experts had been involved in the forensic case or appeared as witnesses for the prosecution.

She rubbed her eyes wearily. To ensure that the task didn't expand too far, she opted to limit her inquiries to investigators alone. She continued for the next couple of hours reviewing Ulrik's and Emil's cases, respectively, noting all the names of detectives who had been in contact with either. It was almost one o'clock when she compared the three lists, finding a handful of officers who had been involved in all three men's cases. Most of them were from Forensics, which was only to be expected since it was the force's most mobile unit. The only two from her own Division represented across all three lists were Karstensen and Henrik.

She knew that the two men were not only the same age but had also followed each other over the years: from Vestegnen to Station City, with both of them eventually ending up in the Division for Crimes Against Persons. However, they'd each had their own career trajectory. Karstensen had elbows so sharp they might as well have been circular saws, while Henrik was far more sluggish. Cecilie couldn't remember a single occasion when he had voluntarily worked overtime. Nor did she get the feeling that he tossed and turned through sleepless nights over his cases. In that regard, he was not dissimilar to Lasse.

She leaned back in the chair. Her preliminary investigation seemed to have been fruitless. If Lazarus was a cop—or had been in the past—then the answer wasn't obvious. Then again, there was one more case. Her own. Lazarus was more familiar with it than he had let on.

She had no great desire to pull the old file out of the archives. She still remembered what had happened at Bellahøj police station with the utmost clarity. Especially the officer who had questioned her. Poul Myers had been his name. A sweet, pleasant guy. Middle-aged. Poul had tried to make sure that the interview had been both dignified and gentle. Which was not always to be expected. Poul had even come to court and had sat in the public gallery throughout the case. He was one of the reasons why she had decided to become a police officer herself. She had never contacted him again, mostly because she had done everything she could to put the case behind her. She figured Poul must have retired long ago. Nevertheless, she opened her email client and composed a message to Katja Sloth, whom she knew from the academy, and who was in Traffic at Bellahøj.

Hi, Kat. Must meet up soon!!! A quick question: Is Poul Myers still there with you? Or do you know where I can find him? Best, C.

When she had sent the email, she checked her phone. Lazarus still hadn't come back to her, and his stubbornness was worrying her. She checked the time. It was almost two o'clock. She knew that if she was going to have lunch before the canteen shut up shop, she would have to hurry.

She took the stairs up to the top floor. The small room was full and the smell of sausages and gravy lingered thickly in the air. Cecilie settled for a couple of sandwiches and some mineral water. When she surveyed the room for an empty seat, she caught Andreas's eye. He was sitting with a couple of colleagues and quickly looked away. Cecilie took a seat by the door. When she was almost done with her lunch, Lasse came into the canteen.

"Guppy," he said, his face lighting up in a big smile. He pulled out a chair and sat down opposite her.

"You not having anything to eat?"

"Been there, done that," he said, patting his stomach. "I've got good news."

"Okay. What?"

"Emil Kam's neighbour, one Kristian Nielsen, stopped by Bellahøj police station today . . ."

"And?"

"You'll never guess what he found in his mailbox." Lasse pulled out his mobile and turned it towards Cecilie.

She put down her food as she tried to appear unaffected. The photo on the screen showed a Global kitchen knife smeared with clotted blood. "Where . . . when did he find that?"

"This morning when he was checking his mail. He was smart enough not to touch it and contacted Bellahøj right away."

"Where's the knife now?"

"Gone for examination. It's one hundred per cent the weapon that killed Emil," he said with a smile, as he looked at the photo again.

"And does the neighbour have any idea who might have put it there?" she asked.

"No. Our colleagues out there say he was pretty shaken up. Which is pretty understandable. First his neighbour gets bumped off, then he finds out the guy was a paedophile, and finally the knife shows up in his mailbox. It's a wonder he hasn't put his house up for sale already."

"When will we get the results back?"

"Within twenty-four hours. They've dropped everything else. Karstensen is over the moon." Lasse grinned. "You done?" he said, pointing to her empty plate.

Cecilie nodded, and they went back to the office together. She was still struggling to accept that Lazarus had made good on his threat. All she could think about was when he would send the video showing her and Ulrik. He had already sent it once to Lasse. Perhaps he had done the same again? She followed on Lasse's heels to his desk. "Does the lab have anything else to say?" she said, looking at his screen where his inbox was open.

"No, I don't think so," he said, looking at her in surprise. "If you want to speak to them yourself, then I'd be happy to forward their email."

She quickly skimmed the list of unread emails on the display and saw that none were from Lazarus. "No, don't worry about it. Just let me know as soon as we get the results back." She sat down at her own desk, opened her phone, and found the last number that Lazarus had called from. Hoping he hadn't changed SIM cards, she wrote a short message:

Sorry for my outburst. We need to talk.

Ten minutes elapsed before her phone rang, showing a number she didn't recognise. She answered as she stood up from her desk. "Cecilie Mars," she said.

There was silence on the line.

"Hello? Lazarus?" she asked in a low voice.

"Cecilie? It's Nikolaj."

"Hi, Nikolaj," she said briskly. "What's new?"

"Well, only that I think we've gone and found her. Sugar."

37

Cecilie put the phone down on her desk and composed herself following the call from Nikolaj. Lasse looked up from his computer. "Everything okay?"

"Yes. More than okay," she replied, trying to smile. "That was Nikolaj. He says they've probably found the girl. Sugar."

"Really?! Great!" Lasse said loudly as he got to his feet. "Pray tell. Where?"

"Rigshospitalet. The emergency department reported an African woman seeking treatment for an infected wound to her breast. The doctor who inspected the injury noted that it was the result of a deep cut."

"Have they held her?"

"She's still hospitalised and under guard on her ward."

Karstensen appeared in the doorway and noted Lasse's enthusiasm. "Have you told Cecilie that they've found the knife?"

"Old news," Lasse said with a chuckle. "Nikolaj has found the witness to Morten's murder. She's currently in hospital. African woman."

"Black?"

Lasse nodded uneasily.

"Has he spoken to her?"

"She hasn't said anything yet," Cecilie said, looking at him.

"Then what the hell are you waiting for?" Karstensen said energetically. Lasse had already grabbed his windbreaker. "Bloody hell, it's nonstop today . . . You coming?" he asked, looking at Cecilie.

"Of course," she replied.

They got caught in traffic on Sølvgade and had to wait in a queue with other motorists who were heading out of the city centre. Lasse drummed the steering wheel impatiently. "I'm bloody tempted to put the flashing lights on," he said, fumbling for the blue lamp on the floor of the Golf.

"I don't think she's going anywhere," said Cecilie, biting her knuckle. She was at the point immediately preceding panic.

"You're right," said Lasse, giving up on his search. "What's the strategy?"

"What?"

"When we question her? What did she say to Nikolaj?"

"It sounded as if she hadn't said anything at all."

"So we don't know if it's her."

"Nikolaj sounded confident. Dark-skinned woman, cut to her breast, sex worker, calls herself Sugar."

Lasse seemed pleased. "This bodes bloody well for the investigation. So how do we get her to talk?"

"No idea," she said, staring out of the windscreen.

He looked at her. "Guppy, you okay?"

"Yes . . . well, no. I'm . . . feeling a bit out of sorts to be honest."

He put his foot down to get across the crossroads at Tagensvej before the light went red. "Maybe we should find you a couple of paracetamols when we get there."

"More my stomach that's playing up. Think it must be something I ate," she said, looking at him with an expression of suffering.

Lasse shook his head. "That's the canteen for you. The food is getting worse and worse." He bit a hangnail nervously. "We've got to push Sugar to find out who she was with out there. But if it was a friend or a colleague, then I reckon it might be hard to get anything out of her." Lasse pulled into the lane to go right.

As they drove down Blegdamsvej, Cecilie reflected on what Sugar might have seen. After all, it had been dark. And she had attacked Morten from behind, out of the girl's line of sight. When they had fought, Morten had been on top of her and must have shielded her from view. On top of all that, Sugar had been hurt and had been occupied with trying to free herself. Maybe she hadn't seen anything at all.

"Shall we?" said Lasse.

Cecilie looked around and realised they had already arrived. Lasse had parked right by the entrance to the emergency department. It occurred to her that she was wearing the same jacket she'd worn on the evening of the killing, and she wriggled out of it quickly.

"Won't you be cold?" he asked.

"I'm already too hot."

They made their way to the entrance of the emergency department. Once they had shown their credentials to the nurse on duty, they went down the corridor to the last room. There were two uniformed officers standing outside the door chatting. As Cecilie approached them, panic began to take hold of her.

Lasse greeted the officers, and one of them opened the door for them. Inside the room, Sugar was lying in bed. Cecilie recognised her right away. She stood in the doorway, her gaze directed at the floor. It occurred to her that she had come to with Morten lying beside her. She had no idea how long she had been in that position. It might have been seconds, or minutes. Sugar might have stood there staring down at her in the meantime.

"What's up?" Lasse whispered.

"I . . . I need the loo," she said, turning back to the corridor.

"Should I wait?"

"No, just get on with the interview."

"Are you sure?"

"For Christ's sake, yes," she said, dashing out of the door.

She found the toilet farther down the corridor. Once the door was closed behind her, she stood at the sink and began to splash water on her face. She found some paper towels in the dispenser and dried herself off. Then she pulled her phone out of her pocket and saw that Lazarus still hadn't replied. She considered whether to write to him but thought that it might seem desperate and would probably have no bearing on the outcome. She waited another ten minutes in the toilet before heading back into the corridor. With Lasse in the room, the two officers on duty had taken the opportunity to head to reception, where they were flirting with a couple of nurses.

Cecilie went to stand by the door to Sugar's room. Through the small window, she saw Lasse sitting on a chair at her bedside. He passed Sugar a tissue from the nightstand. He looked like a concerned relative visiting her. Sugar wiped the tears from her face as she continued to talk.

Twenty minutes later, Lasse emerged from the room. He looked at Cecilie leaning against the wall clutching a paper cup. "Are you okay?"

"On the mend, thanks."

"You sure you don't want to find a doctor?"

"Quite sure, but thanks for asking. What about Sugar? How's she doing?"

"Good, given the circumstances. They've given her antibiotics and taken care of her wound. She's obviously shaken."

"Did she remember anything?"

"Yes, and she was communicative, too. I think it was a relief for her to finally have someone to talk to."

"What . . . did she say about the assault?"

"That Morten persuaded her to go there. He said he wanted to have sex in the open air at the same time as the new moon. She thought it was some romantic thing for him and didn't think anything was up until he hit her and tied her up."

"So it was just the two of them alone out there?"

"Yes. She denied there was anyone else with them."

"And that sounded credible?"

"Yes, I thought so. In fact, she praised the person who saved her. Said they were an angel floating down from heaven."

"Not exactly a description we can use," Cecilie said, looking away.

Lasse smiled. "No, but Sugar also had plenty to say about the person in question."

"She saw him?"

"Her. It was a woman. Older than her, mid-thirties. White, probably Danish. Sugar also described her as small with short hair."

"Still a vague description. Anything else?"

"Not much. She was panicking and concentrating on getting free. She seems to have a guilty conscience about not staying to help. That's why she was relieved to hear that Morten had been killed."

"Where has she been since then?"

"First at Turisthotellet, then out on the street. It was a volunteer from Reden International that got her to go to the hospital."

"Do you think Sugar can identify the woman?"

"Perhaps. I'm going to arrange for her to see the artist. And after that, I wonder if we should have her come in to take a look at our files."

"You think a criminal might be behind the killing?"

"Perhaps. They had the skills, not to mention the courage, to go head-to-head with Morten. I'm thinking it could be someone who knows him and has been following him."

"Who might that be?"

"No idea. Maybe one of his previous victims who got away. Someone we don't know about? Maybe the motive is something else entirely. But if you ask me, it might well be someone from the same background as him."

"That's good work, Lasse. Sorry I wasn't much help," she said.

"Quite alright," said Lasse, putting a friendly arm around her shoulders. "We're a team."

38

Cecilie was back in the backyard. Caught between the dumpsters. Held down on the ground. Him lying over her. Groaning. Sweating. Thrusting. She could feel his weight; she was unable to breathe. She couldn't say anything. He half rose to his feet and she looked at him. She saw that it wasn't Bjarke. Morten had taken his place. The knife was protruding from his neck, and blood was dripping onto her face.

"No!" she heard herself call out.

Cecilie sat up in bed. Her heart was pounding hard and her T-shirt was soaked through. On her nightstand, her phone was bouncing around all by itself. She reached for it. It was gone seven o'clock in the morning and it was Karstensen calling.

"Hello," she said, clearing her throat.

"Cecilie, the report's back on the weapon," he said without any pleasantries. "And it's pretty disturbing stuff. When can you be here?"

"Right . . . right away," she managed to stammer.

"Good, see you shortly," Karstensen said, cutting the connection.

She threw the phone onto the bed and rubbed her weary face. They must have found her DNA on the knife. Had they also been sent the video? If so, why hadn't he just sent a patrol to arrest her? Was it to ensure it was done as discreetly as possible? Were they hoping for a confession before the worst shitstorm in the history of the police hit them all? She looked out of the bedroom window. It was still dark. She couldn't remember Karstensen ever summoning her to the office this early before.

Half an hour later, Cecilie was climbing the stairs. When she reached the third floor, she pushed open the door to the narrow corridor that led to the Homicide Unit. It was still in semidarkness. Outside, the wind was whistling and the rain had begun to hammer against the dark windows, and she felt as if she was still in her own nightmare. When she reached the end of the corridor, she opened the door and entered the Division office. Karstensen was at the far end of the room with Lasse, who was sitting at his computer. To her surprise, Andreas was also there. He was leaning nonchalantly against the wall, his hands in his pockets. The three men stared at her as she made her way towards them between the desks. She put down her bag and then looked at them. It puzzled her that Karstensen had dragged not only Lasse but also Andreas out of bed this early. "So what's up?" she asked, trying to seem energetic.

Karstensen sighed deeply. "We've got the report back on the knife found at Emil Kam's neighbour's house. The report conclusively confirms that it was used to kill Emil Kam."

"Were they able to tell us anything else about it?" Cecilie asked.

"Quite a lot," Karstensen replied, clearing his throat. "They found trace DNA on the knife that doesn't match Emil Kam."

"And not the neighbour either?" she managed to say.

"No." Karstensen glanced at Lasse and Andreas before he continued. "It's the same DNA that was found on Morten Pier Nielsen."

Cecilie projected the most naive look in her arsenal at him. "The same? But how is that possible?"

"Same killer," said Karstensen, holding out his hands.

"And how sure are we that it wasn't a fuck-up with the samples at the lab?"

Karstensen shook his head. "They've double-checked the lot and assured me they're right. Whoever killed Emil Kam also killed Morten Pier Nielsen."

Cecilie used the table for support. "Have we run the DNA?"

"Yes. But unfortunately, we didn't get a match."

"So we're dealing with a killer who hasn't had any run-ins with the law in the past. Or at least not for anything serious."

Karstensen nodded.

"Sugar has given us this sketch to work with," Lasse said, showing the identikit drawing that had been worked up.

The corners of Andreas's mouth quivered. "Not exactly someone you'd want to go on a date with. Looks more like the Tollund Man."

The drawing depicted an androgynous face with bristly hair and small eyes and lips. The identikit was one of the most inferior Cecilie had ever laid eyes on, and she thanked her lucky stars that there was no likeness between it and herself.

"It was dark out there," Lasse said, defensively shrugging his shoulders. "So yeah, I'm not sure what weight we can give to Sugar's observations." He set the drawing down on the desk. "We'll bring her in tomorrow to take a look at the files. Maybe we'll be luckier then."

"Maybe you should question her?" said Karstensen, looking at Cecilie.

"Lasse did a stand-up job at the hospital," she replied quickly. "It seems as if you've already gained her confidence." She looked at Lasse.

"Yes, perhaps," he replied.

"In any case, we need a better description," said Karstensen. "Push her hard. Her type might well hold something back."

"She generally seems cooperative though," Lasse said.

"Yes, well, don't they all?" said Karstensen. He turned to Cecilie. "I'd like you to start looking into some of our unsolved homicides. See whether you can find a similar modus operandi."

She nodded happily, glad to be avoiding a confrontation with Sugar and because the unsolved cases might contain something that would lead her to Lazarus. "And what brings the Prosecution Service to the office at this early hour?" she asked, looking at Andreas.

Andreas pushed himself away from the wall. "The Prosecution Service never sleeps, as you well know," he said with a smile. "Karstensen asked me to review some of our previous vice cases. The most serious ones. All the ones where our charges were not fully accepted."

"You mean the ones you *lost*?"

"Hmm, sort of . . ." he replied in a constrained tone.

Karstensen cleared his throat. "The motive behind these two killings is most likely revenge. It therefore seems obvious to expand the investigation to those cases we're already aware of where the perpetrator may be emotionally involved. I think we're looking for someone who feels that the law hasn't done its job."

"It seems as if you've got a lot to get through, Andreas," Lasse said.

"What do you mean?"

"Well, if you have to go through every case you've lost . . ." he said.

Andreas managed another forced smile. "We are always happy to help the Homicide Unit, *including* solving cases."

Karstensen clapped his hands hard. "Anyway, that's the lie of the land. In all likelihood, we're dealing with a female serial killer who targets sex offenders."

"And we used to refer to them as the weaker sex," Andreas said, smiling.

"Yes. The press is going to have a field day when this comes out," Karstensen said.

"And we'll struggle to answer the phone once all the crazies start deluging us with calls," said Lasse.

"What about the commissioner?" Cecilie asked.

"I'm going to see him as soon as he arrives in his office," said Karstensen, turning to head to his own. "Good hunting," he said, closing the door behind him.

"Coffee?" Lasse asked Cecilie as he stood up.

"A bucketful, please."

"I thought you didn't drink coffee anymore," Andreas said before making for the door.

A moment later, she was alone in the office. She took the fact that Lazarus had only sent the weapon and not the video of her and Ulrik as a sign that he hadn't given up on her entirely. Which was a relief, because as things stood right now, she fitted Karstensen's new profile down to a tee. Just then, her phone buzzed. "Cecilie Mars," she said.

"You're all in so early today," said Lazarus.

"Lazarus?" she said in a low voice, looking around the empty office. "If you're nearby, let me get you a coffee."

"Thanks, but no thanks. What's the occasion for such an early start? Might it be that a certain object has come to light? A possible weapon?"

"I think you already know."

"Well, yes. It's always a pleasure to assist the police in their inquiries," he said, chuckling quietly. "I take it that since you are still in the Division, you must still be in the clear."

"So far, yes."

"You know that I only want the best for you, don't you?"

"If that's true, you have a strange way of showing it."

"Yes, perhaps. But if nothing else, I am calling you in the belief that we can continue our partnership."

"Then let's meet," she said, holding her breath.

"Yes. Let's."

She almost dropped the phone in sheer surprise.

"But only because it is what I want."

"Of course. When?"

"Tonight. I will provide you with further instructions," he said, ending the call.

She was still standing there with the phone in her hand when Lasse returned with two mugs of coffee. "This is the first time I've seen you smiling in ages. Good news?" he asked, pointing to the phone in her hand.

She took her mug of coffee. "We'll see."

39

The Nordvest neighbourhood was being lashed by rain. It was darker than ever. It was almost one o'clock in the morning, and Cecilie was driving along Borups Allé, trying to make out the road ahead of her through the windscreen. But the windscreen wipers were in a futile battle against the floodwaters. She was getting close to the place where the raised carriageways of Bispeengbuen crossed over Borups Allé. This was where Lazarus had sent her.

When she reached it, she found a space in the large car park that spread out beneath the six lanes of Bispeengbuen. Cecilie got out of the car and looked around in the darkness. The sound of cars passing overhead rumbled like heavy thunderclaps. A text message she had received from Lazarus half an hour earlier had instructed her to continue towards the skateboard track adjacent to the car park.

Although she was freezing, she kept her jacket unzipped to ensure she had easy access to the pistol holstered at her belt. She still hadn't decided what she would do when she met him. If she arrested him, it would have serious consequences for her, and she was afraid that he would get off anyway. When it came to the crunch, there was really only limited evidence against him. Even if it were possible to prove through their correspondence that he had incited her to commit murder, it was mostly on her.

She reached the far end of the crowded car park. She looked over her shoulder towards the parked cars before she made her way towards the skateboard track farther ahead. Perhaps the only solution was to kill him? Would she be willing to do that? She doubted it. But what if he resisted or attempted to escape? Would she try to catch him alive?

Cecilie reached the skateboard track with its three crescent-shaped ramps extending up towards the motorway above. She did a lap of the track, checking out the area. Her right hand sought out her pistol in its holster, and she undid it. Once again, she speculated about why Lazarus had agreed to meet. In reality, there were only two options: either he thought he could get her to carry out another killing, or he knew that the game was up. If it were the latter, this meeting meant he wanted to erase the only thing that led back to him: *her*.

"Cecilie Mars!" echoed a voice under the bridge.

She turned around and peered into the darkness. Either he was hiding behind one of the huge bridge piers or he was in among the cars.

"Move straight ahead," he said.

She began to walk towards the row of cars.

"Keep going!" It sounded as if the voice were coming from the rusty dumpsters by the pillar to her right. Cecilie passed the cars and made her way towards the dumpsters.

"Stop!" said the voice when she was around ten metres away from them.

She squinted to try and see better in the dark. The rain running off the motorway above was cascading down towards the dumpsters, forming a wall of water.

"Good of you to come," said a voice somewhere behind the water. The acoustics under the bridge blurred his voice, almost like the digital distorter that he'd used on the phone. Nevertheless, Cecilie could make out something familiar about the voice without being able to put her finger on it.

"Why don't you come out so we can say hello properly?" she asked.

"Because I prefer to keep my distance from you."

"I thought we were going to meet . . . to collaborate," she said while trying to see through the wall of water. "To prove that we could trust each other."

"It's definitely about that, too. More than you could possibly know."

"Why don't we drop this charade?" she said, holding her arms out invitingly. "At any rate, I'd like to greet you properly."

No answer came back.

Cecilie cleared her throat. "Even though we see things differently, I'm impressed by your knowledge, your methodical approach, and your tactical skills." She slowly moved closer to the dumpsters. "Your professionalism almost makes it seem as if you've been in the police. At any rate, you've got the right skills for it."

"So we're on the same page now?" said the voice ironically from the dark ahead of her.

"I'm just saying that while your methods may be extreme, they have unmasked two dangerous criminals and saved countless victims. You deserve praise for that. It's commendable, but . . . well, it's time to put an end to it."

"I was about to say the same thing to you. That you'd be best stopping." There was a click in the dark, like the sound of a shotgun being cocked. "Take that as a friendly warning."

Cecilie stopped in front of the cascade of water. She thought she saw something moving behind it in the darkness, but it might just have been the play of the water creating the illusion. "I'm just trying to find a solution before this ends badly. If we both crash and burn, then the only winners are the crooks. Is that what you want?"

"Bravo, Cecilie," he said sarcastically. "Influence your subject with the right blend of empathy and guilt before making your demands. Sounds like something you learned in the police academy, or on some extension course in psychology. Dreaming of being a hostage negotiator one day?"

"I don't have the necessary patience," she said with a smile. "As I said, I'm just trying to find a solution."

"That's thoughtful of you. I know your heart is in the right place. That's also why I have chosen you."

"Me?"

"Yes. Surely you didn't think this was about the beasts."

"I think you'd better explain."

"Under the silver car to your left you'll find an envelope. It contains all the answers to your questions."

She half-turned and squinted at the silver Audi some seven or eight metres away.

"Go on—the answers are lying there waiting for you," he said mischievously.

Cecilie went to the Audi and bent down to look underneath the car. Lying next to the right-hand rear wheel was an A4 envelope that she carefully removed.

"Open it, Cecilie."

She ripped open the bulging envelope. It contained a stack of documents, photographs, and a bundle of newspaper cuttings. "A new case?" she asked, looking towards the dumpsters and the gushing water.

"This one is different. This is the case that closes the circle for you. This is the case that sets you free, Cecilie."

"Oh?" she said, pulling out the contents. When she saw the top pictures of herself as a teenager, she almost stopped breathing entirely. They were school photos from upper secondary school—from her second and third years. From two completely different worlds. Two completely different girls, inside and out. One grinning at the camera, the other dulled, her gaze extinguished. She flipped through the bundle and found a small newspaper article. Six lines describing her worst nightmare. "Vangede girl raped" said the headline. She found yet another article dated three months after the first. The article described the trial of Bjarke Thomsen, who had been found guilty of rape and sentenced to receive treatment. At the bottom of the pile were several case files, several photos of Bjarke, interview transcripts, and a psychiatric report.

"Do you still have nightmares about that night?"

"Where . . . where did you get all this?" she asked tearfully.

"Does Bjarke still visit you in your nightmares?"

"Answer me. How?!" she shouted.

"You still can't get away from him, can you, Cecilie? Does he chase you relentlessly?"

"Tell me where you got all this from!"

"Do you still feel guilty that you let it happen? That you didn't fight back more? That you let him have his way with you?"

Cecilie pulled the pistol from her holster and stood up. She removed the safety and took aim at the dumpsters behind the cascade of water.

"Tell me where you got this from!"

There was no answer.

This has to end now, she thought to herself as she ran straight towards the wall of water. Each second, she expected to hear the blast of the shotgun. But no shot came. She leapt through the gushing water and landed on the wet ground between the dumpsters. Her gun raised, she stared into the darkness, looking for Lazarus, but he was nowhere to be seen. At that moment, she heard the echo of running feet beneath Bispeengbuen.

Cecilie put the safety back on her gun and returned it to the holster. She'd come close to firing it blindly. Now, when she returned to the case files lying on the ground, she regretted not giving in to her impulse. She looked down at the ground where the photos of herself, Bjarke, and a young man lay. The man seemed familiar. He was clearly a pawn in Lazarus's next case.

40

The ceiling light in the Panda shed a yellowish tinge over the inside of the car. Outside, the rain continued to fall unabated. Over the last quarter of an hour, she had gone through Lazarus's material. She wondered if he had collected the newspaper clippings at the time of the trial, or whether he'd taken them from a newspaper archive. The same was true of the cuttings about Bjarke's string of other cases, and those about the other man, who was called Ronnie. To her surprise, Ronnie was Bjarke's grown-up son, and the two men resembled each other in appearance. Both had the same broad mouths and protruding eyes that made them look feeble-minded.

Now that she saw the photos of Bjarke, she understood that she had been the one who had spent all those years feeding the monster living in her head. In reality, he was a pathetic thing. Nothing more than a louse. She read some of the enclosed legal documents that Lazarus had printed out. For raping her, Bjarke had been sentenced to undergo treatment, which had lasted eighteen months. She still remembered how unfair it had felt when the judgment was passed. She had naively been hoping for a long-term prison sentence—perhaps even life. While she hadn't wised up then, she had over the course of her years as a detective. Here she had seen at firsthand one lenient sentence after another in rape cases.

Following his sentence, Bjarke had spent the same number of months at liberty before his next trial: on charges of consummated rape and robbery against a seventy-six-year-old woman from Husum. The woman had been badly injured, and the court had given him a custodial sentence. He'd done five and half years inside before they had decided it was safe to let him out again. Then there were several smaller cases ranging from shoplifting, document forgery, and drink-driving to public disorder, domestic disputes, and unpaid fines. It had culminated in a domestic violence report from a partner. This time he'd been assessed as suitable for punishment and sent to Vestre Prison.

A few months later, his son, Ronnie, was convicted of rape. Ronnie had already been inside for car thefts, burglaries, drug possession, and credit card fraud. Ronnie's rape conviction had been sensational and had garnered some press coverage. The remarkable element of the case was that Bjarke had encouraged Ronnie from his cell to rape his ex-girlfriend. Yet despite the text messages showing communication between the two, Bjarke had never been charged with being an accessory. Now they were both on release, and according to Lazarus, they had joined forces and were renting a flat in Nordvest. From here, Bjarke and Ronnie were in the process of planning their next crime. A crime they intended to commit together. It was a fantasy that Bjarke had expressed both during the psychiatric evaluation he'd undergone many years before, which Lazarus had enclosed, and in text messages to his son. This fantasy had been further fuelled during the two men's prison sentences. The plan was to break into a home and kidnap a woman. Preferably one of high social status living a carefree life in the suburbs with her husband and kids. They would keep her hidden and systematically degrade her, making her their sex slave. In the letter to Cecilie, Lazarus described what the two men were doing by way of preparation. Lazarus knew that they had found a suitable location to hold their hostage, and that they had already begun to explore the north Copenhagen suburbs for a suitable victim. According to Lazarus, it was only a matter of a few days before they struck. *It is up to you to break the curse and ensure these beasts are put down. Only then can YOU be free.* He hadn't said where they were or how he intended them to be killed. However, he had enclosed a phone number for her to call when *she* was ready. The letter was not accompanied by threats to unmask her, so perhaps he really believed his own line about how this task could free her, or else it was simply his attempt to be conciliatory.

Cecilie quickly checked the phone number, which—as she had guessed—was for another anonymous pay-as-you-go SIM card.

She worked her way through the papers he had included. The court paperwork was in the public domain if you knew where to look for it. The same was true of the newspaper articles, which he could have found in a big library or newspaper archive. On the other hand, the copies of police reports and interview transcripts relating to Bjarke and Ronnie, extracts of their text messages and phone data, as well as the psychiatric assessments on them both, were not. These were all confidential, which once again suggested that Lazarus was someone who had access to them himself or knew someone who did. Although the documents pointed to who Lazarus might be, she could understand why he had felt compelled to include them. It was simply an attempt to document the claim that a crime *would* happen, and to justify the liquidation of the two men as a necessary preventive measure. Given her shared past with Bjarke, Lazarus doubtless felt that he had found the best possible candidate for the job: He had turned the sheep into a wolf.

Cecilie looked through the windscreen at the rain lashing down. She leant her head against the headrest and thought it through. She still hadn't heard from Kat what had become of Poul Myers. A man like that would have both the necessary access and experience, but did he also possess a thirst for revenge?

41

The next day, Cecilie was at her desk in the Division's office and about to call Katja when she heard voices from the corridor. Through the glass wall, she caught sight of Lasse, who was accompanied by Sugar. The girl was wearing the same green satin jacket she'd had on that night in front of Turisthotellet. There was an air of pride about her as she strode towards the exit. Cecilie was relieved to have avoided a confrontation with her. She reached for the phone and called the Bellahøj police station, who put her through.

"Katja Sloth," said a deep bass voice.

"Kat, it's Cecilie."

"Sorry, sorry, sorry," said Katja. "A thousand apologies that I haven't got back to you. I'm the worst."

"It's okay. You guys busy?"

"Like you wouldn't believe. But that's no excuse. You were asking about . . . Poul Myers."

"Yes. Do you know him?"

"Never met him. He was here before my time."

"Okay. Do you know whether he's moved to another station or retired?"

"Neither."

"What does that mean?"

"I don't know how well you knew him, but when I asked around, I found out that he's dead."

"Damn it. I didn't really know him," Cecilie said hastily. "His name came up in an old case." She had never told Kat or anyone else on the force about her rape, and she planned to keep it that way. "Do you know when and how it happened?"

"Cancer. A few years back, apparently. If it matters, I can ask about it again."

"No, there's no need. Like I said, his name came up."

"We have to do something soon. It's been too long."

"Hell yes," Cecilie said. Without offering any further specifics.

A couple of minutes after wrapping up her call with Katja, Lasse came through the door. He came over and sat down heavily on his desk chair.

"What's up?" Cecilie asked.

"Total blank. Sugar sped through the mug book without being able to pick out a single person. It didn't seem like she had any interest in helping either. In reality, I think if she recognised the person from that night, she wanted to protect her." He shrugged. "You can understand why."

"So it's a dead end?"

Lasse nodded.

"What's a dead end?" asked Andreas, who was standing behind her with a stack of case files tucked under his arm.

Cecilie half-turned in her chair and looked up at him. "Sugar is."

"Might have more luck with this lot," Andreas replied. He dropped the stack of case files on her desk.

Lasse got up and looked at them curiously. "Is this every vice case you've lost?"

"I'm afraid there are quite a few more," Andreas said, glancing at them apologetically. "But I'm thinking you could make a start on these. They aren't all ones we lost either. I included a few where the verdict did not—how shall I put it—measure up to the crime in question." He pointed to the stack. "There are also a couple of dubious treatment sentences in there for good measure."

"How do you mean?" said Lasse, picking up the top file and rapidly flipping through it.

"Cases where the accused managed to lie their way to a favourable psychiatric assessment and got off with a treatment sentence. Sometimes Steen Holz—our expert witness—and I have had to fight fiercely to prove to the court that defendants are suitable for punishment. Especially the Terrier's clients. We don't always succeed."

"I remember this case well," Lasse said, reading on. "It's a sordid tale. You think this victim could be our potential killer?"

"I have no opinion," said Andreas, holding his hands up defensively. "All I'm doing is supplying old cases, like Karstensen asked. Then it's up to you to go through them."

"Of course," Cecilie replied. "We'll handle them."

Andreas gave them both a look. "Discreetly, please? Some people have gone through the most monstrous things. The last thing they need is you lot barging in and making accusations."

"We'll proceed with caution," said Cecilie.

"Great. After all, it's the beasts out there we should be going after."

"What?" Cecilie's smile faltered.

"Well . . . the perpetrators . . . the criminals," he said, pointing at the window, as if they were lying in wait beyond it. "Anyway, good hunting," he added, turning around.

Cecilie followed Andreas with her gaze as he headed for his own desk on the far side of the room.

"Should we split it in half?" said Lasse, grabbing a pile of cases. He went back to his chair and began to read the top one.

Cecilie stared at Andreas who was now at his computer, surrounded by the other prosecutors. There was a forest of blue shirts and well-groomed haircuts down there at the point where the Homicide Unit ended and the Prosecution Service began.

Andreas had used the same turn of phrase as Lazarus. But it was unthinkable—it had to be a random coincidence. Or so she tried to convince herself. To use a term like *beasts* about criminals was . . . well, it wasn't something you heard every day. Far from it. She bit her lip as she reflected: manipulative, self-centred, deceitful, controlling, focused, strategic, methodical, smooth, and educated. A character description that was a good match for both Lazarus and Andreas. Given his role, Andreas had unfettered access to all the same reports that Lazarus had given her. That included interview transcripts, court rulings, and of course, psychiatric assessments. Both also had extensive knowledge of police work. Including surveillance, evidence gathering, pathology, DNA analysis, and the very capabilities of NC3.

Perhaps Andreas and his psychologist had lost one case too many and now he was trying to bring about justice by himself? "You're crazy," she muttered to herself.

"What's crazy?" Lasse asked, looking up from the case files.

"Nothing. I just said there was a crazy amount of stuff for us to get through," she said, pointing at the pile.

"Okay," he said, continuing to read undeterred.

Cecilie picked up one of the case files and leafed through it without reading a single word. She couldn't get Andreas out of her thoughts. Even though she had slept with him, she really had no idea who he was. They had deliberately kept everything private except for the shabby hotel room that they both got a kick out of visiting. That was their thing, even if it was mostly a tragic cliché. A cliché that worked well alongside the others that seemed to surround them: his wrecked marriage and her fear of letting anyone get close.

She pulled her phone out of her pocket. The easiest thing to do would be to send Lazarus a message on the number he'd given her and see whether Andreas reacted. She thought it over again before writing a text.

I need more time to make up my mind. Okay?

She looked towards Andreas as he continued to type away undisturbed on his computer, making no attempt to look at his mobile phone. After looking at him for a couple of minutes without anything happening, she returned her phone to her pocket.

"What are you thinking in terms of lunch?" Lasse asked, straightening his back as he sat on his chair.

Cecilie looked over at him. "Lunchtime already?"

"My stomach's rumbling," Lasse said, getting up.

Cecilie peered back towards Andreas's desk, which he had vacated in the meantime. She spotted that his jacket was still hanging on the back of the chair. "I . . . I think I'll hang on a bit longer."

"Okay, see you up there," Lasse said, sauntering off.

When her phone buzzed a minute later, Cecilie took it out of her pocket. She read the message from Lazarus.

Don't wait too long. The beasts are almost ready. Be strong!

She could feel her mouth going dry. It had to be a coincidence. It *had* to be. Shortly after, when Andreas returned to his desk, she quickly looked down at the papers in front of her. Out of the corner of her eye, she watched him. He was leaning back in his chair while removing his phone from his pocket. She expected him to either make a call or check it, but instead, he removed the SIM card from it. He looked around furtively before swapping it for one taken from the inside pocket of his jacket.

Cecilie didn't know what to make of what she'd just seen. It had all happened so fast. Andreas was back at work now, as if nothing had happened. She stood up slowly from her desk and began to walk towards him. She reflected on the times when Lazarus had contacted her at the office, and how Andreas had always been out of sight. She reflected that the answers to her suspicions might be found on that SIM card that he had just put in his pocket.

"Cecilie," he said, looking up in surprise before smiling.

She returned her warmest smile and tried to avoid staring at his jacket pocket.

"What can I do for you?" he said, while continuing to write.

"I was thinking about that dinner."

Andreas stopped typing and looked up at her in surprise. "Yes? What about it?"

"We could do it at mine?"

Andreas blinked. "Er, sure . . . Love to. When . . . ?"

"Tonight, if you're not too busy?" she said, nodding at the screen.

"No, no. Definitely not. What time?"

"At seven o'clock," she said, turning on her heel. On the way back to her desk, she sent another text to Lazarus.

You'll have my answer tonight.

42

Cecilie applied red lipstick to her mouth. She examined the results in the bathroom mirror and saw that her makeup attempt had been a disaster. There was too much and it was too inexpertly done—it made her look like a hooker. If she were honest, most hookers looked prettier than she did right now. She wiped the makeup off her face. Andreas would have to settle for her "natural" visage. Judging by the hungry look he had given her earlier that day, it would probably do. She picked up the phone, which was by the sink next to the holster for her service weapon. It was already quarter past seven and Andreas might arrive at any moment. Cecilie opened the HomeSAFE app and a couple of clicks later she had accessed the alarm system camera fitted in the living room. She was surprised by how good the picture quality was. Unfortunately, the camera couldn't be programmed to record—all it did was broadcast live. Once she had checked whether everything was working, she closed the app and grabbed the holster containing her gun. She searched for somewhere to hide it and settled for putting it behind the toilet cistern. She went into the bedroom with her handcuffs and tucked them under the pillow. There wasn't much more she could do, and as if it were scripted, the doorbell rang at that moment. Cecilie took a deep breath and went to open up.

"Hi," Andreas said, smiling broadly. "Sorry I'm late. Work dragged on."

"That's totally alright. Come in," she said, inviting him through the door.

"Lively area you live in," he said ironically. "Is it safe to park down there?"

"Depends on what you're driving," she replied with a smile. She had noticed that Hassan and the other lads had returned to the neighbourhood, but they were now staying well away from the basketball court.

Andreas grimaced. "Here," he said, proffering a bottle of rosé. "I don't know what you're serving up, but this goes with most stuff. I was in Kjær and Sommerfeldt, and according to them it's the world's best rosé."

Shit, she thought to herself. In her eagerness to prepare her setup, she had entirely forgotten to cook anything. "I . . . I thought we'd order a takeaway?"

"Great," Andreas said.

They went into the kitchen and Cecilie got out a couple of glasses, while Andreas opened the bottle. She found a tray to put everything on and led him into the living room.

"Wow! What a view!" said Andreas, going over to the roof terrace door. "You can see the whole city."

"Yep, not only can I see our own district, but I can see all of Bellahøj and all of Vestegnen, too," she said.

"That's certainly one way of looking at it." He quickly looked around the half-empty living room without passing comment and then sat down on the sofa. "Cheers," he said, raising his glass.

"Cheers," she replied, sitting down beside him. She glanced sidelong at his suit. He had quite literally come straight from the office. Which suited her down to the ground.

"What?" he asked, noticing her staring.

"Nothing." She lowered her gaze and sipped the wine. There was a moment of awkwardness until Andreas asked her how long she had lived there.

"Too long," was her reply. "You've found your own place now, right?"

"Yes, but you know, it's nothing fancy and it's bloody tiny. And it's pretty quiet in the evenings," he added forlornly.

"Quiet? Around your neighbourhood?" she said.

"In the flat mostly, as my daughter's not there. She only stays with me every other weekend, so . . ."

"Okay," Cecilie replied, wondering whether he still had the SIM card in his breast pocket.

He shook his head. "Anyway, I shouldn't be talking about my divorce agonies. Sorry."

"Don't sweat it," she said, sipping from her glass which was already almost empty. "You're not drinking," she said.

He took an awkward sip from his own glass. "You haven't been married, have you?"

"I'm not really the marrying kind."

"Honestly, it's incredible how little we know about each other. Even though we've known each other for what? Going on four years?"

"Yes. And we've had a couple of shags, too," she said, which elicited a smile from him.

"There's that, too." He took a big gulp of wine. When he put down his glass, she refilled it.

"So where did you grow up?" he asked. "You from Copenhagen?"

"Vangede."

"A Vangede girl," he said, smiling.

"Yes."

"Well, I'm from Skovshoved. I moved all of two kilometres from my childhood home to set up what my father now consistently refers to as 'the former marital home.' Sorry." Andreas waved his hand as he found himself sharing yet another divorce anecdote.

A few moments later, Cecilie excused herself and went to the bathroom. After locking the door, she got out her phone and opened the HomeSAFE app. The video footage from the living room camera showed Andreas on the sofa. He glanced hastily at his wristwatch. Even though they had done nothing but exchange pleasantries, she couldn't help but analyse their conversation. Had he been mocking her for being a Vangede girl, just like the headline in the old newspaper article? Or was she imagining things? She swiped out of the app and called the number that Lazarus had provided. She let it ring for thirty seconds without any answer. When she returned to the alarm system app and the image of

Andreas, he was still on the sofa. At that moment, he took his phone from his trouser pocket and checked it. She considered whether she should call again, but instead she sent Lazarus a message.

When can we talk?

She went back to the video and saw that Andreas had put the phone back in his pocket. She waited a little before sending another text.

Need an answer now!

There was no reaction—not from Lazarus and not from Andreas, who was still on the sofa. It was time for plan B. A couple of minutes later she returned to the living room, and Andreas smiled at her. He fastened the top button of his jacket, with the air of someone on their way out.

"What's up?" she said, sitting down.

"I got to thinking that maybe this is a bad idea."

"Why?" she asked, moving closer to him.

"Because you seem a bit distant. That's no criticism," he added politely. "There's also no point getting into something that we'll only regret afterwards."

"We've done it before," she said, stroking his arm. "And we can again."

"Well, yes . . . I just thought that . . ."

"Well, stop thinking," she said, leaning in close to him. She kissed him gently on the mouth. "See, things are much better when we don't think about them." She looked at him seductively.

"Cecilie Mars, you're bad," said Andreas, taking her head in his hands. He stuck his tongue into her mouth, roughly, leaving her almost unable to breathe.

She pulled back from his embrace. "Come on," she said, dragging him off the sofa.

He removed his jacket and allowed himself to be led towards the bedroom. They had barely made it through the door when he tore at the button on her trousers. She pushed him hard in the chest, making him fall over backwards onto the bed.

"Clothes on then?" he laughed, reaching out to her.

She straddled him and undid his top shirt buttons. She caressed his rib cage, letting her fingers slip through his chest hair. Andreas's hands sought out her buttocks, which he squeezed gently.

"Did you miss me?" she whispered.

"Fuck yes," he groaned.

She reached towards his right hand and removed it from her buttock.

"What are you doing?" he asked as she lifted his arm up above his head. She leaned forward and he nipped at her breasts under her T-shirt. She slipped her hands under the pillow and retrieved the handcuffs. In one rapid movement, she pulled them out and clipped them around one of Andreas's wrists.

"Bloody hell. Ouch!" He saw the handcuffs and his face broke into a dirty smile. "Should I consider myself arrested?"

"In a manner of speaking," Cecilie replied, attaching the other cuff to the bed frame. Her hand slid into his trouser pocket, seeking out his phone. When she had it, she got up quickly from the bed.

"What's going on?" said Andreas, looking at her wide-eyed. "What are you doing with my phone?"

"What's the PIN?" she asked.

"You're not having it!" he laughed. "You wanting to take pictures?"

"Just give me the PIN, Andreas."

"No chance. Put that thing down and come back to bed. Things were just starting to get exciting."

Cecilie left the bedroom and went into the living room. When she picked up Andreas's jacket from the floor, she heard him calling to her. She didn't reply, instead searching his pockets. In the breast pocket she found four different SIM cards. It struck her how many times Lazarus had changed numbers. All it took was a stack of SIM cards like these to insert into your phone and then you could remain anonymous. She returned to the bedroom with the phone and the SIM cards. "What's this?"

"What do you mean?"

"What are all these SIM cards for?"

"Work. Not that it's any of your business. What's this all about?"

"Work in what way?"

"Why do you ask? Put that down and come here."

"What do they contain?"

"Confidential material on a whole bunch of cases." He sighed deeply and tugged at the handcuffs, trying to free himself.

"Why are you hiding that on SIM cards?"

"Because that's my choice. Be a good girl and unlock these. I think playtime is over." He rattled the handcuffs.

"Give me your PIN."

"What?" He looked at her in irritation.

"You heard what I said."

"Please open these. This is completely ridiculous."

"First give me your PIN."

He shook his head. "It's . . . it's . . . You've completely lost your mind."

"Very possibly. I could also send them to NC3. The choice is yours. It won't take Ismail long to get into these and your phone."

"NC3? What the hell is this all about? Is that why you invited me home?"

"This is your last chance, Andreas." She put the SIM cards on the nightstand and pulled her own phone out of her pocket.

"You're sick in the head."

"Is that the officer on duty?" she said into her own phone.

"Six-six-nine-two," Andreas moaned in resignation.

Cecilie hung up and slipped her own phone back into her pocket.

She picked up Andreas's and entered the code before scrutinising the list of incoming calls. Her own call was not there. "Did you change your SIM card while I was in the bathroom?"

"I don't know what you're talking about. But now that you've checked my phone, maybe it's time to set me free?" He reached his hand towards her peremptorily.

She didn't reply. Instead, she quickly scrolled through his messages before checking his emails. But she couldn't find anything tying Andreas to Lazarus. She inserted a new SIM card and checked its contents. All the text messages were from someone called Maria. Andreas called himself Lucas, and the tone between the two was decidedly erotic. Among the final messages were a couple of dick pics that Andreas had sent.

Cecilie looked at Andreas in surprise as his gaze wavered. She inserted another SIM into the phone and saw that Andreas was now calling himself Christian and was messaging a woman called Pia. The content was just as erotic as his correspondence with Maria, and the same dick pics were present.

Cecilie went through the final two SIM cards and found the same pattern repeated. Despite Andreas's multitude of aliases, he was clearly not Lazarus. She threw the phone down on the bed along with the SIM cards.

"Happy now? Fuck me, you're the sickest person I've ever met."

"Sorry," she said. "Didn't mean to pry." She got the key for the handcuffs out of her pocket and threw it to him.

"Fuck's sake. Surely you didn't think you were the only one?" Andreas snatched the key and freed himself.

"No. Sorry."

He got up quickly from the bed and retrieved the phone and SIM cards which he put in his pocket. "No fucking wonder you're single," he said, pushing past her.

A moment later, she heard the front door slam. She went into the hallway to ensure that the door was properly locked. Then she returned to the living room and sat down on the sofa. She considered whether to pour herself a glass of wine, if nothing else than to celebrate the fact that she could remove Andreas from her list of suspects. At that moment, her phone vibrated in her pocket. She pulled it out and saw that the number was the same one she had contacted Lazarus on. "Hello?"

"You wanted to talk to me?" he said coolly. "I take it you have a spare moment now that you've seen off the honourable prosecutor. I must say, he did not look happy. I had imagined you to be a good host."

Cecilie cleared her throat. "Where are you?"

"That is irrelevant. Far more important is where Julia Schölin has been taken."

"Who?"

"The woman who was reported missing yesterday. Don't you even read your morning briefing?"

43

Cecilie got up from the sofa clutching the phone in her hand and went to the roof terrace door. The city was illuminated before her in the night and expanded as far as the eye could see.

"Cat got your tongue?" said Lazarus on the other end of the line. "You won't find her by standing at the window staring into space."

He had to be close enough to keep her under observation. She considered stepping away from the window and his field of vision but set the idea aside. "What did you say the woman's name was?"

"Julia Schölin. Thirty-eight years of age, housewife. Married to marketing director Peter Schölin. She was supposed to pick up their nine-year-old son, Emil, from football at 15:00, but she never turned up. Her mobile phone and credit card were left at home. Her car was still on the driveway. The family is worried there's been an accident."

"And where did you get this information?"

"Your morning briefing and the online press coverage. If there's one thing hacks love, it's a juicy disappearance in the nation's whiskey belt."

"And I take it that you think Bjarke and Ronnie Thomsen are behind her disappearance?"

"No, I don't think that. I know for certain, for the simple reason that I saw them kidnap her."

"You didn't see any reason to intervene?" she said sardonically.

"Says the woman who seems to have been too busy inviting the prosecutor to her place so she could get him into bed. Your tarrying has yet again complicated the situation. We could have cleared this up without witnesses. Without loose ends. You could have closed your own circle and made the future better for everyone."

"So what do you think will happen now?"

"What I know *is* happening right now is that poor old Julia is going through the most terrible torture. I dare say you can put yourself in her shoes?"

She felt the knot in her stomach. "Where are they holding her?"

"Should I take that as acceptance of the task that has been assigned to you? Do you wish to rid the world of these two beasts?"

Cecilie surveyed the city and took a deep breath. "I think I can handle them."

"I hope I can count on you. There will be serious consequences should you betray me."

"No threats are necessary."

"That wasn't a threat, it was a prediction. Both Bjarke's and Ronnie's psychological assessments describe them as aggressively impulsive when under stress. It would be most unfortunate if you chose to involve the Special Intervention Unit or the Tactical Unit and we ended up with a major confrontation. Especially for their victim, I dare say."

"I said I can handle it. Do you have an address?"

"I have not only an address but also a mission plan. I suggest you follow the latter closely if you want to get out of this whole thing alive and unseen."

"So where?"

She inserted the key in the ignition and started the Panda's engine. The lads watched from a distance, waiting like lions who had spotted their next meal at the watering hole. Their courage seemed be increasing day by day, and the only question was when their predatory instinct would shut down everything else and unleash their bloodlust.

She left the area and drove past Bellahøj Swimming Stadium on her way towards Bispeengbuen. Shortly after reaching Borups Allé, she pulled over under the vault of the bridge, not far from the spot where she had last parked. She got out of the Panda and made her way past the parked cars, heading again for the skateboard track. Above her, on the motorway lanes on Bispeengbuen, cars were droning along with an ominous rumble. She undid her holster and let her hand rest on the handle of her pistol as she looked around. When she reached the skateboard track, she made her way towards the dumpsters. In the crack between the front two, she caught sight of the same tote bag that Lazarus had left for her in the parkland at Sydhavn. She pulled out the tote bag, feeling its weight. Inside was the sawn-off shotgun and the box of cartridges. At the bottom was a large screwdriver, with its end filed to a point, and a canister of spray paint.

Lazarus's plan was simple: First she was to shoot Ronnie, primarily because he was the stronger of the two men, and then she was to stab Bjarke in the throat using the screwdriver. Once she had killed the two of them, it was up to her to make it look like a showdown between father and son. She picked up the tote bag and retrieved the can of spray paint from the ground. Then she went to the nearest bridge pier, which was covered in graffiti. She was looking for the address as Lazarus had instructed her to, and she found it between the teeth of a Felix the Cat motif. Once she had memorised it, she sprayed over it, just as he had dictated.

Cecilie returned to the Panda and put the tote bag containing the shotgun on the passenger seat. She started the engine and pulled onto Nordre Fasanvej before making her way through Ydre Nørrebro. Despite the late hour, the neighbourhood was a hive of lively activity. Cecilie passed Mjølner Park and then headed into the Østerbro area, which was far sleepier. Soon, she reached the Composers' Quarter where the old houses built by the Workers' Building Society stood in rows. When she reached H.C. Lumbyes Gade, she turned onto the dark street. She pulled over and stared at the yellow-brick terraced houses situated behind leafy front gardens. Cecilie reflected that superficially this was a very idyllic place. She retrieved the tote and got out of the car. She made her way to number 17 where she opened the garden gate and entered. The house, like everything else here, was in darkness; it looked as if the owners were all tucked up for the night. She climbed the steps and knocked on the door. When it didn't open, she knocked harder. After a little while, the hall light was switched on and the door was opened.

"Apologies for the late hour," she said.

Lasse looked at her drowsily. He was wearing a faded Bakken Bears T-shirt and a pair of yellow boxer shorts. "Guppy? What on earth are you doing here?"

"Can I come in?"

Lasse let out a big yawn. "Of course," he said, opening the door wider. "What time is it?"

44

Lasse led Cecilie into the kitchen where they sat down at the long Provence dining table. He leaned back and pushed the door to slightly. At that moment, a large Forest Cat slipped through the gap and made its way towards Cecilie. "Buster!" Lasse said, reaching out for the cat. "That cat is going to be the death of me one of these days," he said, shepherding it back out of the door. "Isn't that true for all stepchildren?" he added, smiling.

Cecilie nodded at him, nonplussed. "Lasse, I need your help."

"Say the word, Guppy. Seems serious."

"And it is. Very." She pulled out her phone and set it between them on the table. Then she played Lazarus's video from the scene of the accident.

"Is that who I think it is?" Lasse said, his eyes glued to the screen.

"Yes, it's Ulrik Østergård. Following the hearing, I kept an eye on him. Mostly because I was worried he was going to do something to Fie. I thought he might try to scare her. Or worse."

"Okay, I understand, although this looks pretty violent," he said, pointing to the screen.

"He made a grab for me, and yes—I panicked."

Lasse leaned back, clearly shaken. "Who . . . who recorded this?"

"An anonymous figure who calls himself Lazarus."

"The one who rose from the dead?" He nodded. "I take it there's a reason why he sent the video to *you*?"

"Yes. Lazarus has been sending me various messages of late, and I've been in touch with him, too."

"What does he want?"

She looked down at the floor. "Lazarus, in his own words, wants to rid the world of all beasts. All the killers and rapists."

"Sounds commendable."

"Yes, except he doesn't believe in the justice system."

"He's a vigilante?"

"Yes."

"Why didn't you mention this sooner?"

"I should have. I know it was wrong of me . . ."

"Either way, this is some serious shit here, Guppy. For Christ's sake, you're risking charges for this."

She nodded. "But . . . it gets much worse," she said, biting her lip.

"How?"

"Emil Kam," she said, pausing for breath. "I . . . I didn't randomly catch wind of him. That was a lie."

Lasse furrowed his brows. "You didn't see him at the swimming baths, did you?"

"Yes, I did. But only after Lazarus sent me details of where I could find him."

"Why didn't you just tell the truth?"

"Because Lazarus is blackmailing me with that video. He wanted me to kill Emil."

"What are you saying?" Lasse gaped at her, his chin practically down to his chest. "Did you . . . kill Emil Kam?"

"Fuck's sake. No! I prevented his death in the first place. Lazarus was planning to stage an accident with Emil's boiler."

"But the murder . . . ?"

"When Emil Kam was released, Lazarus killed him. I had no idea it was going to happen."

"Jesus Christ, Guppy!" Lasse shouted, standing up in agitation. "This is off the charts! What the fuck were you thinking? Withholding that kind of information . . ."

"I know, I know."

"You're a goddamn cop! How the hell could you?!"

"I totally regret it, but I had no choice."

"What are you talking about? You could have bloody well come to me."

"No."

"No? Okay, why not?" He looked at her, wounded.

"Because the weapon used to kill Emil Kam has my DNA on it. Lazarus broke into my flat and stole the knife before using it to kill Emil Kam. He's been using it to blackmail me ever since."

Lasse shook his head in confusion. "The knife that was found at the neighbour's? The one we've got in our possession right now?"

"Yes."

"But if he was blackmailing you with it, why did we only get it now?"

She didn't reply. Lasse wiped his mouth thoughtfully. "Because you said no to the next case? That's why you're here now? Right?"

She took a deep breath. "I only wish that were the case. He blackmailed me into going after Morten Pier Nielsen."

Lasse stared at her. "You're saying that Lazarus also killed Morten Pier Nielsen? That you've known all along?"

"No . . ." She shook her head. "It was me who killed Morten."

"Stop it! This is too much at once." He sat down again, trying to compose himself. "Are you . . . are you sure it's a good idea to tell me all this?"

"Yes."

"You know that I'm going to have to report this? That I might have to . . . arrest you?" A lump seemed to have formed in his throat.

"I know that. And it's okay. I need to tell you all of this." She put her hand over his. "I killed Morten in self-defence. Contrary to Lazarus's plans, I tried to arrest Morten, but he overpowered me. You saw my smashed-up fingers for yourself. He tried to strangle me, and I had no other choice. It was me or him."

"But how the hell did you get yourself into that situation?"

"I had to follow Lazarus's instructions to save Sugar. I had to stop Morten. I had no idea we would find evidence against him at his parents' house. I'd already searched for it at his address on Rådmandsgade."

"So instead you followed the plan of an insane vigilante?" Lasse withdrew his hand.

"No, not quite." Cecilie found the tote bag and showed Lasse the sawn-off shotgun. "Here's the gun he wanted me to use. Lazarus wanted Morten's killing to look like a biker gang execution. The serial number has been filed off, but Forensics might be able to find something on it."

"Get out," said Lasse, examining at the shotgun. "Christ, Guppy. We could have bloody well worked it out. The whole Division would have had your back."

"It's not that simple, Lasse. Without Lazarus, we would never have heard of Emil or Morten. Those two were able to commit their crimes undisturbed for a long time. Morten had already killed three women. I'm not trying to make excuses—but it's a fact. There's also a completely different problem."

"We've already got plenty to be getting on with . . ."

"Lazarus's knowledge and his modus operandi. The more I think about it, the more I'm convinced he's got links to the police. Or has had. He has access to confidential material. Police interview transcripts. Psychiatric assessments. He's had me under surveillance for a long time and his approach is highly professional. Remember the flowers I was sent?"

"Yes. From a secret admirer."

"On the contrary. That was Lazarus sending me a case."

"So you really think he's a police officer?" Lasse said, looking at her sceptically.

"It's likely. I even suspected he might be someone in the Prosecution Service." She looked down at the table.

"Andreas?"

"Yes. But I can confidently rule him out. I'm not necessarily saying that Lazarus is on the force. But he has a good awareness of our methods, and he has access to sensitive information."

"We need to call this in to Karstensen," Lasse said, looking at her phone. "Maybe NC3 can find him."

"I doubt that Lazarus has left any significant traces in the digital or real worlds. Only the ones that he has planted himself, that implicate me. But yes, *you* should trigger a hunt for him as quickly as possible. I only hope that before that happens . . ."

"What?"

"That you can help me."

"With what, Guppy?"

She looked at him for a long time. "A woman was reported missing yesterday. Julia Schölin."

"The Hellerup wife. I saw it in the morning briefing. What about her?"

"She's been kidnapped by two men who are holding her captive."

"I take it that Lazarus told you this? And you believe him?"

"Yes to both. We have to find her before they do her any more harm."

"Of course. Did he tell you where she is?"

"Yes, I have all the information."

Lasse nodded. "Well then, let's pass it on."

"Can't. The two kidnappers are highly dangerous."

"And that's why we have the Special Intervention Unit."

"The last thing we need is them storming the house with their machine guns. You know what they're like. It could have disastrous consequences for the hostage if they end up in a head-on confrontation."

"Sorry, but I don't see any other solution. We have to call this in." He looked towards his mobile phone on the kitchen table.

"Lasse. Listen to me, please. I know one of the perpetrators. If we go down that route, things will end badly. He'll kill her."

"You know one of them?" he said, standing up to get his phone. "How? From a previous case?" He unlocked his phone to make the call.

"He raped me when I was seventeen."

Lasse froze and stared at her. "He did . . . what?"

"You heard what I said."

"But . . . you?"

"Yes, me. Bjarke Thomsen is the elder of the two kidnappers, the other is Ronnie. He's Bjarke's son. A real creep. A chip off the old block."

Lasse sat down slowly. "Fucking hell, Guppy. I . . . I didn't know."

"Lazarus does." She pulled a folder from her jacket pocket and put it in front of Lasse. "You can read about the case if you want. And about Bjarke, who hasn't held back since then."

Lasse opened the folder and carefully removed the newspaper article about the rape to read it. "This is . . . I'm so sorry, Guppy. Damn it . . ."

he said, his voice thick. Lasse glanced through the case files on Bjarke and Ronnie. "Filthy swines," he muttered when he'd read them.

"Lasse, I need your help to rescue Julia and put the two of them away. After that . . . we can sort out the rest of it." She looked down at the table. "So that you can hopefully catch Lazarus."

"I just need to put some clothes on and let Martin know I'm popping out," Lasse said, snuffling loudly.

"Lasse, thank you," she said, looking up at him. "I'm really grateful for your help."

"Don't mention it," Lasse said, turning towards the door. "But why didn't you just go on your own?"

"Because I was afraid I'd follow Lazarus's plan and shoot them. I need you to prevent that from happening."

45

It was two o'clock in the morning by the time they drove towards the address on Tagensvej that Lazarus had written on the bridge column. The streets were deserted, but Cecilie still checked in the rearview mirror to see whether they were being followed. Up to now, she hadn't noticed anything, but she was certain that Lazarus was nearby. Lasse was squashed into the passenger seat in a mint-coloured padded jacket, which prevented him from moving. "You said before that you suspected that Lazarus was one of us. That you thought for a while it was Andreas."

"Which I can definitively rule out."

"Is there anyone else you've suspected?"

"I think by now I've suspected everyone. You turn paranoid when something like this happens."

"What about me? Have you ever suspected me?"

"Not for a second, Lasse." She patted him fondly on the thigh. "You're not really the psychopathic type."

He smiled. "I'm glad to hear you say that. Anything else would have made me sad. So that wasn't the reason why you didn't confide in me until now?"

"No Lasse, not at all. It was more anxiety, stupidity, and a dash of pride. I didn't want you to see me fail."

"Come on, Guppy. You'll always be my hero. No matter what." He shook his head meaningfully. "But that Lazarus is right. The crooks really do get off lightly. It's frustrating."

"Definitely," she replied. "It's not right." She pulled onto Lygten and drove towards Nørrebro Station and Frederikssundsvej. "According to Lazarus, they've set up in a disused warehouse on Svanevej." She looked at the street signs as they passed the side streets.

"It's this one," said Lasse, pointing to a crossroads with an ethnic corner shop on it.

Cecilie pulled onto Svanevej and stopped after they'd passed the large shop window. She looked towards a low white building set back behind a deserted car park. The dilapidated, windowless building was covered in graffiti, and the glass windows in the two doors facing the street had been covered with sheets of plywood.

"One hell of a spot," Lasse muttered. "Perfect for an ambush. You sure we shouldn't bring in Special Interventions?"

"More than ever," she said, getting out of the car. Lasse followed her, stretching to ease his aching limbs. He opened his heavy coat and undid the buckle on his holster. "It looks like there are two ways in," he said, as they crossed the street. "Should we go for the smallest door?" he added, pulling out his pistol.

When they reached it, Lasse got out his lockpicks and crouched by the lock. It took him less than a minute to pick it, and then he gently pushed against the door until it opened. "After you."

Pistol raised, Cecilie stepped through the doorway into the dark warehouse. She switched on her Maglite and shone it around the vacant space. There was a door ajar at the back. She signalled to Lasse to follow her. He took the safety off his gun and followed close on her tail. When they reached the door, she killed the torch and gently nudged it open. Cecilie peered into the room. She caught sight of one figure lying on a sofa and another lying on a mattress beside it. She silently entered the room. There was an array of empty bottles on the floor, and the space smelled of sweat and old booze. Cecilie and Lasse positioned themselves above the two men. She shone her torch at the face of one. The man was completely out of it—the light didn't even register. She swept the beam over the other one, who was much younger.

"Is it them?" Lasse whispered, pistol aimed at the man on the sofa.

Cecilie kicked the young man's leg hard. "Police!" she yelled.

Lasse bent down and shook the other one. "Police! Wake up!"

The two men came to slowly and looked around, dazed. "Wha . . . th'fuck's going on?" said the eldest.

Lasse grabbed the man's collar and pulled him upright on the sofa. He quickly patted down his pockets, which seemed to be empty. "Is it them?" he asked Cecilie again.

Cecilie nodded. "Yes, it's them. Bjarke Thomsen and his shit of a son, Ronnie."

"You can't do this," Bjarke barked.

"Shut up," Cecilie said. She looked around the half-empty room. There was another door at the far end. She went to it and opened it. The small toilet cubicle stank of piss—she quickly closed the door again. "Where is she?" she asked upon her return. "Where have you hidden Julia?"

"Don't fuckin' know who you're talkin' 'bout," Ronnie said, looking down at the floor.

"The woman you kidnapped. Where is she?"

"We ain't fuckin' done nothing," Bjarke said. "This is private property. Get to fuck."

She looked at the two men in turn. Ronnie had inherited his father's traits to an extent that was uncanny. Seeing him was like facing down Bjarke in the backyard all over again. "We know you abducted Julia Schölin from her home yesterday. So where is she?"

"Don't you listen, bitch?!" Bjarke shouted. "We ain't done shit."

"Speak properly," said Lasse, nudging him in the side with his knee.

Cecilie bent down and looked Ronnie in the eyes. "I'm certain that it was your father's idea. You had nothing to do with it. You just got tricked into it. Maybe you were pressured into doing something against your will . . ."

Ronnie's eyes flickered and she could tell that the few brain cells he possessed were starting to work. "I dunno."

"Ronnie. Listen to me. It's important that you do the right thing here. Otherwise we won't be able to help you."

"Yeah, but . . ." He squinted towards his father.

"Ronnie, look at me," she said. "If you don't tell me where Julia is, we'll have to charge you as an accomplice. You'll never see the light of day again. So, Ronnie, what's it to be?"

"Don't listen to that scrubber," said Bjarke. "They ain't got shit on us. We is . . . we're innocent."

"I . . . want . . ." Ronnie waved Cecilie closer to him with his hand and she leaned towards him. He dispatched a gob of saliva at her face.

Bjarke laughed hysterically, slapping his thighs.

"Shut your mouth," Lasse said, shaking Bjarke without making him stop.

Ronnie bared his rotten teeth in a snarling grimace. "We're innocent."

Cecilie wiped her face with the back of her hand. Then she swung the handle of her gun at Ronnie's face. The blow struck his nose, causing a jet of blood to splatter down his front. Howling, Ronnie put his hands to his face.

"The fuck you doin', you cow?!" Bjarke bellowed.

Cecilie stood up and took a step towards him. She took the safety off her pistol and took aim at his head. Bjarke raised his hands in front of him protectively.

"Where is she?"

"Fuck you. That's fucking illegal, innit. The pigs aren't allowed to do that."

"No? Says who, Bjarke? You see any witnesses? Tell me why I shouldn't just euthanise a *beast* like you right here on the spot."

"Fuck . . . fuck you . . ."

"Yes? Or your son?" She pointed back to Ronnie.

"Dad, stop her . . ." Ronnie whimpered as blood flowed between his fingers.

"Do you really not recognise me, Bjarke?" She smiled dangerously. He scrutinised her with his protruding eyes.

"The fuck from?"

"Vangede. You were doing work at our house. Spent all summer drooling over me."

"That I got a hard time believing."

"Oh no, Bjarke. I was seventeen, and you were nasty. You followed me and then you decided to rape me."

Bjarke looked at her uncertainly. "Shit . . . s'you?"

"Yes. Shit. Me." She turned the gun towards him and took aim. He stared at her with the same dead eyes he'd had in the backyard. She could feel him on top of her all over again. Thrusting. Dripping with sweat. If they didn't find Julia, the two of them would soon be at large again, while she'd be in custody, rotting behind bars. All alone with her thoughts. It wouldn't just be the rape in the backyard that would haunt her. It would be this moment: This golden opportunity to execute him would hound her to the grave. She squeezed the trigger a little tighter. At least she would know justice had been done. She felt the spring tightening.

"*Cecilie!*" said Lasse.

She turned towards him.

"Lower the weapon. This isn't the way it should be done." She felt the weight of the pistol and it was as if she could no longer hold her arm out straight. She slowly lowered her weapon.

Lasse pulled out his phone and called for assistance. Cecilie turned towards him, despairingly. It was all over now. Lazarus had lured her out here knowing full well that Julia wouldn't be here. Perhaps he'd thought that the confrontation with Bjarke would be enough to drive her to murder him. He'd almost been right.

"They're on their way," Lasse said behind her.

"Okay," she said, looking around. Why had Bjarke and Ronnie picked this spot? They lived in a flat not far from here, so why get hammered here? Why hide out if they weren't even on the run? She swept the beam of her torch across the floor, looking for clues. For something that would indicate that Julia might have been there. Clothes, blood, something.

"Make sure that Forensics go through this shithole with a fine-tooth comb."

"Sure thing, Guppy. Every single centimetre of it," said Lasse.

She went over to the shabby couch and shone the light around it. Lazarus had said that Bjarke and Ronnie were planning to make Julia their sex slave. The humiliation and degradation of their victim was their motive for the kidnapping—which went against the idea that they had killed her and disposed of the body already. Julia had to be here somewhere. Cecilie wondered whether there were any outbuildings or annexes, but she didn't remember seeing anything. And it didn't make sense. It was all supposed to happen in here. This was where they were meant to return and perpetuate their crime. The perfect, windowless venue without any pesky neighbours. This was their dungeon. She looked at the floor. The basement. Of course. She looked around for a trapdoor in the floor but saw nothing. She allowed the beam of light to linger on Ronnie, who was sitting tensely on his mattress. "Get him up," she said to Lasse. "Get him off that mattress."

Ronnie was about to say something, but Lasse grabbed him by the lapels and yanked him up without any trouble. Cecilie went over and pushed the mattress aside. Where it had been, there was a trapdoor in the floor.

46

Cecilie grabbed the handle and opened the trapdoor wide. The top steps of a steep concrete staircase were visible, leading down into the darkness.

"That's . . . private. You gotta have a warrant . . . or sumfink," Bjarke bellowed from the sofa.

Lasse put one of his large paws on Bjarke's shoulder. "Quiet time right now," he said calmly, with a squeeze. "Understood?"

Bjarke submitted to the pain and said no more.

Cecilie shone her torch down the stairs as she took the first step.

"Shouldn't we wait for backup?" Lasse asked.

She pulled her handcuffs off her belt and threw them to his feet. "Not if you have a handle on the two of them."

He smiled indulgently. "I've dealt with worse."

"You're really gonna be in the shit if you go down there!" Ronnie shouted from where he was sitting on the floor, blood still pouring from his broken nose.

Lasse put his foot in Ronnie's back and nudged him, making him topple forward. "Quiet time for you, too."

Cecilie descended the stairs into the crawl space, which was so low that she had to crouch. The air was suffocating and there was a pungent smell of mould and faeces. She shone the torch around the basement, which was nothing more than a narrow shaft. Some twenty metres ahead of her by the far wall, her torch reflected off a large dog cage. There was a figure huddled up inside. "Julia?!" Cecilie cried out.

The figure didn't respond.

"Julia?" she yelled a second time, moving towards the cage. "Julia, it's the police. You're safe now!"

Still no discernible reaction. Cecilie reached the cage and took in the sight of the naked woman. Despite the bruised face, she recognised Julia Schölin from the picture in her missing person case.

Julia's gaze was empty.

"Julia? Julia, can you hear me?" Cecilie rattled the padlock on the door of the cage to see whether it was locked. The rattling seemed to bring Julia to life, and she lifted her head. "I'm going to get you out of there. You're safe—"

Julia grabbed hold of the bars and began to whimper.

"Calm down. I'll get you out, I promise. But I have to find the key for the padlock. Okay?"

When Cecilie turned around, Julia stuck an arm between the bars and grabbed her sleeve. "Don't go . . . don't go . . . the men . . ."

"Julia, I'm coming back. It's okay. We've arrested them. Do you understand? It's all over now." She carefully prised herself from Julia's grip and smiled. "You'll be free soon."

"Help me . . . help me . . . home . . ."

"Julia, I promise. I'll be back."

At that moment, a shot rang out that resounded hellishly through the basement space. The shot made Julia scream. Several more shots followed.

Cecilie quickly made her way back along the shaft. "Lasse! Lasse!" she shouted as she approached the stairs. When she reached them, she looked up to see a lifeless arm hanging over the edge at the top. There was blood dripping from the index finger onto the top step. In the semi-darkness, it was impossible to tell who it belonged to.

In her eagerness to get back upstairs, she banged her head on the concrete ceiling and emerged into the room above feeling dazed. Bjarke and Ronnie were on the floor. Both shot in the head. Bjarke to his forehead. Ronnie through his cheek and neck. There was a revolver next to Ronnie. Cecilie kicked it away.

"Lasse!" she shouted, making for the door to the next room.

She found him standing by the rear door with his back to her. "Lasse?" she said, going over to him.

He turned around slowly to face her. He tried to say something, but all that came out of his mouth was blood.

"Lasse!" she shrieked.

Lasse's legs gave way as he slipped to the floor with his back to the wall. Under his chin, there was a big, bloody hole where a projectile had gone in. He tried to say something to her, but the blood was gushing from his mouth.

"Take it easy, don't say anything," she said, choking down a sob as she got out her phone to call for help.

Lasse reached out to her, pressing his mouth close to her ear. "Catch . . . him . . ." She could feel the blood streaming down the side of her face.

"Lasse, just keep your mouth shut," she sobbed. "Let me call for help."

"Too . . . late . . ."

"Of course, it isn't. Now just let me . . ." She felt his grip slacken, and then the rattling sound in his throat stopped.

The sound of police sirens outside drowned out her sobs.

47

Rays of morning sunshine shone through the half-open blinds in Karstensen's office. They formed long shadows as they struck the two besuited men standing beside Cecilie as she sat in front of the desk. She was staring blankly at the floor. A crust of dried blood was matted into her hair, and Lasse's blood had stained her left cheek rusty red. Behind the desk, Karstensen was on the phone. At last, he put down the receiver.

"The doctor says she's recovering."

Cecilie looked up slowly at Karstensen. "Julia?" she said absently.

"Yes, they say she won't suffer any lasting impact . . . well, physically, that is," he added quickly. "It seems as if we got to her in time." He smiled gently. "Her family is with her now."

Cecilie tried to stifle her tears. The image of Lasse slumped against the wall, lifeless, wouldn't leave her. "Has Martin, Lasse's husband, been notified?"

Karstensen looked at her worriedly. "That was the first thing I did. Don't you remember me telling you that?"

"Oh, yes," she said, even if she didn't in fact remember either Karstensen's visit to pay his condolences or the hours that had elapsed following Lasse's death. She had a faint memory of the journey to the office in an unmarked police car, but not who had been driving. She also knew that she had then spent a long time in that very office with Karstensen and the two guys from the Independent Police Complaints Authority, but she didn't remember what they had discussed. All she knew was that one of them, John Nyholm—the one with the least hair on his head—had asked her about all sorts of things. She had given answers, mostly in monosyllables, but quite what she had said she did not know. All she could think about was the fact that Lasse was *dead*.

"So let's go through this one more time," said the voice attached to the thinning hair and cheap suit.

"Damn it, John," Karstensen exclaimed. "Isn't this going over the top? Given the circumstances . . ." He pointed at Cecilie.

Cecilie grasped that the "situation" was in fact her, and that it wasn't good. The bloody image of Lasse returned. Lasse was *dead*.

"We're just doing our jobs. We all know that the quality of witness statements only deteriorates with the passing of time."

"Still, she's completely . . . completely . . ."

"I'm okay," Cecilie said. "Just get on with it." She looked up at John. He needed to trim his nose hairs. Lasse was *dead*, and John had more hair in his nostrils than on his head. She smiled blankly.

John flipped through his notes. "You and Lasse Kofoed attended the address on Svanevej where you arrested Bjarke and Ronnie Thomsen on suspicion of the kidnapping of Julia Schölin. Correct?"

"Correct," she heard herself say.

"Did you search the individuals?"

"Lasse searched Bjarke."

"And Ronnie?"

"I searched him," she replied, without remembering whether that was true.

"You said that you searched the premises before entering the basement?"

"We were looking for anywhere that Julia might be, yes."

"And in the course of that search, you didn't find any guns?"

"No."

"So do you have any idea where the gun might have come from?"

She didn't reply.

John raised his eyebrows and made a note beside the others that he had already jotted down. "Was it your decision to enter the basement? Or Lasse's?"

"Mine alone."

"So you asked him to stay and watch the two criminals?"

"Yes."

"Standard procedure is to await backup. Why didn't you follow that?"

"Now see here . . ." Karstensen exclaimed.

"Because I believed that the victim was in mortal danger . . . and it required immediate action. I gave Lasse my handcuffs so that he could . . ." She cleared her throat. "But it seems he couldn't."

John made another note. "You heard shots while in the basement. Do you recall how many?"

"No. I still don't remember the exact number."

"Do you recall hearing different calibres being fired?"

She shook her head. "No. The acoustics in the basement and the victim screaming made that impossible."

"When you emerged and saw Bjarke and Ronnie Thomsen lying on the floor, were they both dead?"

"They definitely weren't moving."

"Did you check for signs of life?"

"No, I was worried that Lasse . . ."

"So they might have died as a result of your failure to intervene?"

"I was concentrating on finding my partner."

"Which is completely understandable," Karstensen interjected, crossing his arms.

John made another note. "Let's skip ahead to that point. He was in the next room?"

"Yes, exactly where . . ." She wiped tears from her cheek. "Where he died."

"Any idea why he was there? As in, why wasn't he in the room with the two men under arrest?"

She didn't reply.

"Cecilie?" John looked down at her.

She still didn't answer.

"I think that's enough for now," said Karstensen. "Perhaps it's time to lay off Cecilie for a bit."

"Very well." John closed his notebook. "As soon as we have the autopsy reports and the reports on the crime scene, you'll be summoned for more formal questioning. Until then, you're suspended from any further duties." He glanced briefly at Karstensen. Karstensen nodded briskly.

"Okay," she said.

"Oh, and there's just one more thing. You said that you gained access to the building in question? But to clarify, you didn't have a search warrant?"

"That is by no means necessary in a case as serious as this. Well-founded suspicion is enough," said Karstensen.

John flashed a placatory smile at him. "Naturally. And that wasn't my point. I was just wondering what prompted the raid."

Cecilie could feel the three men staring at her. "A tip," she replied tersely.

"A tip from who?" John asked.

She looked away. "A witness who saw the two men with a woman they were dragging into the building."

"Is this something that the witness called the emergency control room about?"

"No. They called me."

John made yet another note. "We'd very much like that witness's details as soon as possible."

She didn't reply.

"Gentlemen," said Karstensen, standing up and pointing towards the door.

"We'll be in touch," John replied, bidding Cecilie farewell.

Karstensen escorted John and his colleague out of the office. When he had closed the door behind them, he turned back to Cecilie. "Off to home with you."

"Yes," she said, standing up. "Thanks."

"It's nothing. Those arseholes have no idea what it's like being a proper police officer."

She nodded and made her way to the door.

"Cecilie?" Karstensen called out to her.

She turned to face him.

"It might be worth getting on to the police federation as soon as you can. Get some legal representation before John gets too much of a head start. You never know how things will go."

Cecilie passed Lasse's desk, where his empty mug with the Bakken Bears logo was languishing. She sped up and hurried out of the office and down the empty corridor. This was all Lazarus's fault. Lasse had paid the price for her failing to obey Lazarus's order to liquidate the two men. Lazarus had taken matters into his own hands, just like he'd done with Emil Kam. He must have had the building under surveillance and seen them arrive. Then he'd broken in carrying a revolver that he'd used to kill Lasse. Most likely, he'd shot Lasse first and then used his service weapon to execute Bjarke and Ronnie. Bjarke and Ronnie must have been too shocked or too under the influence to react. Then, unarmed and with a bullet in his throat, Lasse had tried to set off after him. *Catch him.* Those had been his last words. She began to cry again.

48

Five days had passed. All through the fug of zombie tablets. Some new ones this time, which were still in date. All the same, they didn't seem much different from the ones that Cecilie had taken before. They slowed her down, both in her own thoughts and in the physical world. But the most important thing was that they kept her obsessive thoughts at bay, thoughts which quite literally threatened to pull her into the abyss each time she approached her own roof terrace. The tablets were her strait-jacket and shackles. Right now, she was in the Panda wearing sunglasses and turning the key in the ignition without anything happening except a few clicking sounds. She pounded the wheel with her hand, knowing full well that this was not the day for her to arrive late. She turned the key again, and this time the starter let out a croak. She pulled out her phone, first checking the time and then her messages. Lazarus was still maintaining his silence. The bastard. She had tried calling him on all the numbers he had used, only to find that none of them were in service any longer. She tugged at the knob for the bonnet and got out of the car. In contrast, the press had not been shy. The Julia Schölin case had been a real treat for them. A story that had it all. A kidnapped house-wife from the suburbs miraculously found. Two murdered kidnappers. Father and son to boot. Not to mention the heroic cop killed in the line of duty. The pièce de résistance was her own past and the rape case. A case that linked her to one of the perpetrators. Her suspension had only fuelled the speculations about what had really happened in that building on Svanevej. Cecilie suspected that both Lazarus and John Nyholm had anonymously tipped off the media about her old case.

She stared towards the basketball court where hip-hop music was blaring and spotted that the lads had returned. They still hadn't started catcalling her, but she reckoned it wouldn't be long before they plucked up the courage. Cecilie opened the hood and stared at the engine. She checked the ignition coil and yanked at the cables between the power distributor and the spark plugs to make sure they were properly attached. Then she checked the battery and noticed that the cables attached to the positive terminal were loose. She didn't have any tools, so instead she used her fingers to tighten the nut.

"Hi," said a faint voice.

Cecilie looked over her shoulder and spotted Fie standing behind her with her bicycle. "Hi," she said, pushing her sunglasses up her face. Despite the smile, Fie still had the same tortured look in her eyes. "Everything okay?"

Fie nodded quickly. "Mostly. I'm going back to sixth form soon, so . . ." She shrugged. "Hopefully, it'll be good again."

"That's great," Cecilie said.

"I did like you said."

"Oh? What?"

"Talked to someone. A shrink. Her name's Mona. She's a total sweetie."

"I'm glad to hear that, Fie. Really, I am."

Fie stood there looking at Cecilie, who began to tighten the nut. "I . . . I read about that case. It's good that you saved that woman."

Cecilie nodded. "At least she's alive."

"It was . . . total shit. The thing with your partner."

"Yep. Total shit." Cecilie turned the nut until her fingers ached.

"Did you know him well?"

Cecilie closed the bonnet and looked at the girl. "Yes. He was my best friend."

"He looked like a really nice guy in the photos in the papers. Didn't seem like a cop, y'know?"

"I get it. He was so much more than that."

"Just like you," Fie said, smiling.

"No, he was nothing like me."

"How do you mean?"

"Nothing." She felt the lump in her throat. "He didn't deserve to die," she said, going to the driver-side door. "Be seeing you, Fie."

Fie cleared her throat. "Do you remember what you said to me at the hospital?"

"What did I say?"

"That I wasn't to blame. That it was his fault."

Cecilie surveyed the car park. "This one is different."

"Okay. But . . . but it helped me. See you later," said Fie, getting onto her bike.

"Fie?" Cecilie called out.

Fie stopped and looked back at her.

"Thanks," said Cecilie, feeling her eyes stinging.

"Can I ask you something?"

"Of course."

"The guy who raped you that time . . ."

"What about him?"

"Would you have preferred him to end up in jail?"

Cecilie shook her head briefly. "I honestly don't know."

"That's how I feel about the guy who attacked me." She nodded curtly and departed on her bicycle.

Cecilie got back into the Panda and turned the key again. The engine coughed into life. She checked the time and saw that she was late.

49

The spire of St Jacob's Church rose into the steely grey sky, which was threatening to subject them all to a deluge. Cecilie entered through the open door on Østerbrogade. A couple of alert press photographers by the door recognised her right away and took a couple of quick snaps before she reached the sanctuary of the church.

The pews beneath the high-vaulted ceiling were filled with officers in uniform. Sitting in the front rows closest to the white coffin were Lasse's close family. The pastor, an aging, grey-haired woman, was delivering her sermon as Cecilie quietly made her way to stand at the back.

It was completely unreal that Lasse was up there in a sealed coffin. She kept expecting him to appear at her side at any moment to crack an inappropriate joke about the whole thing. Simply to watch her struggle to maintain her mask. That was how she wanted to remember him—as the only person in the world who could make her laugh so much tears came to her eyes.

"Cecilie Mars," said a low voice at her side.

She cast a sidelong glance at John Nyholm, who had his hands clasped together. He still needed to trim his nose hairs. She turned her gaze back towards the pastor by the altar.

"I've issued you with a summons to a meeting on Monday morning. You still haven't responded."

"I'll be there," she said without looking at him.

"Good. I've got lots of questions for you."

"Why don't we leave them for Monday?"

At that moment, the organ roared into life, and the congregation began to sing "Always cheerful when you go." Neither Cecilie nor John joined in the singing, and part way through the second verse, he leaned over to her and whispered: "I must admit that the reports we've received have been most interesting. Especially when compared with the preliminary statement you provided."

She tried to ignore him as she searched in vain for an empty spot in the pews in front of her.

"*Gunshot residue*," John added, unprompted. "I've always thought that gunshot residue analyses are rather in the shadow of witness statements, fingerprints, and, of course, DNA testing. Sort of like an unloved stepson."

"I'm sure that they share your fascination with them down in the lab," she replied, taking a step away from him.

John moved with her automatically. "At any rate, they've found all sorts of interesting things."

"Such as?"

"The gunshot residue on Bjarke's hand comes from the revolver that we recovered, but there's so little of it that it's doubtful whether he fired it."

"And?"

"Perhaps someone wanted to make it look like he fired the gun, and applied the gunpowder particles after the fact?"

She glanced at him without saying a word.

"It doesn't stop there," he whispered, smiling at her coolly. "The gunshot wound to Bjarke's forehead had burn marks around the point of entry, which suggests that the shot was fired at close range. Execution style."

Cecilie shook her head.

"What's even more peculiar . . ." John paused for effect. "Is that there was no gunshot residue on Lasse's hands worth mentioning. Even though ballistics shows that it was his pistol that was fired and killed both perpetrators." He smiled again. "All that from mere *gunshot residue*."

She looked towards the coffin surrounded by an ocean of flowers and clenched her hands. What she wanted more than anything was to lamp John.

"It vexes me that we didn't do a gunshot residue test on you," John said.

"Why would you have? I didn't fire my weapon."

"No, certainly not your own."

"What the hell are you insinuating?" she snapped.

A couple of uniformed officers in front of them turned around and scowled at them. Cecilie looked at them apologetically.

John lowered his voice: "I'm not insinuating anything. I was merely informing you of the results of the gunshot residue analysis. And what those results allow us to infer."

Fifteen minutes later, the funeral drew to a close and Lasse's coffin was borne down the aisle, followed by his family. Cecilie lowered her head as it passed her by, in an attempt to shut it all out. The rows of officers followed it slowly towards the exit. Cecilie deliberately remained in the background, hoping she wouldn't have to speak to any of her colleagues. The only downside was that John stuck by her.

"Not quite the same turnout at Bjarke and Ronnie Thomsen's funeral," John said. "It took place this morning."

"And?"

"I thought you might be interested." He looked at her for a long time.

"You can think what you like," she snarled, pushing through the queue for the exit. But it was impossible to evade John.

"I've had the opportunity to review your latest cases, and an interesting pattern emerges from them."

She turned to face him. "What do you mean by that?"

John gently took her arm and drew her aside.

"Three dead sex offenders. The first in a car crash with *no* witnesses. The next two homicides committed by persons unknown. And that's not forgetting Bjarke and Ronnie Thomsen."

"We have multiple unsolved cases, unfortunately. What's your point?"

"Did you know the girl that Ulrik Østergård molested? Fie Simone Simonsen?"

"I think you already know that I was acquainted with her. We all live in the same area and she trained in my self-defence class."

He nodded.

"How is that of any relevance?" asked Cecilie.

"Because I suspect you and your dead partner of carrying out vigilante justice and murders on several occasions."

Cecilie took a step towards him and stared him in the eyes.

"What the hell are you thinking, blackening his memory like that?"

"It's not *me* blackening his memory," John replied, buttoning his suit jacket. "Perhaps you ought to give some consideration to telling me what really happened."

"I already have done."

"I mean in every case. See you on Monday at eight o'clock sharp. And don't be late, or I'll have you picked up." John strode past her and made his way out of the church.

Cecilie looked around the empty pews. She felt as if she couldn't breathe. She couldn't let it happen. She couldn't let John arrest her before she'd got hold of Lazarus. Lazarus had tried to manipulate her into carrying out his acts. He'd shaped her into his own personal avenger. Perhaps he was right? Perhaps she harboured a darkness that she wasn't aware of? If so, it was time to let go of it. She had a score to settle with him over Lasse's death. Inappropriate as it was, she offered up a silent prayer that she would get Lazarus.

50

Cecilie shrugged off her leather jacket in the hallway. In her pocket, the zombie tablets were rattling in their jar, reminding her that it was high time she took another. She resisted their call, hanging her jacket up instead. She knew the consequence of bouncing on and off her medication was a combination of paranoia and violent nausea. All things considered, there was no delusion that could surpass the situation she found herself in, and she could stand the nausea, too. A perfectly satisfactory swap for ensuring she had a clear head.

She went into the living room and sat down on the sofa. The sound of the wind rattling the door to the roof terrace made her look over at it. Outside it was getting dark. For a brief moment, she considered checking whether there was someone outside, but she stopped herself. In three days' time, she would be held to account by John and his pack of bloodhounds. She hadn't been given that time out of consideration, to allow her to grieve for her loss. It was solely because John wanted time to investigate her without bringing charges immediately. The conversation in the church had been nothing more than a stress test, offering a taste of what would soon strike her down like a sledgehammer. John Nyholm was just as calculating and just as intimidating as Lazarus.

At that moment, another gust of wind rattled the terrace door, and she quailed, but the door withstood the pressure. She reflected on the profile she had drawn up when she suspected Andreas. Despite his controlling

behaviour, Lazarus seemed to be the slave of his own emotions. The killings of Emil Kam, Bjarke, and Ronnie indulged his emotional and uncon-
trolled nature. A need to kill that outweighed the plan he had made with
her. If she had had to describe him in a few words, it would have been as
a bloodthirsty, self-righteous shit self-satisfied with his own intellect, who
wanted to control his surroundings. There had been something ritualistic
about the way that he had involved her. Perhaps rituals themselves were
important to him? Perhaps he used them consciously or unconsciously
to control his own unstable mind? That kind of person craved knowledge. The idea that Lazarus might come from an academic background
resurfaced. Maybe he was a fallen angel? If he wasn't on the force or
in the Prosecution Service, but still had access to confidential information, there was only one place left to go: defence attorneys. Although the
idea seemed unrealistic, over the years she had seen plenty of them lose
their licences. It was mostly in biker gang cases where they made asses
of themselves by passing on confidential information or smuggling things
like mobile phones into prison to pass to their clients. Paranoia eventually won out, and she got up from the sofa and went to the roof terrace
door to make sure it was locked. She leaned her head against the window
and stared at the night sky and glowing city. Could Lazarus really be a
defence lawyer? The thought became less and less improbable the longer
she stood there. It was an old cliché that defence lawyers remained unaffected by their clients' guilt—that regardless of the gravity of the crime,
they would defend any criminal at all simply to ensure the rule of law.
In fact, the most serious cases affected them the same way they affected
everyone else. Possibly even more so. You saw as much when examining
the suicide rates for the profession. Perhaps one of them had reached
their limit? Perhaps one of them had been the victim of a crime and that
had changed their view on the rule of law?

She turned around and leaned against the terrace door. The glass
felt cool against her back. What about Phillip Vang? The Terrier? He'd
had both Ulrik and Emil as clients. She wasn't sure whether he'd also
defended Ronnie and Bjarke. The Terrier was an arrogant little shit with
boarding-school manners. He housed psychopathic traits and gallop-
ing delusions of grandeur in a body smaller than Napoleon's. He was

insanely sharp, strategic, and cynical. But was he also capable of killing? And if so, what had made him change his view on his clients? She didn't know his background well enough to know what might have made these four cases personal to him. But if her suspicion was right, there would without doubt be other deaths among his clients, whether they took the form of murders, accidents, or something else entirely. The wind tore at the door, making it seem as if it would fly open and drag her out into the night. That would almost have been a relief. She knew just who to contact to find out more about the Terrier's old cases. Whether he was willing to help was another matter entirely.

51

The five-storey blocks of flats in the Nordhavn district were reflected in the dark waters of the inner harbour. Cecilie had never been to the residential area that had appeared with surprising speed in the old industrial quarter. She parked the Panda and went to the main door, where she found the name on the intercom.

"Yes?" said a metallic voice from the speaker.

"It's Cecilie."

"Ye-es?" the voice repeated, this time surprised.

"Are you alone? And can I come up?"

The intercom buzzed in reply and she entered the stairwell. Two floors above, Andreas was waiting for her in his doorway in socks but no shoes. He wore a crumpled T-shirt that added to the homely look. "You're just about the last person I expected to come calling. If you've come to apologise then I accept."

"I haven't."

"Okay," he said, taking a stepping to one side so she could come in. "Now that you're suspended I guess you no longer have your handcuffs."

"You can rest easy on that point," she said, stepping into the hallway.

"Can I offer you something?" he said, leading her to the living room.

"Thanks, but no thanks." The whole apartment smelled of fresh paint, and there were unopened moving boxes on the floor between designer furniture that still hadn't found its place. "Sorry about the mess. Take a seat," he said, settling on a pouffe.

She sat down on a silver Philippe Starck and looked at him without saying anything.

"It was a beautiful funeral," he said, attempting to fill the silence.

"Yes." She looked down at the scoured floorboards.

"It's a damn shame about Lasse. I always liked him. How are you doing?"

"I'm a wreck."

"I can imagine." He let his gaze drift over her one more time. "I . . . saw you at the church. With John Nyholm."

She raised her head. "I was not voluntarily in his company."

"He's like a dog with a bone. But he's good. Do you know what they're going with? Disciplinary or . . . ?"

"I won't get off that easily."

"How do you mean?"

"I'm up to my neck in shit and John and his damn bone have decided to bury me once and for all. We're talking jail time."

"Jesus, Cecilie." Andreas put his hand to his mouth. "I barely dare ask what you've been up to."

"I need your help, Andreas," she said, looking at him.

"Okay. But before you say another word, just remember that I'm part of the Prosecution Service. They can call me as a witness and ask about what you've told me."

"Yes, sure, I know that it can be used against me." She silenced him with a hand gesture. "I've got three days. Well, two really. Before the hammer falls. Once that happens, there will be nothing you can say or do that can make things any worse for me. Believe me."

"Okay." He seemed shaken. "So how can I help?"

She took a deep breath and began the story that she had been preparing on her way over. "Lasse and I were working on a case in secret. The short version is that it's about an anonymous tip off I received from someone calling themselves Lazarus. A man who pointed us in the direction of previously convicted sex offenders before then killing them himself. The details are rather complicated, but you're aware of all the cases already.

The killings of Emil Kam and Morten Pier Nielsen, and likely as not Bjarke and Ronnie Thomsen."

"But . . . but these are cases that I've been involved in," he said in surprise. "Does Karstensen know anything about this?"

She shook her head. "Initially, only I knew about Lazarus, until I told Lasse. I'm certain that Lazarus was responsible for his death. That's why I need to find him before John messes it all up. Do you understand?"

"I . . . I . . . No," he said, looking at her angrily. "Why wasn't I informed? Why wasn't Karstensen?"

"Because at first we believed that Lazarus was one of us. That meant we had to tread cautiously."

He looked at her in amazement. "Was that why . . . that night at yours . . . did you think . . . *Me?*"

She grimaced apologetically at him. "I was keeping all my options open. Karstensen was also on my list of suspects if that's any consolation."

"I can't say it is," he said. "Do you have any evidence for this?"

"Not much. Lazarus is good at covering his tracks and incriminating others," she said, pointing to herself.

"There's evidence incriminating you?" He stared at her, speechless.

"Yes, but that's not important right now."

"Oh, isn't it? Really?"

She nodded. "I need your help finding Lazarus."

Andreas scratched his head. "So I take it you have other suspects?"

"Yes. Phillip Vang, the Terrier."

"The Terrier? Are you serious?"

"One hundred per cent. He's been in contact with all the men killed."

"Yeah, but . . ."

"I need to take a look at some of his previous cases. And that's where you come into the picture."

"Stop right there, Cecilie. It doesn't make sense. Why would a defence lawyer kill his own clients?"

"There are precedents. Especially that jealousy killing in 2007."

"This is something else entirely. You're talking about a vigilante appearing for the defence."

"We all have our doubts about whether justice is done. In his capacity as a defence attorney, Lazarus may be burdened with feelings of guilt, a thirst for revenge, or something else entirely."

"I doubt the Terrier has ever been burdened with guilt. What on earth has made you focus on him?"

"Apart from his dead clients, he matches the profile."

"Sounds desperate."

"Regardless."

Andreas sighed deeply. "Okay, I will admit that the Terrier is unscrupulous enough to come up with just about anything. He doesn't hesitate to lie in court or to coach his clients ahead of psychiatric assessments so that they act crazy." Andreas shook his head. "If you knew how many times we've tried to overturn those assessments."

Cecilie interrupted him with a hand gesture. "I already know that the Terrier has defeated the Prosecution Service countless times. What I need to know is how many of his acquittals and convictions have subsequently died. We can start by checking whether Morten Pier Nielsen was one of his clients."

"I know for sure that he was."

"Good. That's us one step further on. What about Bjarke Thomsen and his son, Ronnie, and their cases?"

"Bjarke's cases?" Andreas glanced at her anxiously. "You think there are others?"

"I'm sure that there are cases other than the one involving me, even if the papers have been feasting on that one of late," she said coolly. "Once we're done with Bjarke and Ronnie, we can check the Terrier's other cases where he represented sex offenders."

"How many days did you say you had? This is going to take weeks. The Terrier's had hundreds of cases like that."

"Then we focus on the ones in the last couple of years. If nothing catches our eye, we can always go back further." She pointed imperiously towards the PC in the corner of the room.

"You really mean it?"

"I need this, Andreas."

He shook his head dramatically. "This calls for a serious glass of rosé."

He got up and went into the kitchen. A minute later, he returned with a bottle and two glasses. He raised the bottle. "Supposed to be the world's best . . ."

". . . according to Kjær and Sommerfeldt." She smiled reluctantly and let him pour it. "Shall we?" she said, nodding at the computer.

Andreas spent the next couple of hours on the Prosecution Service intranet searching for cases in which Phillip Vang had been their opposition. Andreas and Cecilie were both surprised to discover how many defendants in vice cases Phillip Vang had represented. Over the years, he had handled more or less all the cases for Emil Kam, Morten Pier Nielsen, and the Thomsens. When Andreas extended his search, he found out that as a young legal clerk, Phillip Vang had worked for the Smedtoft & Partners practice which had provided the defence in Cecilie's case. Andreas identified a total of nineteen rape cases that appeared relevant, and which had all taken place within the last three years. In most of them, it had been him facing down Phillip Vang. According to Andreas, the majority had ended in treatment sentences because Phillip Vang had coached his clients ahead of their psychiatric evaluations. Ten of the convicts were at large again, and in three cases the perpetrators had died within the last year. It took a while for Cecilie to find out the causes of death, but at last she succeeded. She looked down at her notepad. "Lars Andersen, suicide. Mikkel Lund, burned to death in his home. Thorleif Holmblad, drowning accident. No witnesses in any of the three cases. All three cases were closed."

Andreas leaned back in his chair and yawned. "It's not like we've turned up any cast iron evidence, but . . ."

"But the pattern is there," she said. "The Terrier is linked to every case. That gives us a total of seven dead clients within a year, if we count Emil Kam, Morten, Bjarke, and Ronnie. That must be a record in itself."

"Eight dead clients."

"How do you mean?"

"You forgot Ulrik Østergård. There were no witnesses to that either when he died in a single-car road accident."

"No, we can't rule him out either," she said, looking away.

"But I still have a hard time picturing this. What are you going to do?"

"Confront him."

"Is that really wise?"

"I don't have time to do much else."

Andreas drained his wine glass. "Is there anything I can do?"

"Visit me in prison."

"That's not funny." He took her hand and squeezed it gently.

52

Cecilie scrutinised Phillip Vang's pearl white Maserati Levante parked outside Café Victor. The huge SUV seemed intimidating, and she struggled to imagine how the little man could even get into it. She peered across the street towards the railings and flower boxes that semiscreened the outdoor tables. The planting wasn't so high that it prevented passersby from seeing who was sitting at the tables. The old yuppie stronghold still managed to accede to its patrons' desire to be screened yet visible.

Helped by the sound of Phillip Vang's loud voice, she spotted him sitting with an obese biker in a white leather waistcoat and with face tattoos. As she drew closer to the table, she saw Phillip Vang receive a thick envelope that quickly vanished into the pocket of his powder blue suit.

"Now run along and do your homework, Finn, and it'll all be fine," Phillip Vang said, dismissing the man with a hand gesture.

The biker stood up and dug into his pocket, looking for change.

"No, no. The cola is on the Terrier. Run along, and I'll see you in a couple of days."

The man mumbled thanks and shambled away. Phillip Vang shook his head before digging into his steak lunch steak.

Cecilie pulled out the chair and sat down opposite Phillip Vang, who looked up.

"Bon appétit," she said.

Phillip Vang stopped chewing and put down his cutlery in surprise.

"Another one you're coaching on how to get through the psychiatric assessment? He looked stupid enough already," remarked Cecilie.

Phillip Vang struggled to swallow his food. "I . . . I don't know what you're talking about."

"Isn't that how you get your clients off, or secure them a more lenient sentence?"

He took his glass of red wine and sipped. "Who said that? Andreas? Or that psychologist. The *expert witness*?" he said, inserting air quotes around it. "If so, it's only because they're sore losers."

"So it's not true? It'd be a pretty smart move on your part."

He looked at her in surprise. "Am I on tape?"

She opened her jacket and tapped her pockets to show that he wasn't.

"Anyway, what I have to say about that is no secret." He leaned towards her. "Do you realise what I'm up against? It's not like you lot, with the powers that be behind you. The Terrier operates solo." He pointed meaningfully at himself. "So when the Prosecution Service starts tooling up with all sorts of expert witnesses to rip the psychiatric assessments to shreds, you can bet your bottom dollar it's payback time. As it happens, I can give you a million other examples of when they've tried to influence the court with their so-called *experts*. I dare say you've popped by the city court a couple of times yourself?" he said rhetorically. "And I'm still stitching the lot of you up." He made a vulgar gesture with his hand.

"You seem proud."

He leaned back in the chair. "Of course, I bloody am."

"Even if it means another creep goes free?"

"I like winning. It gives me a hard-on." He took a toothpick from the cup on the table and began to pick at his teeth. "I heard you were suspended. I heard that the Independent Police Complaints Authority is sniffing around your old cases. You come to see whether I'm free?"

Cecilie chuckled. "I'd rather defend myself."

"Suicide? Yes, I suppose that would suit you nicely. But then why are you here? This doesn't seem like a regular haunt of yours," he said, measuring her up with his gaze.

"Your clients seem to have a habit of dying when they are released."

"What a shame," he said indifferently. He cast the bloody toothpick down onto the plate. "It's bad for business."

"Is that all you have to say?"

"Well, repeat business is my bread and butter. You really must stop shooting them."

"Emil Kam and the Serpent weren't shot. Lars Andersen was hanged; Mikkel Lund burned to death in his home. And that's not forgetting Thorleif Holmblad."

"Who?"

"Thorleif. Your client on two occasions. The first time he was sent down for paedophilia and got three and a half years. The second time, you got him off on a charge of incest. Then he happened to die in a drowning accident in Lake Arresø. No witnesses."

The Terrier smiled. "Oh, yes. Wee-wee-Thor. I remember him. He always talked my ear off when I visited him in the cells. Loved talking about all the stuff he'd done. Some really sick stuff. And with his own daughter, at that." He grimaced.

"And what did that do to you?"

Phillip Vang looked at her as if he didn't fully understand the question. "I thanked my lucky stars that he got it all off his chest with me instead of doing it in court. When the daughter ended up topping herself during the trial, the case pretty much won itself." He held out his hands. "But you're telling me he drowned afterwards? I can't say I ever saw Wee-wee-Thor as much of a swimmer. Big fan of juvenile urine on the other hand."

She tried to suppress her disgust at the Terrier. "Have any of your other clients died?"

"Well, I'm not exactly on their Christmas card lists." He got out his wallet and waved to the waiter. "I see where this conversation is going."

"Oh? Where's that?"

"Despite your suspension, you're still playing the detective. Why might that be if one is permitted to ask? Is it because there's a connection between the cases? Or is it simply your *feminine* intuition?"

"How was the food, sir?" the waiter asked, presenting the bill.

"Rarer next time. I don't mind if it's still breathing," Vang said with a chortle. He passed a five hundred kroner note to the waiter and signalled that he could keep the change.

"And what if I am investigating a connection?"

"Then you're more desperate than a single mother on a Friday night. Which is something that's never given me a hard-on."

"Don't we all share an interest in preventing crime?"

He shook his head. "I don't think you heard me when I said that . . ."

"Yeah, yeah, you get a hard-on in court. I heard you. But women don't do it for you. Phillip, the only men who talk about their dicks are the ones who aren't well-endowed, and the ones who like taking it up the arse. Both are tedious to hear about, so why don't we change the subject to something other than dicks?"

He stared at her wide-eyed. "So what is it you want to know?"

"You were right about a connection." She looked at his wine glass covered in greasy fingerprints. "As part of the murder inquiries into the deaths of Emil, Morten, Bjarke, and Ronnie, we've found the same matching DNA in each. In other words, we know it's the same killer." She looked him straight in the eye and hoped he wouldn't see through her bluff.

"The same killer? But you haven't identified them?"

"Not yet. But my guess is that it's someone empathetic, someone with a tremendous sense of justice, and someone who sees this as the final resort against a failed justice system. Something you can hardly blame him for . . ."

He sat in silence staring at her and then eventually replied: "A rather surprising statement to make."

"Nevertheless, that is my position." She smiled cheerfully.

"Bloody hell. It's almost too funny."

"Is it?"

"Well, no. It's actually tragic that the police aren't more talented." He picked up his glass, spat into it, and passed it over to her. "If that's not enough for your DNA analysis then you know where to find more." He pushed back his chair and stood up to leave.

"Lazarus?" she said, awaiting his reaction.

He looked at her wearily. "Who?"

"Lazarus. Does the name mean anything to you?"

"Dead man resurrected by Jesus. Not dissimilar to those zombie movies my kid loves. Why do you ask?"

"No reason," she said, sighing.

"Give me a call if they start grilling you." He found a business card and slid it across the table. "In your case, there's no need to fake the psychiatric evaluation," he chuckled.

"Fuck you."

"I thought we weren't meant to be talking about dicks any longer?" he said before leaving.

She followed him with her eyes as he struggled to scramble into the white SUV. If the Terrier was Lazarus, then she was the Virgin Mary. Truth be told, it was unlikely either of them would end up in heaven.

53

Cecilie walked along the dark path leading from the car park to her stairwell. She had spent the last few hours wandering around, which hadn't reduced the maelstrom of thoughts in her head. If it wasn't the Terrier, then who the hell was it? When she reached the basketball court, a figure emerged from a bush. Her hand slid instinctively down to her belt where she usually kept her pistol. At that moment, she heard a sound behind her and she spun around. Several figures appeared, all with their hoods up. They had her surrounded, the little shits. She tried to spot Hassan among them.

"We've been waiting for you," his voice said behind her. Cecilie turned around.

Hassan slowly pulled the hood off his head.

She screwed up her eyes and toughened herself. "I've got no time for your shit. I thought I told you to stay away."

"You did," Hassan said.

"So what part of that didn't you understand?" She looked around at them as she surveyed her surroundings. There was no way out. No help to hand. The door to her own stairwell behind the chubby lad seemed to be miles away. "You really want to pick up where we left off?"

"Not at all. No one wants to meet some slut-cop on her period packing heat," Hassan said with a wry laugh.

The others laughed, too.

"Then piss off." She put her hand to the side of her jacket where her service weapon was normally inserted in her belt. She sensed the lads' nervousness. Except Hassan.

"You were a badass last time. Respect for that. Proper bitch."

"Well, I haven't changed since then, Hassan." She smiled dangerously at him.

He shook his head. "That's not true. There's a lot happened since last time. You know, our boy Brush . . ." He pointed to one of the others. "Brush is a smart lad. He reads all sorts of shit online. All I do is stare at fucking porn all day." He guffawed mockingly, and the boys around him did the same.

"Maybe you can still get yourself an education, Brush," she said.

"Maybe he can," said Hassan. "Like I said, dude's fucking smart. So smart that he read about you online. You're a real celebrity bitch now. Dead famous. Picture 'n all. That's why I want your autograph."

"I want your autograph on my cock," said a voice behind her.

Raucous laughter followed.

"You know what he read about you? You know?"

"No, Hassan. What did Brush read?"

"He read that you'd been in a shoot-out. How your partner, some gay cop, got wasted." He smiled. "I'd love to bump off some asshole cop. But then again, it's totally easy. You know why?"

"I think I can guess."

"Because they're all poofs."

More harsh laughter around her.

"You done?"

"Me?" He pointed at himself. "No, no. I'm just getting started. Brush read loads more. Well loads more. Brush read that you'd been . . . suspended. First thing I thought: Fuck me, what's that? Thought it was some fucking venereal disease. Thought it was kinda weird to write about how you had AIDS or whatever? So you know what I did?"

"No, Hassan. But I can't wait for you to tell me."

"I fucking googled it!" he said, his voice filled with pride. "That's how I found out what it meant."

"Good for you."

"It means fired. And you know what? It hit me like a baseball bat to the head that you ain't no cop-bitch no longer. You're a regular old white bitch." He shrugged. "And now that you're not a cop-bitch anymore, you know what I was thinking? That you ain't got no gun neither. Am I mega right or what? They taken your gun, ain't they?"

"You ain't got a gun, so now we gonna smash you," said a voice behind her.

She shook her head. "Hassan, Hassan, Hassan. It really is splendid that you've been able to do an online search all by yourself, but . . . *suspended* doesn't mean fired. It means leave of absence. Time off. I'm still a police officer." She raised her jacket slightly without exposing herself. The movement alone was enough to make a couple of the lads step back.

"You're lying. She's fucking lying," said Hassan. They all looked at him uncertainly.

"I swear she's lying." Hassan took a step towards Cecilie. When he reached out towards her, she kicked him in the balls. He crumpled with a bellow of pain. The others seemed to be paralysed as she strode past them.

"Get . . . her!" Hassan groaned.

She ran down the path. Behind her, the lads swarmed after her. She grabbed the keys from her pocket. She tried to find the one for the main door. If she got inside, she stood a chance on the narrow stairs. They wouldn't be able to jump her there. She held out the key. Inserted it into the lock to open it. At that moment, someone pulled her hair from behind. She spun around leading with her arm. She hit the kid in the face with her elbow. She felt something give way. Heard him grunt. The next two were already on her. She lashed out with a kick at the first. Hit him in the side. He seized her leg. The other put a fist in her face. Her vision went dark. She fell onto the paving stones. Blood was running from her nose. More came. They kicked her from all sides. She tried to defend herself with her hands. The kicks still found their way through. A couple of them tried to stamp on her head. She felt like an insect they were trying to crush. Hassan came over. The others stepped back slightly. "Fucking bitch," he said, delivering a blow to her stomach. The kick winded her. Several more followed, and she could no longer breathe.

"Beat it!" said a hoarse woman's voice. "I'll call the cops!"

"Fuck you, bitch!" one of the lads shouted back.

Hassan stopped kicking, and Cecilie saw all the lads staring up at an old woman at the window on the second floor.

"That bitch be filming us."

"Come on," said Hassan. "The bitch is finished anyway." He made to leave, the gang following him.

"Are you okay? Should I call an ambulance?" the woman shouted down to her.

Cecilie looked up at her as she tried to get to her feet. "I'm . . . okay . . ." Then it all went black.

54

The morphine made Cecilie's lips tingle, while at the same time her body felt weightless. At least it was an intoxication that removed her from the miserable state she found herself in. A nurse was standing over her, about to stitch up her forehead. The laceration she'd suffered ran some five or six centimetres down towards her left eye, which that was completely closed. In addition to the injuries to her head, two of her ribs were broken, so Cecilie had had her whole left side taped up. She was struggling to breathe; it felt as if Morten was sitting on top of her again. A young male doctor entered the room and came over to them. Cecilie had already been examined, but in her befuddled state, she could not work out whether it was the same doctor as before.

The doctor quickly inspected her record on his iPad. "Cecilie, I think we're going to keep you in overnight for observation." She was about to nod, but the nurse was holding her head firmly and tugged at the needle with the suture.

"If you're feeling relatively comfortable, given the circumstances, then I'll inform the police that you're ready to be questioned. How does that sound?"

"I am . . . from the police . . . I should probably report it myself," she replied hoarsely.

He smiled. "Sorry, that's not how it works. We're obliged to report this, as I'm sure you're aware."

She was about to say something when there was a commotion in the emergency department reception area. A moment later, a stretcher with a dark-skinned man on it was carried past the doorway by two paramedics. They were followed by four police officers and an assortment of men in black hoodies with gang logos on their chests. The officers tried in vain to subdue the man's rowdy comrades. A female doctor popped her head around the door and whistled for her colleague. "Jakob, you coming? Gunshot wound to the leg. We need you."

The doctor raised his eyebrows and looked wearily at Cecilie. "That's the third one this week. Just occasionally, I find myself wishing they were slightly better shots," he said, and ran out the door.

"There we are," said the nurse, applying a plaster over the stitches. "You just ring the bell if there's anything you need," she said, pointing to the button on the wall.

"Thanks," said Cecilie, turning her gaze to the ceiling.

From the room next door she could hear agitated voices, and Cecilie almost felt as if she were back home in Bellahøj. The morphine had made her drowsy, and she was just nodding off when her mobile phone buzzed. With difficulty, she turned over onto her side and looked at the nightstand, where the phone was spinning on the spot. She reached out and felt pain radiating all down her one side. With the tip of two fingers, she managed to get hold of the phone. "Cecilie Mars."

"Cecilie? Where the hell are you?" said Karstensen.

"At the . . . emergency department."

"What are you doing there?"

"Long story. What's up?"

"That shit John needs to talk to you."

"I know . . . Eight o'clock Monday morning. I've promised not to be late."

"Forget about Monday. They want you in now."

"What do you mean?" she said, disoriented.

"It's serious. I had to pull rank to stop them from dispatching a patrol car to pick you up. I promised you'd come in of your own accord."

"A patrol car? I'm not with you . . ."

"They want to arrest you."

"For what?"

"They . . . John says they've found highly incriminating material."

"In relation to Bjarke's and Ronnie's deaths?"

"No. Something else entirely. A previous case. I pushed John and he said something about a video they'd been sent anonymously."

Her mouth was dry. "What kind of video?"

"One in which you are apparently shown committing violence against the victim of a traffic accident." He snorted down the line. "I know it sounds crazy, but that's what I got out of John. Do you have any idea what it's about?"

"Not a clue," she said in exhaustion.

"Okay. But you have to come in as soon as possible. They're sitting outside my office bloody waiting. The whole lot of them."

"I'm coming," she said, hanging up.

So Lazarus had finally decided to bury her alive. Cecilie Mars, the failed protégé. Perhaps it was the fault of the morphine, but the thought was liberating. She attempted to smile and felt her jaw ache. "Well, well, you win," she muttered, sitting up in bed. She felt the room spinning around her, and she had to support herself on the rail to prevent herself from sinking back into bed. Those little bastards had properly done her over. Luckily, she didn't need to worry about running into them any longer. John Nyholm would make sure that she was put away for so long that the lads would either have shot each other to smithereens or be in the slammer themselves. The irony was palpable.

She heaved herself out of bed and looked for her shoes. Moving her head made the nausea increase. Why hadn't she simply asked Karstensen to send John to the emergency department? If he wanted to interrogate her, he could join the bloody queue in the corridor. She bent down and reached for her shoes. Perhaps in her state she could postpone the interview? Or maybe she should have taken the Terrier up on his suggestion of a psychiatric assessment? She sat down heavily on the floor to put on her shoes. She felt like a child as she struggled to tie her shoelaces. The Terrier had said she wouldn't even have to cheat on hers. She smiled at the thought. Cursed his stupid little lawyer's snout. For Christ's sake— just how many times had he trounced them in court? Maybe hiring him made sense? Get the Terrier to smash—no, *fuck* John. As he'd so vulgarly said. Him, the Prosecution Service and all their expert witnesses. The Terrier wanted to fuck the lot of them. The image of a gang bang that appeared in her mind's eye was not pleasant.

The shot gangster was screaming in the room next door. She put her hand behind her looking for support. She reflected on the doctor's remark that the gangsters ought to take some target practice. Lazarus could not have agreed more. She slowly got to her feet, her legs swaying uncertainly. She felt stiff as anything and like she had a hangover at the same time.

Coat under her arm, she shuffled towards the open door. When she reached the corridor, she saw the officers still had their hands full keeping the wounded gangster's comrades under control. She made her way towards the counter at the far end and asked the member of staff seated there to call her a taxi. Judging by the looks the patients in the waiting room gave her, she must have looked all in. A couple of minutes later, a taxi arrived, and the driver gaped at her in the same way. At least she would put the fear of God into John when he saw her.

The taxi went via H. C. Andersens Boulevard, where they ended up stuck in rush hour traffic. The driver apologised, but she assured him that she was in no hurry. She looked through the window at all the other motorists, thinking to herself that Lazarus was hiding out there somewhere. She had been so close to him—not just physically, but also to revealing his identity. And she'd managed to fuck it up. She'd had all the pieces in front of her, but she hadn't managed to put the jigsaw together properly. It had cost Lasse his life. The grief she felt was like a void in her stomach. It hurt even more than the going-over the lads had given her. She felt tears trickling out of her swollen, closed eye. She felt her hatred of Lazarus rising to new heights. He would not get away. It wasn't fair. He would pay for what he had done. She couldn't let this happen. Not when she was so close. In the midst of her despair, it slowly dawned on her: *He knows us, but he's not a cop. He's deeply involved in the cases, but not in legal practice. He watches us without being one with us. He has our knowledge without being able to follow us. He is heard but never understood. Never understood.* The latter suddenly made renewed sense.

"Turn around!"

The driver looked at her in the rearview mirror as if she were a half-wit. "Madam, I cannot," he said, holding out his hand. "The traffic is insane."

"Then take the next turn. We're going the opposite direction."

"Opposite? Where to madam?"

"Bellahøj."

55

Twenty minutes later, Cecilie opened the boot of the Panda and looked down at the tote bag containing the sawn-off shotgun. The thud of hip-hop was emanating from the basketball court as demonstration of the fact that the lads had retaken their territory. *They can fucking have it*, she thought to herself as she shoved the tote to one side. Lying in front of her were two case files, each with an elastic band around it. The bundles contained copies of Ulrik Østergård's and Emil Kam's complete police records, respectively. She tucked the files under her arm and dropped them on the passenger seat before getting in behind the wheel. In reality, she didn't feel up to driving, but then again she didn't much feel like hanging around either. The yobs had eyes everywhere, and it wouldn't be long before they spotted her. She turned the key in the ignition and started the car.

She drove in an arc around the full Bellahøj neighbourhood, ending up down on Bellahøjvej where she parked up outside Bella Grill bar just a couple of minutes later. Above the entrance, attached to the grubby white façade, was a neon sign reading GRILL. Cecilie pushed open the door and went inside. The stench of old fried food hit her like a wall. Various customers were standing by the counter waiting for their orders. She edged her way past the queue and made her way to the back half of the venue, where she found a vacant table. It wasn't long before the restaurant's aging proprietor came over to her. He wiped down the waxed tablecloth with a damp dishcloth that smelled of vinegar.

"Long time no see, Inspector," he said, smiling through his white stubble.

"You're not wrong there, Kurt," she said.

Kurt wore the same open-heeled black wooden clogs and speckled blue apron that he always did. He frowned, scrutinising her bruised face. "Injury in the line of duty or . . . something more personal?"

"Bit of both, I reckon."

"You should take better care of yourself. Having anything to eat?"

"No, just some peace and quiet to work," she said, pointing to the bundles of papers. "You still serve beer?"

"Hof, right?"

She nodded.

Kurt disappeared before returning a minute later with her beer. She thanked him and took a sip from the bottle. The cold beer did her good. Cecilie leafed through Emil Kam's cases and it wasn't long before she found what she was looking for. Then she went through the stack of Ulrik's cases, skimming them, too. She pulled a pen from her pocket and circled his name: Steen Holz. Expert witness for the Prosecution Service. She remembered the first time she had met him. Andreas had introduced her to him that night at the sports bar. She had later bumped into him a few times in court, and his name had cropped up in several of the cases they had reviewed at Andreas's.

She took another sip of beer and pulled out her mobile. For a moment, she considered whether she should call Andreas. But she didn't know whether he was waiting for her along with John and the others. Instead, she did a search online for Steen Holz, pulling up a couple of photos of him. His winning smile and calm eyes meant that he was far from the cliché of a psychopathic killer.

She found a website for his private clinic, which was located at a fashionable address in the city centre. It was called the Anxiety Clinic. The name made the corners of her mouth quiver. The website described which psychiatric disorders Steen Holz was able to treat. These ranged from ADHD, depression, and post-partum psychosis to anxiety and bipolar disorders. It was also possible to book private consultations for everything from couples therapy to dealing with stalkers and psychopaths, whether at home or in the workplace. She felt like an obvious candidate for all his forms of consultation.

Cecilie continued to search online and discovered that Holz was a man of firm opinions. He had written a string of controversial opinion pieces in the national press. These included one in which he had said that many unemployed people, especially in immigrant circles, faked mental illness to receive benefits. In another piece, he had outlined how easy it was for criminals to circumvent the justice system through coaching ahead of their psychiatric assessments. Both articles had garnered a lot of attention and whipped up a shitstorm around him. She also discovered that Steen Holz had been a member of the Medico-Legal Council from 2009 to 2015, when he had been dismissed. Both from the council and from his role as a consultant in the psychiatric ward at Bispebjerg. This had apparently been on the grounds that he had released a controversial book titled *The Extreme Consequence*. Cecilie searched for the book's title and found various references to it. The book argued that criminals should be subjected to forcible medication to prevent them from committing new crimes. Cecilie read that a number of experts and politicians had renounced him as a result. In one newspaper interview, Steen Holz had accused them all of having blood on their hands for as long as they stuck with an inefficient and outdated justice system.

Kurt had apparently spotted that her beer was empty. He appeared and set down a new bottle at her side.

"Thanks," she said, leaning back in her plastic chair.

"I'm closing up soon, but you're welcome to stay until I'm done cleaning up."

"That's sweet of you. What do I owe you?"

"Just pay me next time," he said, returning to the counter.

She found a crumpled fifty in her pocket and put it on the table. There was no reason to cheat Kurt of his payment.

If only she had looked into Steen Holz sooner, she might have had a chance of uncovering his involvement in a string of legal cases. And she might have been able to investigate his time in the psychiatric ward before he'd been fired. She might even have found witnesses or evidence to suggest that he was Lazarus. But time had definitely gotten away from her, and by failing to voluntarily hand herself in to John she had further incriminated herself to boot. Now they would definitely be coming to pick her up. She was on the bloody run.

Fifteen minutes later, she said goodbye to Kurt and got back into the Panda. She wouldn't be able to go home. All that awaited her there were the lads or the cops. She needed to find a car park to hide herself and the Panda in.

She knew there were a couple of places near Steen Holz's practice, which fitted in nicely with her burgeoning plan to be his first patient in the morning.

56

The underground car park on Adelgade slowly began to fill with commuters arriving from the northern suburbs. The exclusive fleet of vehicles, largely comprising German makes, made her rust-speckled Fiat Panda parked in the back row look even more wretched. The sound of a car door slamming woke Cecilie, who stretched in the reclined driver's seat. The night had allowed her a couple of hours of uneasy sleep, and it took a moment for her to remember where she was. She returned the seat to the upright position and made eye contact with an older man in a suit. The man gave her a disapproving look and pressed the lock button on the key to his Porsche Panamera an extra time. Cecilie ran a hand through her hair and examined her reflection in the rearview mirror. Her left eye was barely swollen now, and she could see with it again. However, the eye socket was a shade of blue-black; she looked like a raccoon. She found her phone and saw the reams of text messages that had arrived from Karstensen, John Nyholm, and Andreas. Despite the different tones in the messages, they were all asking her to get in touch. She checked her voice mail, where she found Karstensen had left three messages and Andreas one. Karstensen's messages were full of snorts and groans and half-veiled threats that *now* was her last chance to come in of her own accord. Andreas was more subdued. But his message that *we're worried about you* told her that it had been sensible not to involve him in her plan to pay Steen Holz a visit. She was alone now, like never before.

Cecilie got out of the Panda and walked through the car park, heading for the exit. When she emerged onto Gothersgade, she found a café on a corner and bought herself a black coffee and a croissant. As she devoured the croissant, she checked the news and the police morning briefing on her phone and noted that they still hadn't reported her missing. She drained her paper cup and made her way towards Sankt Annæ Plads. Ten minutes later, she was standing in front of the entrance to a fashionable building with a white façade. The signage by the intercom told her that the clinic shared an address with two child psychologists, a life coach, and a law practice. She buzzed and was admitted.

The front office for the three psychologists on the first floor was decorated in bright colours and featured soft furnishings and a play area that filled most of the space. The young woman on reception looked at her injured face but then smiled kindly at Cecilie as she stepped up to the counter.

"I'm here to speak to Steen Holz," Cecilie said.

The receptionist looked at her computer screen. "And what's your name?"

"Cecilie Mars."

"I don't see an appointment for you today, Cecilie."

"Could you let him know that Inspector Cecilie Mars from the Homicide Unit would like a word with him? I dare say he'll find the time."

"Just a moment," the receptionist said. She had stopped smiling. She turned around and went down the corridor, disappearing through the door to the last office. A couple of minutes later she returned to reception. "Dr. Holz will see you now."

Cecilie entered Steen Holz's bright, well-presented office. The psychologist was standing in profile by the tall window, looking calmly down towards the square below. The strong light concealed his face, and instead she noticed his slim figure.

"Steen Holz?" she said, taking a step closer.

He slowly turned towards her and smiled calmly. "How did you find me?"

His question surprised her. "I . . . with difficulty, I must say."

He came over and looked at her with his piercing blue eyes. "Really? Most of my clients find me online or they're referred on by their own doctor." He held out his hand. She took it. It felt cool, but not in an uncomfortable way.

"Won't you sit down?" He pointed to one of the two Wegner chairs positioned at a small table, and he took the other.

Steen Holz wore a light suit and a white shirt with a mandarin collar. The smile on his slightly tanned face was winning, and sitting there completely calmly, he reminded her of a newly returned missionary. "So how did you find me, Inspector Cecilie Mars? Or may I call you Cecilie?"

"Cecilie is fine, Steen. I found you through Andreas Bostad at the Prosecution Service."

"Oh, yes, Andreas," he said, nodding. "How's he doing? I've heard on the grapevine that he's just divorced?"

She shook her head quietly. "I'll have to disappoint on that one. I don't know him in a personal capacity."

Steen Holz glanced at the plaster on her forehead. "Are you visiting in a personal capacity?"

"Not really, no."

"That sounds cryptic."

"Not at all. I gather from Andreas that you've been an expert witness on a few occasions?"

"Yes, that's right."

"Do you remember how many cases you've done?"

He looked thoughtfully at the ceiling. "Quite a few by now. Around twenty, I think. Why do you ask?"

"And what kind of cases has that been in connection with?" she asked quickly.

"Both homicides and cases relating to violence and vice."

"And in what way did you assist the Prosecution Service?"

"I assessed whether the accused was suitable for punishment."

"So basically, whether they were off their rocker or not?"

"Quite. To be off your rocker or not off your rocker, that is the question," he replied cheerfully.

She nodded. "And what makes you an expert?"

He pointed to the diplomas on the wall without looking towards them. "Those, and nigh on thirty years' professional experience in psychiatry. Including a role on the Medico-Legal Council for six years." He squinted at her roguishly. "But something tells me, Cecilie, that you've already done your research. Perhaps you'd like to tell me about the reason for your visit?"

"Of course," Cecilie said, smiling cautiously. "We've been investigating a number of murders lately and we think the same man is behind all of them. These include the murders of Emil Kam, Morten Pier Nielsen, and those of Bjarke and Ronnie Thomsen."

"The names don't ring any bells."

"But you were called as a witness for the prosecution in some of their previous cases."

"Oh, yes." He nodded quickly. "It's starting to come back to me. If I may ask, what exactly leads you to believe that it is the same killer?"

"Modus operandi, evidence, various coincidences. I can't go into any more detail about them."

"And why come to me?" he said, holding out his hand nonchalantly.

"I thought that with your experience you might be able to help me profile the killer."

"Profile? A serial killer?" he said, smiling.

"Yes."

"That's not really something I do."

"It occurred to me that you had the necessary experience." She kept her gaze fixed on him, trying to read him. But Steen Holz didn't give anything away.

"Determining whether or not someone is, ahem, off their rocker or whether they are merely pretending to be is an entirely different matter to profiling. Furthermore, that kind of perpetrator is unusual. I don't know of many precedents. Are you sure that you're not dealing with random connections in your investigation?"

"We're pretty sure."

Steen Holz adjusted his trouser crease before continuing. "You said *man*. Why not a woman? In my experience, women can be highly motivated, verging on pathological, but they're better than men at hiding their psychopathy."

Cecilie sensed a mischievous glint in the otherwise cool eyes.

"We're certain that it's a man," she said, looking away. "As I said, there are a couple of details I can't go into . . ."

"Of course. I understand. But in any case, he must be rather adept if you haven't yet apprehended him."

"Or lucky . . . so far."

"So what's your own assessment of him? I'm curious to hear it."

She cleared her throat. "Will this remain between us?"

"Of course. Nothing you say will leave this office."

"Good. We've received a number of tips from someone who calls himself Lazarus."

"Which one?"

"I didn't know there was more than one Lazarus."

"Two, according to the Bible. The one that Jesus resurrected, and the other, a poor man who appears in the parable of the rich man and whose name means God's helper. He's the one to listen to if you don't want to suffer torment in the realm of the dead," he said, without batting an eyelid.

She cocked her head. "You seem to . . . know a lot about this?"

He held out his hands in resignation. "My father was a priest. Some of what he preached has stuck," he chuckled. "So what's your own assessment of Lazarus?"

"He's clearly intelligent and well educated, possibly from an academic background. He's eloquent. Furthermore, he's familiar with how the police work. Judging by his messages to us, he harbours tremendous hatred of the justice system. It seems as if he is pursuing justice in line with the Old Testament: an eye for an eye, a tooth for a tooth."

"Sounds like just my sort of guy," Steen Holz said cheerfully. "And you've been able to trace the text messages from him, have you?"

"Which text messages?"

"You said . . . messages. I assumed they were texts or emails?"

She paused before responding, attempting to interpret his slip of the tongue. But he seemed calm. "We've got people looking into it. The whole NC3 is involved."

"Interesting," he said with a shrug. "What other impressions have you formed of him?"

She narrowed her eyes. "The very fact that he's contacting us clearly indicates a morbid form of narcissism. This is a man who is dreaming of being caught and getting his message out to the world. Judging by the content of his messages, he seems like someone with low self-esteem. A pathological liar with psychopathic traits. He has no empathy, remorse, or guilt. I suspect he's a sexual deviant, although he may be impotent. His whole game may be a form of sexual gratification."

Steen Holz winked at her. "Perhaps you should have become a psychologist instead of a detective."

She smiled disarmingly. "These are just my personal views. In reality, he's no different to the other killers we're hunting. Just another callous piece of scum."

Steen Holz didn't reply. He merely stared back at her coolly.

Eventually, she held out her hands. "Anyway, as I said, I'm here to find out whether you would draw up a profile of him? Let the expertise speak for itself rather than relying on my guesswork."

"Hmm, well . . ." he replied dryly. "I would really require access to all the material you have on him."

"Obviously we'll have to clear that before I can hand it over. As I said before, there are details of the investigation that can't be allowed to get out."

"Of course," he said, standing up. "I take it that I'll be hearing from you?"

"Yes," she replied, following suit.

He looked at her, both hands jammed in his pockets. "I must say that I am surprised to see you."

"Why?"

"Well, I haven't been able to avoid following this case in the media."

"Which one?"

"The most recent one with Ronnie and his father, Bjarke." He shook his head. "A couple of real beasts."

She stared at him. The word he had used seemed carefully chosen. "And?"

"I read somewhere or other that you'd been suspended. That your case was being investigated by the Independent Police Complaints Authority. Is that true?"

She nodded. "It's just routine. It's what happens in any case where a service weapon is fired."

His gaze ran down her body, as if seeking out a pistol in the same way that Hassan had done outside her building.

"But now I'm back again," she said.

"How reassuring."

"Yes. We need to give it everything we've got to catch this cop killer. That's also why I came here today."

Steen Holz looked at her in surprise. "Wasn't there talk of an exchange of fire between the officer and the two kidnappers? I seem to remember reading that."

She shook her head dismissively and lowered her voice to a confidential whisper. "As I said before: Lazarus is a narcissist who thinks he's untouchable. It was clearly a setup. He killed all three of them."

"Really? That hasn't been made public."

"There's lots that hasn't."

Steen Holz smiled uneasily. "Must be hard losing your partner."

"Yes, but right now, it's also my greatest motivation," she said, proffering her hand. When he took it, she noticed that his hand had become warm and clammy in the course of their conversation.

He squeezed her hand tightly. "How many people know about . . . Lazarus?"

"It's just . . . a small group."

"I see. Good day to you," he said, releasing her hand. When he opened the door for her, he smiled at her kindly.

57

Cecilie sat staring vacantly through the windscreen towards the row of cars opposite her in the underground car park. The encounter with Steen Holz had begun to eat her up. She pounded her fists on the steering wheel. "Bloody fucking hell," she snarled through gritted teeth. Steen Holz was Lazarus. She was almost one hundred per cent certain of it. She was tempted to go straight back there, shove the double-barrel of the sawn-off shotgun down his throat and pull the trigger. *Bloody fucking hell.*

On the whole, he had remained calm, but he had been sloppy at a couple of points. She'd seen it in psychopaths before when questioning them. They always felt smarter than everyone else, and it was generally this arrogance that was their eventual downfall. She wondered whether Steen Holz had been gasping to reveal that he was Lazarus. She was sure it would have delighted him to reveal all the details of his plans. "Bloody fucking hell."

She pulled out her phone and searched for the video of herself and Ulrik. She rewatched it in the desperate hope that the contents could somehow be explained away. But given the way it had been edited, it clearly showed her kicking him and then absconding. She reread all of Lazarus's messages to her. Together with the emails he had sent and the case files he'd given her, they were proof of his existence. But she also knew full well that John Nyholm only had eyes for her. There would be no great incentive to explore these leads. There was no need to start muddying a case by investigating avenues of inquiry which, if she was reading Lazarus correctly, would all meet with dead ends. John and the top brass would settle for the physical evidence against her and consider the case closed as soon as she was convicted. She wondered whether Karstensen or Andreas would be more responsive. Whether in the longer term, once the smoke had cleared, they would come back and look into the case. Perhaps there was something in Lazarus's documents that would lead them to Steen Holz. All she could do now was retrieve the documents at home and pass them to Andreas before she handed herself in. If the yobs showed their faces and tried anything, at least she had the shotgun to threaten them with. *Bloody fucking hell*, she thought to herself as she drove out of the car park. It was unbearable for it to end like this.

Cecilie pulled out onto Adelgade. The rain was pouring down, and she stopped at the crossroads with Dronningegården. She was about to continue ahead when she spotted a patrol car approaching along Dronningens Tværgade. The officer at the wheel looked indolently towards her as he rolled through the intersection and headed on towards Rosenborg Castle Gardens. Either she was not wanted yet, or they were two cops who hadn't been given enough doughnuts and praise by their superiors. Shortly after, as she turned onto Sølvgade, a text message arrived. She grabbed her phone and read the message.

Cecilie Mars. I think we should meet. While there is still time. Lazarus.

Cecilie pulled to one side while considering what had made Lazarus contact her now. What had changed since her visit to Steen Holz. She wondered whether Lazarus really had plans to meet her, or whether it was just an attempt to play for time. She replied quickly.

Time is up. I hope they catch you.

She didn't have to wait long to hear back from him.

It isn't like you to give up ahead of time.
I must apologise for the state of affairs. I wish to help you.

Lazarus's apology took her by surprise. The only logical reason for his behaviour was that he had devised a new plan. She reflected on how important it must be for him to see it through.

If that's true I think you should hand yourself in.

His answer came promptly.

Drop the impertinence, Cecilie.
It does not become you, and you can't afford the arrogance that you are currently shrouding yourself in. I am the only one who can help you out of your tricky situation. The only choice you have is between meeting me or the Independent Police Complaints Authority.

She couldn't compute why Lazarus wanted to meet. Why save her when he had given her up himself by sending the video to John Nyholm? Why expose himself now when he had done everything to stay under the radar? There was only one answer to those questions: She had found him. Steen Holz was a man under pressure. If so, she wanted to apply some more.

I'll choose John Nyholm every time. I'm sure he'll be amenable when I tell him about you.

When five minutes had elapsed and he still hadn't replied, she grew worried that she had gone too far. She was contemplating whether to write again to defuse the tense situation when he replied.

If it is of your own choosing, then I cannot offer you salvation from your own demise. However, I predict that you will remain tormented by Lasse's death for the rest of your life. Only I can tell you what truly happened that night.

She shook her head at this pathetic attempt. Damn it, she'd been there herself. She'd heard the shots fired. She'd held Lasse as he'd died in her arms. What did Lazarus imagine he could add that she would want to hear? Nevertheless, it struck her that he was very good at getting under her skin. She sent him a new message.

When and where are we meeting?

Lazarus replied immediately.

Good choice, Cecilie Mars.
I will let you know shortly.

She was certain that Lazarus's intention in meeting was to ensure that she didn't speak to John Nyholm. The only question was whether he was planning to shoot her, cut her throat, or something else entirely. If Steen Holz was Lazarus, the obvious thing to do would be to watch him. She turned the car around and headed back to Sankt Annæ Plads. A little while later, she found an empty spot not far from Holz's practice that gave her a clear view of the main door to the building. Through the pouring rain, she saw that the lights were shining on every floor, including in Steen Holz's office where the curtains were half drawn.

She wondered where he was planning to meet her. Probably somewhere secluded that he had intimate knowledge of. One thing in her favour was the fact that now she could follow him and remove the element of surprise. She was considering whether to retrieve the shotgun from the boot when her phone began to make a chiming sound. It was an unfamiliar sound and seemed like an alarm. She fished her phone out of her pocket and looked at the display. It was the HomeSAFE app warning her of an intrusion. A short message said that the alarm on her front door had been activated and that she should contact the police. There was a link prompting her to call 112 at the top of the screen. She made her way through the menu to see the live footage from the living room camera. When she finally found it, a black screen appeared with the words "No connection." A moment later, another message informed her that the alarm had been disabled. She gazed towards Steen Holz's windows, where the lights were still on. What the hell was he doing at her flat? Had he tried to surprise her there? She quickly sent him a text.

Waiting for your reply! Where are we meeting?

A couple of minutes later when he hadn't replied, she found the phone number for the clinic and called it. She could tell that the voice on the line was the same receptionist she had spoken to earlier.

"Cecilie Mars. Is that Steen Holz?"

"Sorry. I'm afraid Steen Holz has left the office for the day. Can I take a message?"

Cecilie hung up and started the Panda.

She sped down Sølvgade and then onto Øster Søgade, setting a direct course for Bellahøj. She concluded that her visit must have unsettled him, and that Steen Holz had probably left shortly after she had. She continued along Åboulevard, using all four lanes to get past other motorists. If Lazarus wanted to meet in her flat, then that was fine by her. What was he thinking? That he'd hurl her off the roof terrace? Another staged accident? If so, she'd show him—using the shotgun. A couple of minutes later, she pulled into the car park situated between the grey blocks of flats in Bellahøj. She drove between the rows of cars and parked close to the path leading to her own stairwell. As she turned off the engine and was about to get out, she heard the first yells. They came from all sides. From the dark figures emerging from the rain, heading for her car. They weren't wearing hoodies like the yobs. Instead, they wore helmets and bulletproof vests. Submachine guns raised, the members of the Tactical Unit surrounded the Panda and took aim at it as if it were a dangerous animal. Behind them, she glimpsed John Nyholm and a couple of his colleagues. She realised that it hadn't been Lazarus who had triggered the alarm—it had been John and his entourage. At that moment, the mobile on the passenger seat buzzed. She glanced at the display. It was a message from Lazarus with an address. It seemed familiar, but she couldn't place it. Then she realised where she had last seen it. It was the address on the business card she'd been handed at Café Victor.

Bloody hell. How could she have been so mistaken? She'd been a moron. The Terrier was Lazarus.

58

The Tactical Unit leader standing in front of the car yelled at her to get out. She thought she recognised the voice, but the window had fogged up completely and it prevented her from seeing who it was. It was probable that she knew half the officers who were outside, their machine guns raised. All things considered, John Nyholm must have managed to get them whipped up into quite the frenzy since he had control of more or less all the cavalry.

Cecilie turned off her phone and slipped it between the passenger seat and the centre console. Forensics would definitely find it, but it would hopefully buy her a little time before NC3 cracked it. She carefully opened the door with one hand, sticking the other one in the air in surrender. Before she was able to set foot on the asphalt, the door was yanked open and she was pushed to the ground. She felt the weight of the officer putting a knee in her back as he forced her arms behind her. There was the whine of plastic zip ties being put around her wrists. The officer told her she was under arrest, and together with a colleague he heaved her up off the asphalt. They pulled her away from the car, which was already being examined.

The operation had attracted a number of spectators, who were watching the spectacle from a distance. She heard the lads catcalling from the strip of grass over by the basketball court. Just then, John came over. The pouring rain made his thinning hair stick to his scalp. "I'll be damned if I understand why you're making things harder for yourself."

"I'm sure there's plenty more that you don't understand, John," she replied.

"I'm sure. Although, following a search of your flat, I'm somewhat the wiser. That's quite an archive you've been keeping on your victims."

"I've got no idea what you're talking about."

"There's extensive material beyond the stuff that ties back to your own case. I can see how painful it must have been for you." He appeared to be feigning empathy. "You were determined to have your revenge over all these years."

"Like I said, there's a lot you don't understand."

"Gun!" shouted the officer standing by the boot of the Panda. He carefully opened the tote bag, revealing its contents to John and the other officers nearby.

John looked back at Cecilie. "Who was next on your list?"

She didn't answer, averting her gaze to the ground.

John signalled to the officer, who led her over to the dark blue Passat belonging to the Independent Police Complaints Authority. The officer put her in the back seat and locked the door while he stood outside. She twisted the zip tie at her wrists and found it was loose, although she couldn't wriggle free. Shortly after, John and his pallid colleague trudged back to the car and got in. From his seat behind the wheel, John turned to look at her. "Damn it, you really have pulled the wool over all our eyes."

She silently turned to look out of the side window. Outside, a couple of patrol cars had arrived and as John pulled away, they obediently followed.

"Where are we going?" she asked.

"For questioning. But I think we'll use the back way in so that there's no need for you to pass the Homicide Unit and be confronted by your colleagues."

She nodded in silent thanks.

"On the other hand, I am counting on your cooperation so that we can get to the bottom of all this."

"There's always a catch."

He didn't reply.

She leaned back and surveyed John in the rearview mirror. She could just about see him smiling. This was surely a big day for him. One of the ones he would remember. As he sat there behind the wheel, he was probably already dreaming of his promotion and his new corner office. She turned her head and stared out of the back window looking for the patrol cars following, but in the downpour she could no longer see them among the other vehicles. They were approaching Bispeengbuen, and John stopped at a red light not far from it. She looked at the nearest door and saw that it was locked. She knew the central locking system was controlled by a button on the driver-side door. The light switched to green and John headed up onto Bispeengbuen. They reached the summit of the bridge arc where the road began its sharp downward trajectory. She anchored both her feet to the floor and raised herself half out of her seat. Then she brought her tied wrists down around her buttocks and sat down again.

"Stay still!" John shouted back at her.

His partner reached out towards her legs, but she kicked his hand away.

"Fuck! You bitch."

Cecilie drew up her legs and shifted her hands up in front of her stomach. She reached for the handbrake and applied it. The Passat's rear wheels locked and the car skidded. John pawed at the steering wheel. In a panic, he put his foot down on the accelerator, sending the car towards the outer crash barrier. The violent collision made the car ricochet across the carriageway towards the inside lane. It hit the concrete barrier sideways on and then came to a standstill. There was a squeal of brakes from the cars behind followed by some loud bangs from a couple of them crashing into one another. In the Passat, the released airbags hung there like white flags, fluttering. John Nyholm and his partner were in a daze, trying to pull themselves together. Cecilie could hear John gasping for breath. She reached forward and made contact with the central locking system button by John's armrest. Then she opened the back door. She saw his partner's gun half protruding from its holster and the walkie talkie hanging loosely at his belt. Quickly, she ripped them both loose and took them with her as she leapt out of the door. She began to run down the inside lane. The rain was lashing down and she almost slipped on the slick tarmac. John shouted at her. She half-turned around to see him staggering along behind her. Beyond him, the flashing blue lights of a couple of patrol cars were visible as their sirens sounded on the wind. Cecilie sped up, running for all she was worth. She was looking towards the nearest set of traffic lights, some four hundred metres from the end of the bridge. It was a distance she had no chance of covering before the patrol cars caught up with her. She slowed down and looked over the concrete barrier. It was twelve or thirteen metres to the car park below. Even if she landed on top of one of the vans below, she would be badly hurt. She looked back.

John had drawn his gun and was perhaps fifteen metres behind her. The patrol cars were right on his tail. Cecilie tucked the gun and the walkie talkie in her belt and used her bound hands to help herself hop up onto the edge of the concrete barrier.

"Don't do it, Cecilie!" John yelled. He signalled to the cars behind him to stop.

The two cars slowed down while positioning themselves to block the road.

Cecilie continued her tightrope walk along the narrow strip of concrete above the car park below. Her bound hands made it difficult to maintain her balance. She swayed a few times and stopped.

"Cecilie, stop. It shouldn't end like this."

She looked back towards John. "No? Then how should it end?"

"A fair . . . investigation," he tried to say.

She smiled back coolly. "And you promise that?"

"I . . . I promise we'll take everything into consideration."

"That's not good enough. He killed Lasse. And the others."

"Who did?"

She looked down into the abyss at her side. "Lazarus."

John shook his head. "Then why don't you just get down? We'll go to the station . . . and you can tell me all about it. Nice and easy."

"Sorry, John, but that's just not going to be possible." She moved her feet a few centimetres closer to the edge.

"Cecilie!"

"If I can't, well . . . you have to find him, John. Find Lazarus." At that moment, she leapt off the barrier and disappeared into the darkness.

John threw himself forward, but it was too late.

59

Cecilie fell three or four metres, hitting the top of the skateboard ramp that rose up beneath the bridge. The collision with the wooden surface forced her legs up towards her chest and squeezed the air from her lungs. She toppled onto the steep ramp, rolling over and over down it before landing heavily at its base. She lay there gasping for breath. The rain was falling through the gap between the two bridges above her. She tried to stand up. Her entire body ached, but she hadn't broken anything. Far above on the bridge she heard the officers shouting to one another. They were shining their torches down towards the car park. Cecilie got off the ramp and hobbled under the bridge towards the nearest car. She put her bound hands around the wing mirror and began to wriggle her hands back and forth. Eventually, she managed to expand the strip enough to free her hands. Not far away, a patrol car accelerated. On the walkie talkie at her belt, she heard the officers talking among themselves. More were en route to assist in a search of the area. She pulled the pistol from her belt and checked: The magazine was full. Then she ran, leaving behind Bispeengbuen as she headed for Østerbro and for Lazarus.

60

The sixteen storeys of the Copper Tower office block at Amerika Plads rose into the night sky. The patinated metal cladding on the building's exterior made it glow in the dark. It was a fitting palace for the lawyers working inside it, and especially the Terrier. There was just one light on in the large windows, in a single office on the top floor. Cecilie headed for the wide entrance and peered into the dark lobby. She pressed the buzzer. There was a loud click and the door opened. She made her way inside and past the deserted reception area. A brass plaque behind the counter listed the law firms in the building. Not unexpectedly, she found Phillip Vang listed on the top floor.

She headed for the lift and took it up to the sixteenth floor, accompanied all the way by a quiet bossa nova. When she reached her floor, she got out and drew her gun, clicking the safety off. She moved down the corridor, looking into the dark, empty offices. At the end of the passage, she stopped outside a door that was ajar. A band of light escaped from the room onto the floor. Using the muzzle of her pistol, she pushed the door so that it slowly glided open. She was met with the dazzling glow of a desk lamp angled at her from a desk at the other end of the room. She shielded her eyes from the light and saw the outline of the Terrier behind the huge desk.

"Feel free to turn that light out," she said, aiming the pistol at him.

Phillip Vang did not respond.

"I must admit that your message surprised me." She took a step to the side, out of the blinding light.

He turned his head towards her and muttered something or other. She kept her aim steady as she slowly approached the desk from the side. When she reached it, she saw that he had been gagged with his own yellow tie, and that his forearms were taped to the armrests of his chair. He was bleeding profusely from his right ear, which had been half cut off. At that moment, she felt the cold steel of a knife blade against her neck.

"Be so good as to hand it over," said a voice behind her, as a gloved hand reached for her gun. Cecilie handed it over and received a shove in the back which sent her flying towards the desk. She turned around and saw Steen Holz. He wore a blue overall and accompanying hairnet. There were protective plastic overshoes on his feet.

"You took your time getting here. Phillip Vang—or should I call him the Terrier—has been expecting you."

She looked coolly at Steen Holz without answering. It was clear that she was part of a plan that he had concocted. A plan that involved him leaving no trace of his presence.

"I thought you would come storming in with that shotgun I gave you. But this thing here will do just as well, I suppose," he said, raising the pistol towards her. "I thought they confiscated your service weapon long ago. So how did you lay hands on this?"

"I stole it," she replied.

Steen Holz clearly didn't believe her and laughed.

"How's it going to be staged this time?" she asked. "I wound Phillip, but just before he dies, he manages to shoot me with my own weapon?"

"Something like that, yes."

"No one's going to buy that."

"I've gotten away with deaths in circumstances that were considerably more suspicious. What really matters is tying up the loose ends. You have to create a scenario with just the bare minimum of plausibility. It's not that the police are lazy as such, but my experience tells me that they have plenty to deal with and are quite happy to accept an easily solved case."

"Perhaps. But why on earth would I kill him?"

"Because he's responsible for all those beasts that go free. Despite being aware of their horrific crimes, despite him knowing that they will go on to commit them again. He has spent years creating new victims—all for the sake of money."

She flashed an ironic smile at Steen Holz. "He's a defence lawyer. He's just acting in his clients' interests. What did you expect?"

Steen Holz shook his head. "For everyone to follow the rules of the game. That's how we uphold the rule of law. That's how we ensure there is justice. Without it, the wicked are victorious." He moved around the desk to a position behind Phillip Vang. He put the knife against Vang's ear and cut the final sinew holding it to his head. Phillip Vang writhed in the chair and howled through the tie stuffed in his mouth.

"Stop!" Cecilie cried out.

"I haven't even started yet," Steen Holz said calmly, taking aim at her with the gun. "First his ears, then his eyes, and finally his tongue. He'll drown in his own blood. A fitting punishment, don't you think?"

"You're as sick as the criminals you go after."

"You wound me, Cecilie," he said sarcastically, shifting the knife to Phillip Vang's left ear. Phillip Vang tried desperately to move his head, and Steen Holz let him flail. "I've followed all his cases. Followed all the people he helped to avoid just punishment."

"All the cases that you and Andreas lost."

"Well, among others."

"Perhaps you should have done more to prepare, instead of letting him take the brunt now?"

"Oh, Cecilie, don't waste your sympathy on him." He smiled at her. "I have been considering paying a visit to Andreas. I've frequently found myself wishing to mete out a suitable punishment to him for his incompetence and laziness. He spends more time thinking about copulating than his work." Steen Holz smiled. "But then again, he has proven himself to be useful. He's always been communicative and never the sort of person to change his passwords. Imagine being able to survive on that basis alone," he said, turning the knife in his hand. "But that might still change."

"So that was how you gained access to our archives? To our pending trials? To my case?"

"Someone had to clean up after him," Holz said, glancing at Phillip Vang.

"Have there been other cases?"

"You mean other than the ones involving you?" A crooked smile appeared on his face. "My dear Cecilie, it's been a long and arduous struggle for me. It began long before you revealed yourself to me."

"How many?"

"Not anywhere near enough."

"I've counted two fatal accidents and a suicide among his clients in the last year alone, and then there are the new cases that you were involved . . ."

"Then you haven't counted them all." He rested the blade of the knife between Phillip Vang's ear and his scalp. Then sliced.

Phillip Vang screamed as blood spurted from the half-cut-off ear.

Steen Holz moved the knife back to cut again.

"So why me?" Cecilie said.

He looked up from the knife. "Initially because of Ulrik. I had been following him for a while before he raped that girl you knew. It was at the preliminary hearing that I noticed your fury when they released him. Your deciding to follow him—I saw that as a sign. Like one of the Valkyries being sent down from heaven. It was as if my prayer for a soul mate had finally been heard."

"Soul mate?" she said sceptically. "I didn't kill him."

"No, you fled in a panic. That disappointed me. I had thought you would snuff his life out. Instead, I had to take matters into my own hands."

"You?"

He nodded. "I punched him in the chest where you had kicked him. It was very straightforward. But I could hardly show that in the video I sent." He nudged the loose ear with the knife. Phillip Vang sobbed.

"When did you find out about my old case?"

"I'm meticulous in my research. That's why Bjarke was also my gift to you. I truly wanted to set you free, Cecilie. I am still convinced I would have succeeded if you had trusted me." He sighed deeply. "But instead, you chose to embroil your partner." In a sweeping motion, he cut the ear off and let it fall to the desk. Phillip Vang roared in pain and tried to get free. Steen Holz looked down at him. "You never listened to reason or the screams of your clients' victims. I think this is how *Cecilie* would have punished you. Had she had the courage. Had she followed her instincts." He turned his gaze to Cecilie. "My only mistake was to believe that you could be turned. That we could shake the police officer out of you. It pains me that it must end this way." He raised the gun and took aim at her.

She stared him down coolly, fearlessly. "Once a cop killer . . ."

"You're thinking of Lasse." He nodded. "I promised to tell you about the circumstances of his death, didn't I?"

"You can tell me what you like."

He smiled. "Lasse was a smidgen ballsier than you. By the time I arrived, he had already put his gun to Bjarke's head. Quite literally." Steen Holz turned the gun towards Phillip Vang and put the muzzle to his head as if to illustrate his point.

"You're lying. Lasse would never have done that."

"On my word of honour. Lasse said to Bjarke: 'This is for *Guppy*.'" Steen Holz shrugged. "Who knows? If he hadn't heard me coming and reacted to that, he might have squeezed the trigger. Unfortunately, that's not quite how it went."

"No, you killed him."

"Not willingly. As I explained previously, my mission is solely to liberate the earth of beasts. Time for the eyes, I think," he said, squinting at the Terrier.

Just then, the sound of sirens rose from the street outside. The sound intensified, indicating they were approaching rapidly. Steen Holz turned the pistol on Cecilie, as he took a step backwards towards the window, where he stared down at the blue flashing lights illuminating the night.

"You won't get away. Not this time."

He looked back at her. "What . . . how?"

Before she could answer, there was a blaring sound from under her coat. Steen Holz waved the pistol to indicate that she should open it fully. She pulled down the zipper, revealing the walkie talkie on her belt. "You . . . you . . ." he stammered, speechless.

"I told them where to find me, just before you buzzed me in. If they've been listening properly, I should think it won't be long before the Special Intervention Unit arrives, too."

"You . . . you disappoint me, Cecilie."

"Maybe it's time you laid down your weapons. You won't want to be waving them around when they come a-knocking. Not that it makes any difference to me whether you live or die." She reached for the pistol.

"Yet again, you fail to live up to my expectations!" he bellowed, spittle flying from his mouth. "You could have made a difference! Do you understand?! You could have been so much more than a victim!" He took aim at her head. She directed a circular kick at the light on the desk. It flew towards Steen Holz, striking his arm. The light bulb blew, and for a second the office was shrouded in darkness. "I'll kill you!" he shouted, and the gun went off, the flashes illuminating the room in a series of stark interludes as he fired blindly.

Down in the street, there was the sound of squealing brakes. Cecilie ran past the huge window, glancing down quickly. There were two black Range Rovers beside the patrol cars down by the entrance. The heavily armed members of the Special Intervention Unit were storming out of the open doors of the vehicles. "Give up now, Steen!" she shouted.

Steen Holz spun around towards her and fired the gun. The bullet hit the window, shattering it, and Cecilie threw herself to the floor.

Steen Holz looked at Phillip Vang in the desk chair. "Feel powerful again, little man? Think you've won?"

Phillip Vang moaned and tears ran down his cheeks.

"Just like all those times you've stood up in court and lied." He turned the chair a half revolution so that Phillip Vang was facing the filing cabinets. "Look at your work, little man. Look at your Sodom and Gomorrah. Look at them for the last time." With a powerful blow, Steen Holz thrust the knife into his chest. Phillip Vang's body tensed into an arc and he emitted a death rattle. At last, he fell back into the chair, lifeless, and Steen Holz pulled out the knife.

"Cecilie? Where are you hiding?" he called, brandishing the gun in the dark. At that moment, the walkie talkie rattled on the far side of the office. "They might be on their way, but no one can save you now." He moved slowly towards the dark silhouettes of the sofas. The walkie talkie became louder, the bursts of sound close to each other this time. "Still on your own, just like when Bjarke raped you. A victim who couldn't fight back. A lamb in the middle of a pack of wolves." He rounded the first sofa and passed the low coffee table, making for the sofa opposite it. "Despite your best efforts, you were never able to free yourself," he said, stepping forward. He pointed the pistol downwards in the dark as he held the knife up protectively in front of him. The walkie talkie with its luminescent display was lying on the floor. It blared again, and Steen Holz snorted. At that moment, Cecilie's fist hit his neck. His legs gave way and as he sought the support of the sofa the pistol dropped from his hand. He landed heavily on the floor, clutching the knife. Cecilie put her foot on his hand and stamped. Steen Holz let out a groan and released his grip on the shaft. She planted her knee in his back and retrieved the knife from the floor. "You killed Lasse." She grabbed his hair and forced his head back. "The only person who has ever meant anything to me." She pressed the knife to his throat.

Outside in the corridor, the lift chimed and a moment later the sound of running footsteps followed as the officers raced down the passage.

"He screamed like a little girl when I shot him," Steen Holz groaned. "Just another pathetic victim. Just kill me."

Cecilie pushed the knife harder against his throat, and a fine streak of blood appeared. "There's nothing I'd rather do." At that very moment, the office door flew open. The red laser sights of the officers' automatic weapons swept the room.

"But I'd rather see you rot in jail," she said, sticking the knife into the floor right before his eyes. She raised her arms above her in surrender as she stood up. The dots from the laser sights danced across her body and face.

"Down on the floor!" the leading officer shouted.

Hands up, she followed his order, crouching down to her knees. Out of the corner of her eye, she saw Steen Holz fumbling for the gun on the floor. A moment later, he took hold of it and he swung it around. He aimed at Cecilie and fired. There was a loud report, and a searing pain in her chest made her crumple. The room was immediately filled with the sound of a volley of shots, all aimed at Steen Holz. When the officers stopped, he lay motionless on the floor with gunshot wounds to his face and upper torso. One officer kicked the pistol away from him, while another shook his head dismissively. "Target is down."

The unit lead who was standing by Cecilie bent down. "Have you been hit?"

"Fuck, yes," she groaned.

61

They came to pick her up three days after she was admitted to Rigs-hospitalet. Two young officers, one with a moustache, the other with a thick Aarhus accent. It felt to Cecilie as if the officers graduating from the police academy were getting younger by the day, but she had to admit to herself that she was probably becoming an old rat. A maimed one at that. The doctors had kept her in the operating theatre for four hours as they fought to stop the internal bleeding caused by the bullet. A couple of centimetres lower, and Steen Holz would have hit her heart. She had found herself thinking about the emergency department doctor who had jokingly wished that gangsters would improve their aim. She had to admit, she was grateful that Danish psychologists had a similarly poor aim.

The officers put her in the back seat, but without any handcuffs and without locking the door, which were both good signs, albeit not signs to be interpreted as a hero's welcome. She guessed that John Nyholm was already waiting impatiently for her arrival. Quite where she was bound after that remained an unknown. Most likely, she'd be transferred to the custody cells ahead of her preliminary hearing.

"Does it hurt?" asked the officer with the moustache.

"Only when I breathe."

The officers chortled, and she couldn't help but join in. Mostly because it had been a long time since she'd heard laughter in a patrol car. Not since she'd been in the car with Lasse, whose notoriously loud outbursts of laughter could make a whole car rock.

Twenty minutes later, the officers escorted her up to the fourth floor where the top brass had their offices. She wasn't clear what business they had up there, and her surprise was not diminished when one of the duo knocked on the commissioner's door. Never in her career had she spoken personally to Volmer Bangsgaard—not even when she had been promoted. The officer closed the door behind her and Cecilie looked around. Bangsgaard had taken up a position in front of his desk, arms crossed. Beside him were Karstensen, John Nyholm, and Andreas, their faces all pinched with seriousness.

"Cecilie Mars," Bangsgaard said by way of greeting, pointing her to the chair in front of them. "I gather you're physically in the clear?"

"Yes, they seem to have patched me up alright." She smiled slightly and took a seat.

None of the four men smiled back. Bangsgaard turned to Karstensen. "What's the situation vis-à-vis the investigation of Steen Holz?"

Karstensen cleared his throat and blinked nervously. "We've carried out a number of searches. These include at his clinic, as well as his residence in Charlottenlund. At the latter, we found weapons, electronic equipment, and an array of documents and other effects. All of these confirm that he was the killer in a string of murder cases—in addition to being the culprit in a string of *other* cases that have now come to light, and that we will investigate. NC3 is examining the hard drives and mobile phones we found at the address."

"So we're sure we've got our man? And that he was also behind the killing of detective Lasse Kofoed?"

"There's no doubt about it."

"Steen Holz himself confessed to it in radio communications that we recorded as part of the recent operation," Karstensen added.

John Nyholm nodded briskly. "That aspect has been established. But as far as our investigation is concerned, we are looking into the involvement of Inspector Cecilie Mars in these cases," he said, nodding towards her.

"Is it the view of the Independent Police Complaints Authority that charges can be brought?" Bangsgaard asked.

John shrewdly suppressed his smile. "Yes. We are more than convinced. We face extensive investigative work in relation to the deaths of Ulrik Østergård, Emil Kam, Morten Pier Nielsen, and . . ."

"In what way?" Bangsgaard interjected.

"There are a number of details that must be clarified in terms of what the inspector did on her own account, but also in terms of what she omitted to report, including her ongoing contact with the killer."

Andreas cleared his throat. "May I add that Steen Holz's identity was not known at that time, and that Cecilie—that is to say, the inspector—independently investigated the issues that came to light on an anonymous basis. In that respect, she merely investigated matters as she saw fit. Which cannot in itself be regarded as misconduct."

Karstensen let out a grunt. "That's as may be, but it took place without any form of consent from her superior, me." He patted himself on the chest.

"Quite frankly, it is also the least serious offence in the entire, wide-reaching cluster of cases," John interjected.

Andreas smiled slightly at Bangsgaard. "If I may add one further thing, the reason that the investigation was shrouded in the utmost secrecy was that the inspector strongly suspected that the anonymous vigilante was in fact on this very force. She thus found it necessary to handle the inquiry by herself—until such a time as she sought the assistance of Lasse Kofoed. His tragic death clearly indicates the forces she was up against—how carefully she had to tackle this."

John looked condescendingly at Andreas. "The conversation between Steen Holz and the inspector in the office of Phillip Vang revealed a special bond between them. This must be interpreted as complicity."

"Hardly," Andreas said. "No one disputes that Steen Holz had an unhealthy obsession with Cecilie—that is to say, the inspector—but this can hardly be to her detriment." He turned his gaze pointedly towards Bangsgaard. "In the case of Morten Pier Nielsen, as well as that involving Ronnie and Bjarke Thomsen, she was the direct reason why their victims escaped."

John turned to Andreas in irritation. "Just whose side are you on?"

Andreas looked back at him. "I'm just telling it as it is."

"Is that so? Because Holz was your man? Because you allowed him to remain a security risk?"

Andreas put his hands on his hips. "Steen Holz wasn't *my* man. He worked for the Prosecution Service as a whole. That he was able to illegally gain access to confidential information isn't something you can pin solely on me. But feel free to raise it with the Director of Public Prosecutions."

"That's just what I intend to do!" John snarled. "Believe me, Andreas . . ."

"I take full responsibility for my actions," Cecilie said, looking at the commissioner. All eyes turned to her. She cleared her throat before continuing. "There are several things I wish I could have done differently. I'm sorry for that. Naturally, I'm at the Independent Police Complaints Authority's disposal. And I would like to assist in the investigation insofar as that is possible."

A satisfied smile played across John's face.

"But if I may add something . . ." she said, looking down at the parquet.

"Which is?" the commissioner asked.

"When it comes to rapists like Ulrik Østergård, paedophiles like Emil Kam, serial killers like Morten Pier Nielsen, monsters like Bjarke, who trained his own son to rape . . . well, we're fighting an uneven battle. This should not be taken as an excuse for my actions. Far from it. But there is no one who can know for sure that they are safe out there."

John Nyholm sighed heavily. "Let's get back on topic." He looked significantly at the commissioner.

Volmer Bangsgaard thrust his lower lip out thoughtfully as he planted his hands in the pockets of his grey suit trousers. After a moment, he let out a gentle sigh. "This meeting never took place."

"What does that mean?" John asked.

"It all stops here. We're going to wipe the slate clean," he said, looking at Cecilie.

"But . . . what about the investigation?" Karstensen asked.

"We have a dead killer. You said the items found in his home confirm his guilt. There's no need to dedicate any further resources to this."

"Very well," Karstensen said.

"That's . . . this is completely unacceptable," John said indignantly. "This . . . I'll . . . I'll take this to the top!"

"Is that so?" Bangsgaard said, looking at him coolly. "Of course, that is your right. But here's the thing, John. You need to square this with yourself: Which is biggest? Your balls or your ambitions?"

Andreas slapped his hand to his mouth, hiding a smile.

"Un . . . unacceptable," John replied. He stormed out of the door, slamming it behind him.

Bangsgaard sighed deeply. "If I know John, he'll return to the fold in due course. Karstensen?" he added, looking at him.

Karstensen held his hands out. "The Homicide Unit is to consider this case closed as a result of the meeting that never took place." He glanced coolly at Cecilie. "But there's no rush for you to come back. Your conduct has by no means been forgotten."

She rose from her chair and said goodbye to the commissioner and Karstensen. When she turned to Andreas, she smiled cautiously at him.

62

The sun shone over Nordre Fasanvej as motorists queued along it, their windows rolled down. Despite the fact that it was only ten o'clock in the morning, the temperature was verging on twenty-five degrees. The weather forecast had warned this might be the hottest day of the year to date. But beneath the raised arcs of Bispeengbuen, the daylight barely penetrated, and the expansive car park remained hidden in darkness. Police tape fluttered around the three ramps of the skateboard area, fencing it off. The uniformed officers were enjoying the cooler temperatures under the bridge while they kept unauthorised parties at a distance with a lazy eye. Behind the cordon, three members of the forensic team in blue overalls were securing evidence using small yellow flags. Several cartridge casings lay on the ground between pools of clotted blood. One forensic technician was taking photos of a body in a hoodie that lay on the centre skateboard ramp.

Cecilie raised the tape and carefully slipped underneath it into the crime scene. Her blue T-shirt was already soaked through with sweat, and she removed her Ray Bans to wipe her brow with the back of her hand. On her tail was a younger, ginger-hair detective. He wore an oversize bulletproof vest which threatened to drown him.

"Watch where you put your feet, Troels," Cecilie said, pointing to the yellow flags ahead of them.

"Yeah of . . . of course," he replied, following at her heels. "This isn't my first crime scene," Troels added as he looked around uneasily.

"Excellent," she said, making a beeline for the skateboard ramps. "Where did you say you were from again?"

"Hobro."

"Well then, you'll fit into Nordvest just fine," she said, smiling. "Welcome."

"Well, I'll be damned. Cecilie, you back?" Ole Madsen said, laughing loudly.

"Yep."

"You're looking sharp. And who's this chap?" Ole nodded at Troels who had caught sight of the body and seemed unable to tear his gaze away.

"Troels. New detective. From Hobro."

Ole smiled.

"What do you have for me?" Cecilie asked, pointing to the hoodie-clad corpse.

"Young man. Gang related, if we take the logo on the top at face value. So far, I make the count eight shots. Mostly to the torso. One to the forehead. Full-on execution. Probably yesterday evening or in the small hours."

Cecilie stepped cautiously onto the ramp and crouched beside the body. She scrutinised the shot that had blown the top of the man's head clean off. "Hollow-point bullets?"

"Yes. Someone wanted to make sure he died. At any rate, this is not your bog standard drive-by."

"Was he really . . . executed?" Troels asked.

"Looks that way," she replied, standing up. "Our boy Hassan must have been running off at the mouth."

"You . . . you know who he was?"

She nodded and put her sunglasses back on. "One of the local yobs who had risen through the ranks to be a full gang member. I guess some-one needed to send them all a message."

"A message?"

"Yes, Troels. About who is boss around here." She put her hands on her hips and surveyed the area. She inhaled through her nose, still able to discern the smell of gunpowder lingering on. It was a smell that made adrenaline course through her. She crouched over Hassan's body and peered towards Nordre Fasanvej, the sun reflecting off car windscreens. She spotted four girls in skirts and trainers. The girls were laughing loudly as they rode off on their bicycles, loaded up with towels and beach bags. Cecilie thought she saw Fie laughing among them, but perhaps that was just wishful thinking down here in the darkness.

ABOUT THE AUTHOR

Michael Katz Krefeld (b. 1966) is one of the most-read Danish crime authors, and his critically acclaimed books have been awarded several fiction prizes. He is best known for his bestselling crime series featuring Detective Ravn, which has thrilled readers across the globe. Having begun his career as a screenwriter, Krefeld tends toward fast-paced and highly unpredictable thrillers. The fight against evil and personal sacrifices made for the greater good are typical recurring elements of his work.

DISCOVER
STORIES UNBOUND

PodiumAudio.com

Made in United States
North Haven, CT
04 December 2023